BAD LANDS

SELINA ROSEN
LAURA J. UNDERWOOD

FIVE STAR

An imprint of Thomson Gale, a part of The Thomson Corporation

THOMSON

™

GALE

Detroit • New York • San Francisco • New Haven, Conn. • Waterville, Maine • London

LIBRARY OF CONGRESS CATALOGING-IN-PUBLICATION DATA

Rosen, Selina.
   Bad lands : a Holmes & Storm mystery / Selina Rosen, Laura J. Under-
wood. — 1st ed.
     p. cm.
   ISBN-13: 978-1-59414-473-8 (alk. paper)
   ISBN-10: 1-59414-473-7 (alk. paper)
   1. Forensic scientists—Fiction. 2. Psychics—Fiction. 3. Reality television
programs—Fiction. 4. Serial murders—Fiction. I. Underwood, Laura J. II.
Title.
PS3568.O7746B33 2007
813'.54—dc22

                                                        2006038267

First Edition. First Printing: June 2007.

Published in 2007 in conjunction with Tekno Books and Ed Gorman.

Printed in the United States of America on permanent paper
10 9 8 7 6 5 4 3 2 1

"To all those fans who wouldn't leave us alone until we
finished this book—
And to Lynn just because she DOES do so much for the
authors on many levels . . ."

CHAPTER ONE:
MAGGIE

The alarm clock is burning the hours into my retinas every time I look at it. Currently, it's reading 3:15 A.M. *Hell,* I thought, *it's going to be one of those nights.* Time moves slowly when you're lying alone in a king-sized bed with a head full of wild thoughts.

Normally, I'm not such a worrier. Even when John died five years ago in the SUV wreck, I was practical enough to think of the distance of the skid marks in the snow and calculate that he probably died on impact. One gets into such habits after working as a forensic scientist for twenty-five years.

I'm semiretired, now. These days, I'm more of a crime scene consultant, someone who stands over the newer crew and tells them what they are doing wrong. The book I wrote titled *The Parapsychology and Phenomena of Crime Scenes* got some frowns from my colleagues, but is still paying a nice royalty. Between that and John's life insurance, I was able to go on comfortably, see my son wed and my daughter start college.

So life's a little lonely, but for the most part I can't complain. I even have a contract for a new book.

And that's part of the reason I am lying here with the blankets thrown off and the AC turned down low enough to freeze an Eskimo. I want desperately to do this book on paranormal activity at the scenes of mass murders, and I have a lot of research still to go. And one particular scene I want desperately to explore.

Towards this end I did something . . . Well, that I probably shouldn't have done, and now I've got to figure out a way to tell my friend Vivian what I have "volunteered" her for.

I don't think she is going to like it.

The whole thing started because I wanted to go to Knight Island. I'm told the old Spanish name for the place was La Isla de Sangre, or Island of Blood, quite appropriate when I think about it. Years ago, the place was purchased by a man named Garret Knight who gave it his name. It had originally been a fancy resort when it was built in the fifties, one of those places where the rich and beautiful go to squander their money. But something terrible happened during the off-tourist season—a mass murder in which one of the guests went nuts and murdered the ten people who were on the island at the time before he hanged himself.

No one bothered to tell Knight this when he bought the place. He tore down a lot of the old stone resort and built a fine, fancy mansion for himself and his family out of the old hotel. Then out of the blue, twenty years to the day, Garret Knight went bonkers and butchered his family and servants before killing himself.

That was twenty years ago. I just know the place is full of psychic energy. It would be the perfect location to research my new book, but the heirs are being jerks. They won't let me go to the island for anything less than a hundred thousand dollars— like I could come up with that sort of money.

That was when I learned that Lynx Network was planning to film one of their "reality TV" programs there. They were going to send several couples to Knight's Island to "live" among the spirits of the island's bloody history, and the ones with the courage to remain would get a million dollars. As much as I dis- like reality TV, I was not going to pass on such an opportunity.

The money was not my motive. I wanted to do the research.

They were going to have scads of equipment on hand that I could never afford to rent, let alone own. So I filled out all the forms online, read everything carefully, and learned that the producers were looking for "diverse, romantically involved" couples. Vivian and I could be diverse. No one would ever have to know we were not really a couple.

Vivian is going to think I'm crazy.

The clock now reads 3:27.

Maybe I am crazy. Pushing fifty, I find my body taking a vacation from its former, fit self. No, I'm not getting fat, but there's a spread that was not there before. Forensics is not exactly highly active work. You're on your feet a lot, but then you're on a stool staring at microscopic specimens or on your hands and knees scraping bits of evidence off the ground, not exactly athletic work.

I quit doing "fleshies" after John died and cut back to part-time work. Identifying what was left of him after the wreck had taken the last of my resolve.

Just as finding my best friend Cassie had started me on the road to research.

I was all of nine. Cassie lived down the street from our old house in Virginia. She was not exactly the sort of friend my parents approved of. Her family lived on welfare, and her brother had been in trouble with the law. Friendship does not recognize such differences. Cassie was taller than me, and she kept some of the older girls from beating me up in school, all because I didn't make fun of her for having a harelip. In fact, I thought it was rather fascinating. Cassie was a wild child when it came to life. Me, I was as sedate as applesauce, the smart kid with the grown-up outlook on life. My parents were British immigrants, and they raised me a little stiff and introspective. But Cassie, she had lived a hard life and at nine, she was as tough as nails.

Too bad she didn't live to see womanhood. I suspect she would have been one of those feminist activists. She had a good head in spite of her home life. And she was smart and a dreamer as well.

But she was dead at nine, and I still cannot get the image out of my head after forty years.

I found her. That's right. It was early on a Saturday morning. I had been told I could not go down there to play with her. Cassie and I had planned to run off to the woods and play. We were not supposed to go to the woods. My mother thought children who went into the woods never came out again.

I crawled out of bed early that day. Dew was still on the lawn. My mother wasn't even up yet. I slipped out the back door, crossed the fence and started down the street. Cassie lived about two blocks away in an area where the houses were shabby. "Other side of the tracks" is what my mother called it.

Now, I know why the night before, when Cassie and I walked home from school together, and we got to her house she had looked uneasy about going in. We had stood on the sidewalk, talking about the woods, making our plans. Then Cassie's dad, wearing a sleeveless T-shirt and pants that he belted down under his belly, had leaned out the door, taken his cigar from his mouth and spat, "Get your little ass in here, missy!" in a manner that made me wonder what was going on.

So there it was, early morning, and I was sneaking out to play. I cut through a couple of yards and managed to avoid the Bensons' wiener dog when it charged out of the door flap and yapped at me.

Cassie had always told me to come to her window when I wanted to get her attention. I don't think she was ashamed to have me come to the door as much as she was afraid that her brother would answer it. He had a reputation in high school for getting what he wanted from any girl he met. I was too young to know what he was getting, but I had my suspicions. Girls talk as much as boys do about these things.

I slipped up to the window, tapping lightly to get Cassie's attention. Seemed like an hour passed, though now I know it was no more than five minutes, and she didn't respond. Frustrated because I wanted to get into the woods before my mother knew where I had gone, I rapped a little harder and halfway expected Cassie's parents to come shoo me away. But no one came. Puzzled, I went around back. Maybe they were all in the kitchen . . .

The back door was ajar slightly. I stepped up on the cinderblocks that served as a porch and whispered, "Hello." Nothing. Not a word of response. Carefully, I pushed the door in, but it refused to go far. So I slithered through the opening like a little rabbit wriggling through a bunny hole, popped in rather suddenly, and fell because the floor was slick with crimson coagulation.

I had never seen a dead person before, and when I first got to my knees and looked at the blood on my hands and clothes, I was confused. Then my eyes followed the trail to the back of the door, a headless corpse in a flower print dress and yellow apron lie there. One hand stretched toward the door as though she had tried to open it at the moment of death.

I don't know why I didn't feel sick. Shock, maybe. I just don't know. I got up, and felt a strange chill in the air. The house reeked of blood and bowels, and there was a trail of blood from the corpse to the next room. I followed it, not sure of what I was going to find.

The next room was some sort of dining area, and there on the table sat a row of heads. That's right. They were lined up as neat as you please. Six of them in all. Cassie's parents, her baby brother, her uncle, a girl I didn't know, and Cassie. A light bulb had been rammed into a hole cut into the top of each one.

Blood spattered everything.

But for all that, what had my attention was something that to this day I have never been able to explain. The bulbs had a dim glow to them, as though some energy was pulsing inside each one. I kept blinking, thinking it was my imagination, but no. Pale lights swirled in each one.

I backed away then, stumbled, and sat down hard in someone's lap. The stiffness of a wooden knife handle popped me in the neck. An arm flopped down around me, a hand covered with blood. I screamed then for the first time, struggling to escape the weighty grasp. Falling to the floor, I rolled over and looked up to find Cassie's older brother in the chair. The knife was plunged into his throat. I screamed again and ran.

Later, I learned that Cassie's brother had been an addict and had gotten a bad batch of drugs. Apparently he had taken them, killed his family in a PCP induced madness, and then killed himself.

Overnight, I was famous, the little girl who had discovered the brutal mass murder scene. I kept telling the police about the light in the bulbs, but they just shook their heads. My parents paid for some pretty fancy therapy.

I had nightmares about it for months. In those dreams, the bulbs would glow bright white and the faces of the dead would appear in the brilliance, looking like angels.

To this day, I wonder if the bulbs glowed faintly because there was just enough light trickling through curtained windows, or because some part of the spirit of the dead had made it do so.

It was a defining moment in my life and the one that set a course not just for what my career would be but my preoccupation with paranormal activity at crime scenes. I became fascinated with the lives and crimes of various murderers when

I was in high school. Read every book I could get my hands on about forensics and famous crimes. I had to hide most of them, of course. My parents didn't approve, but I didn't care at that point in time.

I went off to college, got a degree and met John. He was taking a degree in forensics as well, and we hit it off as the old saying goes. I hadn't quite finished my PhD when we got married, but I finished my degree and went to work for the local authorities. In the beginning, I was doing fieldwork and lab work, and that was when I started to notice things. Like sometimes there are cold spots around bodies. And sometimes, one would see things flit from the corner of the eyes that would not be there when you turned to look. I became convinced that there was something happening that I could never quite put a finger on—sort of like those glowing bulbs.

Two children later my life became more routine than I liked. I was never much of a housewife, but I could cook. John didn't seem to mind as long as the bed got made. We could afford to hire someone to dust and do laundry and look after the kids when we were working.

I was still having the nightmares about Cassie, and that was when John suggested I write. He was a big believer in self-therapy. Besides, I had enough field experience as a forensics scientist to know how to gather research material. And since I liked to read, I was sure I would like to write.

It was work, however. But I wrote the book, figuring it would only appeal to a small scholarly audience, and was rather surprised when it gathered such a huge audience of ordinary folks while the intellectual community scoffed at it.

So naturally, the publishers wanted another book from me. It was in my contract.

Then John died and my world took a slight tumble. That book became my new child. John Jr. married his fiancée the next year. Then Anne went off to college.

If it wasn't for Vivian's friendship, I probably would be insane right now.

I met Vivian at a murder scene a year after John died. The force had hired her to draw pictures of suspects from eyewitness accounts. Her pictures looked uncanny. Almost like photographs. It amazed me that anyone could get that much detail out of the vague descriptions most witnesses give. I started to suspect there was more to Vivian's artistic skill when I saw her off to one side of the body, her lips moving as though she were talking to someone.

Had I not seen her do this more than once, I would never have put two and two together. So I confronted her with it, and to my surprise, she confessed.

After that, I made sure she and I worked cases together. I was seriously interested in using her skill to further my research. Working with her I wrote my second book, *What the Dead See*. Through it all, we became friends. I was an only child, and Vivian became like a younger sister. She was bright, tall and athletic. I was short and matronly, though not in a bad way.

Surely she won't begrudge me this chance. She knows I've been trying to get on Knight Island for the last six months, and now I have the perfect opportunity.

I roll over and glare at the alarm clock. 3:56 A.M. glares back at me. I close my eyes and try to go to sleep.

Yeah, Vivian was not going to like what I had done. I'd have to be careful how I told her about it.

See, I fixed it so the producers would think that she and I were lesbian lovers.

Chapter Two:
Vivian

The alarm goes off. I hit snooze hard enough to kill most alarm clocks, which is of course why I spent an extra twenty bucks and got a better one than the three previous ones, which had died rather badly. It finally dawned on me that I wasn't saving money if I was replacing them every two weeks.

That's the way I am about most things—it takes me a while to learn my lesson.

Anyway, I reach over to grab me something warm and fleshy and realize I'm in bed alone. My nearest and dearest ex, Tammy, had just left me for some fat, greasy Latino girl who worked on the docks, or maybe she was a trucker, doesn't really matter, same difference, right?

To put it simply I have shitty luck when it comes to my women. They say unlucky in cards lucky in love. Well, I'm here to tell you that's a crock of shit because I can't play cards worth a damn, either.

I try to go back to sleep at least till the alarm goes off again, but that isn't going to happen because by then I'm depressed, so before that damn alarm can start screaming in my ear again I shut it off, sit up, and reach for my smokes.

That's when I realize just what a shitty day it's going to be. There aren't any cigarettes, because once again I have let Maggie talk me into trying to quit smoking.

Now, I'm not a dumb-ass, I know smoking is bad for me and that I have a lot better wind and feel better when I'm not smoking. But, dammit! When you wake up in bed alone wondering how you screwed up this time you just want a crutch.

That's why I went and got a beer out of the fridge.

Now, Maggie'd shit a great gaseous turd if she knew I'd just replaced my early morning smoke with my late, after-jogging beer, but what she doesn't know I'm not going to have to hear her bitch about for three or four hours.

I drink the beer down and then mainline a pot of coffee. I look at the clock and it's nine, so I'm behind schedule and I hate being behind schedule. I blame the fact that it takes longer to drink a beer than it does to smoke a cigarette. Or at least it takes longer in the morning.

I braid my hair, get out of my boxers and tank top and into my gym shorts and another tank top and start out the door. I'm almost there when I notice there is dust on the top of the ceiling fan blades, and I'm thinking this day just gets better and better. I clean the ceiling fan and head on out.

Now, I work Monday, Tuesday and Saturday nights from 7:00 P.M. to 2:00 A.M. tending bar at the Show & Tell Club about a block from my apartment, so I'd never have to get up at 7:30—except maybe when the cops call me—but I learned a long time ago that if I didn't get up early the whole day got wasted; besides, it's the best time of the day to jog down to the beach and have a run, and I'm also only about two blocks from the beach. The club I work out at is only three blocks away, so you guessed it, I spend the bulk of the money I make on rent.

But I really like my apartment and I can sometimes go weeks without having to start my car, which is a good thing because that Tercel ain't gonna live much longer.

That day I jogged on down to the beach and I started my usual run. I'm starting to feel less depressed about Tammy and the cigarette, and even the dust on the fan—then I hit it. Now I'd run that beach hundreds of times and never hit it before, but that morning I did. Someone had died there, and they hadn't died well. The vision of the last thing the victim saw flooded my head, and as often happens—when it's such a violent and unexpected vision—when it ended I was on my knees with no memory of how I'd gotten there. This murder had been so vile, and the vision so intense, that I threw up the coffee and beer I'd had for breakfast.

Naturally this incident sent me down to the police station to see if and when there had been a mutilation on the beach. It could have just happened, or it could have happened years ago. Signature energy—or whatever the hell it is—like that doesn't usually dissipate very quickly.

I spent most of the early part of my life trying to stay away from such places, because they've always screwed with my head like that. But right after I dropped out of med school, or was it law school? Maybe it was right after I quit my psychology courses . . . It doesn't really mater, anyway this girl had been killed on campus—a girl I knew—and I knew I could find her killer. I went to where they'd found her body, and I knew exactly what the killer looked like. I told the cops that I was a really good artist and that I'd like to help. As fate would have it their sketch artist had the flu, so they let me give it a try. I talked to the witnesses, but I didn't really listen, I just drew the person I'd "seen."

Long story short, that's how I got that job. A few years later Maggie figures out what I'm doing, and before you know it I'm being drug all over the country to some of the sites of the most brutal murders and killings in history.

That's mostly how my life runs. Whatever I try hardest *not* to do I inevitably wind up doing. You'd think I would have learned by now, but like I said it takes me a long time to learn a lesson.

Anyway, I'm down at the station telling the cops what I saw and where I saw it. By now they all know that I'm psychic—or whatever the hell I am—and I've solved enough cases for them that they don't question me at all, just load me into a car and haul me down to the beach.

"So, what horse in the ninth?" Jim asks, looking over his seat as he talks to me, which isn't too cool since he's the one that's driving.

"I've told you turds about a billion times. I'm not that sort of psychic. If I was, do you really think I'd always be so dog-dick broke, or go out with women who all turn out to be bitches?" I look up and see the dumb-ass is about to run into the side of a truck, so I yell, "Watch out truck!"

Jim barely misses the truck then says, "See? You *can* use your psychic ability to read the future."

"It's called watching the damn road. You might try it sometime," I say, and his partner Moe laughs his ass off. I like Moe. When he isn't being a cop he belongs to a motorbike club called Psycho Pigs, which is comprised of other cops who ride bikes. He never asks me which horse to bet on or thinks I'm holding out on everyone. In other words, Moe has a brain.

We get out at the beach. "Did you mark the spot? How are you going to find it?" Jim asks.

I smile, "Oh I'll know." I don't tell them how.

We get to it, and Moe looks at me and smiles. He knows how I've marked the spot.

"What now?" Jim asks. It was the first good question the stupid bugger had asked. Talk about ass-backwards, we had a picture of the suspect but no dead body, not even a missing person report. No idea in fact who the victim might be, whether they had died yesterday or twenty years ago. You couldn't call a forensics team out to look for evidence to a crime that might not have been committed, and the only evidence that we had was my vision—which wouldn't hold up in court.

"You dig on the spot and I'll look around for clues," Moe

said, and I could see his shoulders shaking with well-concealed laughter as he walked away.

Jim didn't hesitate. He just shrugged, made that look like it was all a big waste of time, put on rubber gloves, dropped to his knees and started digging.

"Keeyrist, Storm! What did you do, mark the spot with your piss?" Jim asked.

"Actually I puked," I said fighting a grin. As much as I liked Moe I didn't really care for Jim.

"God dammit, Storm!" He slung down the fistful of wet sand he'd had in his hand.

"Just chill, Jim, all I'd eaten was some coffee and a beer . . ."

"Coffee and beer," Moe laughed, walking up with an evidence bag in his hand.

"Breakfast of champions," I said. "What you got?"

Moe handed me the bag. I wish he hadn't. It was a small knife, and not just any knife, but *the* knife. I swayed but didn't fall over. It was the murder weapon, and for Moe to have found it that quickly so close, it could mean only one thing—the murder was recent.

"Dammit, Storm, you ain't gonna hurl again, are ya?"

"If you find what I think you're going to find where you're digging, a little puke is going to seem like a welcome breath a' fresh air."

The body had been cut at the joints and buried in the sand on the beach. When the forensic people got there they said the corpse was about one week old and that the murder probably hadn't taken place on the beach, but I knew it had. I wondered how it could have happened and nobody had seen, then I remembered there had been walls. I drug Moe aside.

"The guy used a tent. He killed her in the tent."

"That explains why nobody saw, but why didn't anyone hear anything?"

"It was late at night. She was dazed. I got the feeling that she wasn't really able to scream, like maybe she'd been drugged."

Moe nodded. They let me go. The official record would read that I'd found the body while running on the beach. Sooner or later someone was bound to put two and two together and figure out that I sure did find more than my fair share of bodies.

I went home and took a good long bath. I felt filthy, and my head started pounding the way it always did when I'd had a "vision." I realized I still hadn't eaten anything, but I'd bought a pack of cigarettes when I'd been out.

I know, I know, but the flesh is weak.

I popped a cigarette in my mouth and lit it as I went to check the refrigerator for food. A box of Pop-Tarts and a slightly used fast food hamburger looked back at me. I ate a couple of Pop-Tarts for lunch and had the burger for dessert. I washed it all down with a cheap-ass cola.

I had just finished this feast and cleaned up the mess when the front doorbell rang. "Who is it?" I hollered as I started for the door.

"It's Maggie."

Damn. It would be Maggie. I sniffed the air. You could definitely smell cigarette.

"Wait a minute, Maggie! I'm on the can," I yelled. I went and grabbed the can of disinfectant off the kitchen counter and sprayed it around the living room and kitchen, put it down and headed for the door. Then I saw the pack of cigarettes and the dirty butt in the ashtray. I hid the cigarettes under the couch cushions and ran in and flushed the butt, thus continuing my ruse that I was on the can. I stashed the ashtray under the sink, washed my hands—just because I can't go into the bathroom and leave without washing my hands—then I headed for the front door and opened it.

"Come on in, how you doing, Maggie?" I fully expected Maggie to jump my ass and tell me that she knew just what I'd been up to. I pride myself on being a champion bullshitter, but I can hardly ever pull one over on Maggie.

I was a little surprised when Maggie just walked in without saying anything and sat where she normally sits on the couch. I'm guessing maybe she's heard about the corpse I found since she still occasionally works for the coroner's office, but oh no, that isn't the case at all. "Want something to drink?"

"No."

Now Maggie isn't like me, rattling all the time, but she isn't exactly a woman of few words, either, so now I know something's up. I think maybe she's mad that I didn't call her when I found the corpse. As I often do, I expect the worst, and this time I ain't wrong. I just guess the wrong thing. "The kids all right?"

"Yes."

"The baby?"

"Yes, fine." Maggie smiled at me then, one of those "I need you to do something for me and you aren't going to like it" smiles.

I sit down because I figure I'm probably going to need to. "What the fuck is it? And I think I should tell you I'm having a particularly shitty day."

"I figured that out when I heard you hiding your cigarettes and trying to get rid of the smell," she said with a smile.

I laugh then because I can't help myself. She's my friend, my best, and she knows me better than anyone else. "Couldn't you just once pretend to buy my bullshit?"

"I'm not quite the actress that you are."

"All right, Maggie, just tell me and ruin what's left of my day."

"Well . . . you know the Garret Knight estate?"

"Yes," I say, trying to keep my voice steady. I hate even the thought of this place, and had been secretly, and at times not so secretly, hoping that the estate wouldn't allow us to study the place. When they told us they wanted one hundred thousand dollars and I knew Maggie didn't have it, I did a fucking dance of joy. I'm dreading what she's going to say next because I'm thinking maybe she got a grant to do the research, but no, it was so much worse than that.

"Lynx Network rented the estate for a reality show they're going to do. You and I are going to be contestants."

I'm guessing there was steam coming out of my ears. "I don't remember signing up for anything like that, Maggie!"

"Listen before you go off. They're going to supply all this really expensive ghost-busting type equipment, the stuff that I could never in a million years afford. Spectrometers and Rectal-probe-annihilators . . ." and a whole lot of other crap I could give a shit less about but which makes Maggie cum in her drawers. "There's a chance we could win a million dollars."

I get up and start pacing then because I'm pissed. "I can't believe you did this without even asking me . . ."

"I knew you'd say no, and I figured we'd never get such a great opportunity again. Besides, I figured what were the odds that we would get picked from all the thousands of entries they would get . . ."

"Oh, yeah, because everyone's just dying to go to a haunted resort where not once, but *twice,* a perfectly normal person went ape-shit crazy and killed a bunch of people . . ."

"Well, there actually *were* thousands of entries."

"That being the case I'm wondering just what you told them that tipped the scales in our favor."

Maggie's face scrunched into a knot then as if the next words she spoke were being dragged from her. "They said they were looking for a very diverse group of people." She just ended it there, as if she couldn't quite finish what else she had to say.

"So you told them what?"

"Well, that I was a forensic pathologist, which is true, and that you were a bartender, which is true . . . and then I told them that we were a couple." She told the last part real fast as if she thought if she said it fast enough I wouldn't actually hear what she said and kill her.

I stopped pacing and just looked down at her. I wanted to be really pissed, but the idea of me and Maggie together was so funny I just started laughing, and the more I laughed the funnier it was till I had to sit down or fall down. Maggie laughed too, at first, then when I just kept laughing she stopped.

"Ah . . . what's so funny?" she asked.

"You and me." I could hardly breathe, so talking was a real effort. "Together." I started laughing even harder.

"Why is that so funny?"

If it was possible I laughed even harder.

"Well?" she demanded.

At this point I was afraid I was going to puke again I was laughing so hard, so I worked at calming down. "Nothing personal, Maggie, but you just aren't my type."

"And why not? Is it because I'm nearly fifty? I mean you'd sleep with a rock if it smiled at you, and suddenly I'm not good enough for you."

The offended tone in her voice only forced me to start laughing all over again. I just didn't know how to quit after that.

Maggie just sat there tapping her foot and waiting for me to calm down which took me a good ten minutes.

"I'm sorry," I said finally as I wiped a tear from my eye. "It's just so . . ." I almost started laughing again, and Maggie saying,

"Now don't start that again," was really no help.

I wound up thinking about the dead body I'd found that morning just to calm myself down.

"Do you honestly believe that anyone for even a second is going to buy you and me as a couple?" I asked.

"Well, I don't see why not. I know I'm not the typical blond-headed, big-titted bimbo you usually go out with, but I'm not exactly chopped liver, either."

I had to fight the laughter again, and then I decided to screw with her head as badly as she was screwing with mine. "I'm sorry, Maggie, take offense if you want, but I just can't see you eating pussy."

Maggie turned a very delightful and fulfilling shade of red and changed the subject.

"We've only got two weeks to settle things with our jobs and work on our story."

"I haven't said I'm going to do it, Maggie. You realize what a place like that is going to do to my head."

"Yes, and I know that as much as you hate it, you also enjoy figuring things out as much as I do. You know as well as I do that ghosts can't hurt us. Think of it this way—you're always bitching about money problems, and this could be your chance to end all that. Those other people are going to get scared because they aren't us. You and I have seen horrible things, so it takes a hell of a lot to scare us. If we go, we'll win. We'll get to split a million dollars."

She was right. I did know that the dead couldn't actually hurt you, at least not do more than give me a splitting headache, and she was right about the money thing, too. If anyone could stick it out there it was me and Maggie. Hell, it would probably be fun. I nodded, and she jumped up, ran over, and hugged me. I looked down at her and said, "So . . . when are you going to tell the kids about us?"

"Oh, shit! I haven't even thought about what to tell the kids yet."

CHAPTER THREE:
MAGGIE

The ancient Chinese have a philosophy that we have children so we will have someone to look after us in our old age. Modern American parents know this is not the way it works. You raise your children in the hopes that they will one day get out of your house and let you live in peace.

That is not to say that I do not love my children. I didn't spend all those hours in labor, screaming obscenities at their father, because it was fun. I like to think that my children are special. John Jr., who recently got a nice position in an engineering firm, made me a grandmother about a year ago. Anne has finally decided that her calling in life is to be a lawyer. She got a scholarship and just started her second year at Harvard. It's nice to know my little hooligans are finally turning into decent adults.

Still, if I thought telling Vivian what I had done was going to be hard, faced with the prospect of telling my children, I came to realize that an insanity plea might be my only salvation. *Oh, you know your mother. She's just one of those eccentric writer types. We're all crazy.*

I had to tell them. There was no way I could simply disappear for two weeks without arousing a lot of suspicion. After all, I was still a forensics consultant for the police. If I disappeared, John Jr. would have one of his "protective" moments. Since his father died, John Jr. has taken it upon himself to be the man of the house, in spite of the fact that it's not his house and he no longer lives here.

He has his own home, and his own wife, and if he wants to rule that roost, fine. But I can take care of myself, I don't need his constant fussing and worrying. Thank God, Anne is a little more sensible.

At any rate, I had to tell them, and I decided that the only safe way to do so was to invite them all over for dinner. I asked Vivian to join us, wanting her there for support, but she told me that she had to work. It was a Wednesday night, so I knew it was a boldfaced lie, but I felt like I'd better not push things as far as Vivian was concerned. So I was on my own, trying to fix a halfway decent meal that would appeal to both my offspring without one of them thinking I was favoring the other.

This is a near impossible task and forces me to make an eight course meal.

Anne arrived first and helped me with setting the table. She is a little taller than me, and has her father's eyes. John Jr.—who looks exactly like his father did the day I fell in love with him—was late, apologizing because he and Ruth could not find a sitter for little Adrian. So Ruth opted to stay home with the baby, though I sometimes wonder if Ruth just doesn't want to visit her husband's mother. Really, I have tried not to be an interfering mother-in-law. I'm much too busy to run my children's lives. Still, I suppose sometimes I express my opinion when no one really wants to hear it, but then doesn't everyone?

John Jr., however, tells me it's because I cannot keep from discussing some of the cases I deal with. Ruth apparently has a weak stomach.

He finally arrives, and we all sit down to our meal.

"So, Mom," Anne says in her usual crisp manner. "Do you plan to wait for dessert before telling us why we're here?"

I frowned at her. A lot of good that did, Anne is very much like me, analytical and as stubborn as a rock when she's on the track of something.

"Is there some rule that says a mother can't invite her children over for a meal and a pleasant discussion?" I asked.

"I knew it," John Jr. said, and shook his head as he glared at Anne.

"Knew what?" I said, and fixed him with a puzzled look.

"Anne said you were up to something *weird.*"

I looked at Anne who merely smiled and winked. "I didn't say she was up to anything weird," she protested. "I said that it seemed weird that she would invite us over like this when we both know she couldn't wait for us to get out from under her feet."

"Excuse me. What wicked tales have you been telling your brother this time?" I tried to look like the affronted matron as I spoke.

"Must be something *real* weird then," Anne said.

I shook my head. "Okay, I asked you here so I could let you know that you shouldn't worry about me if I disappear for a couple of weeks."

"Ooooo, now it sounds mysterious," Anne said.

John Jr. fixed me with a look of disapproval that matched anything his father could have done. "Mother, what have you been up to?"

"Research," I said flatly. "You know I am working on another book, and well, I just got an opportunity to go do some investigating that will assist me and . . ."

"You're going to be on *Chicken Out* and go to Knight Island," Anne said.

"Are you psychic?" I asked.

"I saw the copies of the applications on your desk . . . and the airline tickets to Cancun," she said. "And besides, that was all you talked about when we had lunch last week. How the Knight family had refused you the right to go to the island unless you came up with a ridiculous sum of cash and . . ."

"Hold on," John Jr. said. "You're going to be on that stupid reality TV show Lynx produces?"

"Yes," I said. "It was the only way I could get to the island and do my research."

"But Mother, Ruth watches that show. You're single and they only accept couples on the show."

"Well, yes." I glanced at my plate. "I am going as a couple."

"I always knew you were a little schizoid, Mom," Anne said and patted my hand. I resisted the urge to be juvenile and stick my tongue out at her.

"How can you go as a couple?" John Jr. insisted. "I mean . . . Dad is gone, Mother and . . . Are you seeing someone? Is that what this is really all about? Are you trying to tell us that you've got a boyfriend?"

I took a deep breath. Here was the part I had dreaded more than anything. "I am going with Vivian."

"You're a lesbian!" John exclaimed as his jaw dropped.

"No, I just said I was to get on the show," I answered.

Anne let out a guffaw. "Oh, Mom, that is *so* rich! You and Vivian!"

Her humor was a little infectious. I smiled as my face went red. "Well, yes, I know, it is a little outrageous, and I won't tell you what Vivian said, but . . ."

"Have you lost your mind?" John Jr. snapped so suddenly, neither Anne nor I were prepared. We both looked at his seething expression. "You are a widow, for Christ's sake! A woman of respect with a fine career in forensics behind you, a successful writer, and you're going on television with a . . . a . . . ."

"Dyke?" Anne said.

"Bartender," he shot back.

I bit my tongue rather than laugh.

"And what's wrong with Vivian being a bartender?" Anne said.

"Nothing . . . except that she works in that sleazy bar full of . . ."

"Gay people? Really, John, your attitude is so fifties sometimes," Anne said in disbelief.

"It's not that," he said and shook his head. "I've nothing against Vivian. I mean, she's always been okay . . ."

"For a dyke?" Anne said and wagged a finger at him.

"Stop twisting my words, Anne. Mother has her reputation to think of . . . and ours as well. What are people going to say about us?" John Jr. gestured to himself and Anne without looking at me. "I mean, did you bother to even think about that, Mother?"

I will admit I had been sitting in my chair, feeling a tad stunned by all this. "Of course," I said, frowning at him. "Why do you think I decided to tell you about it instead of running off and letting you find out when the show aired?"

"You were going to leave without telling us?" he said, rounding toward me.

"No, but you're making me wish I had," I said.

"Mother!" he cried. "Everyone's going to think you're gay."

"So? Are you not even a little aware of how important this is to me?" I said. "I've been trying to get on that island to do research for a long time, and I finally get the chance, and my only son has no more respect for me than to cast aspersions on my friend's sexual preferences."

"It's not Vivian's sexual preferences that are worrying me, Mother. It's your refusal to see the danger you could be placing yourself in. And the harm it could do to your reputation. I mean . . . what if something *did* happen to you while you were there? What if you got sick? What if you were kidnapped by South American guerillas?"

"In Cancun?" I said. "Were you paying attention in geography? Knight Island is just off the Yucatán Peninsula . . . nowhere near Nicaragua . . ."

"That's not my point!" John Jr. said, and his face was turning a ripe shade of plum now. "What if you go there and someone kills you?"

"You are such a worrywart, John," Anne shot back before I could. "She'll be with Vivian, for Christ's sake. And you and I both know Vivian can probably kick anyone's butt."

"Oh, yeah, like she can deal with people with guns and knives and . . ."

"All right!" I cried, throwing up my hands. "John Anthony Holmes Jr., you should be ashamed of yourself. I am still your mother, and I am perfectly capable of taking care of myself, and if I want to go to Knight Island with Vivian, I will go!"

Anne applauded. John Jr. sat back, folding his arms over his chest. In that moment, I swear, he looked just like his father, and it sent a little twinge of remorse shuddering through me. I looked away from him.

"Mom," Anne said. "You go right ahead. I'll look after the house while you're gone."

I fixed her with one of my matronly stares. "No parties," I said.

She smiled. I glanced back at John Jr.

"Well, who's for dessert and coffee?" I asked.

"Me!" Anne said, raising a hand.

John Jr. nodded. "Fine, I'll have some too," he said.

So, that's it? I thought. *No apology? No regrets?*

Serve him right if I *did* get kidnapped by Nicaraguan terrorists.

CHAPTER FOUR:
VIVIAN

Maggie gets me up at 5:00 in the friggin' A.M. because she wants to make sure we don't miss our 11:00 flight. I think she is insane, and I tell her so in no uncertain terms.

"Are you packed?" Maggie asks in that tone of voice that says that if I'm not already packed I'm just trying to screw up her day. Oddly enough, she expected me to be awake and ready to go when she got there. She's that excited about "Our little adventure."

"Yes, Mother," I say and head off for the bathroom and a shower I hope is going to wake me up. I bitch mostly to myself, but sometimes loudly enough that Maggie can hear me, the whole time I'm in the shower because as much as she just can't wait to go to the haunted island of death, that's how much I don't want to go and interface with the victims of the freaked-out psychotic dead guys.

I'm really not very good with names, place or personal, so I tend to give everybody and everything names I make up that I can remember until I've got the real one in my head. The only problem with this system being that I sometimes slip and call people the names I make up for them. Shallow, ugly, red-headed chick still won't talk to me. Go figure.

Anyway, Maggie just couldn't wait to start the adventure. The proof of that being that she was the one waking me up. Usually when we're doing something together, it's the other way round.

I start screaming loudly when I step out of the shower and stub my toe on the toilet. This, too, is somehow Maggie's fault I'm sure, so I yell at her.

"God damn it, Maggie! Wake me up in the middle of the night . . ."

"It's early morning," she corrected with a scream from the living room, "and I'm sure that whatever you've done is more the fault of your own carelessness than it is my waking you up a little early."

I just start mumbling then. I was so mad in that moment that I think given half a dollar I would have willingly killed her. I didn't really want to admit the real reason why I was so mad. I blamed it on the fact that she hadn't gotten my permission to use me in her whole—let's call it what it is folks—*experiment.* I blamed it on the fact that she was breaking up my routine, and I'm a person who likes routine, who needs it. It's unstructured routine by some people's standards to be sure, but it's my routine and I don't like to screw with it. But all that was just me blowing smoke up my own ass and everyone else's. Truth was—and I can admit it now, so maybe I've grown—I was just scared shitless.

The energy at crime scenes is never particularly pleasant. Ghosts—if that's what you want to call them—never give you a straight answer. You get glimpses of things. If they say anything at all it's vague and riddle like. I'm usually seeing things through the eyes of the victim; I'm feeling their dying emotions, sometimes hearing their dying words, seeing the last things they see. It's never a happy experience.

Now it's true, Maggie wasn't lying, I like solving the puzzles every bit as much as she does, maybe even more because I feel like I have a personal stake in solving a crime. In ways I really couldn't explain I feel like I'm a victim, too, because I've been forced to relive that crime.

This, however, was something different. First off there was no one to catch, no real puzzle to solve, except maybe why this island drove people bum-fuck crazy. Which, to my way of thinking, was a really good reason not to go there. Twenty-two people had died there, and unlike battlefields—which she had also drug me to, by the way, in doing her research for *Bad Lands*—death had not been swift and impersonal. Two of these people had taken their own lives, and let me tell you, that leaves behind an energy that's most nasty. The other twenty had been brutally—and from what Maggie had told me, *slowly*—mutilated, which was going to have left a signature that would be overpowering. I was afraid there would be no place on the island, and certainly no place in the house, where I could go to escape it. Usually if I know I'm walking into a crime scene I can control myself a little, but this might just be too much, and . . .

Well, I was scared to death that I was going to come off as a flake or worse yet, a big-assed weenie on national television. That I might "chicken out" and lose the money, in which case there was no reason at all for putting myself through the shit.

Maggie was right, we'd both seen terrible things, this should be a walk in the park for us, but somehow I just knew it wasn't going to be. So maybe I'm more psychic than I think.

I got dressed and walked into the living room with my suitcase in one hand and my backpack with sleeping bag on the top in the other, and Maggie sighed a sigh so loud that it couldn't be ignored.

"What? I packed everything on their little list. Yours, too, for that matter."

"Viv, you can dress casually without being a total slob," she said.

I laughed and decided to try and get in a better mood. "This from the woman who makes little trails through her living room."

"My house isn't that dirty . . . Would you look at yourself?"

34

I did. I was wearing white canvas high tops with black socks, jean cutoffs and a black tank top. I shrugged as if I couldn't imagine what she was talking about, but the truth is I knew damn good and well how sloppy I looked. I just couldn't give a shit less.

"You're a thirty-year-old woman . . ."

"Twenty-nine, I won't be thirty for six more months."

Maggie smiled then. "And how long do you intend to be twenty-nine?"

"At least as long as you plan on being forty-nine, honey," I jabbed her right back.

"Touché," she said, then frowned, letting me know that she hadn't forgotten what she was bitching about. "Do you even own anything besides cut-offs and tank tops?"

"That reminds me. I need to buy some more jeans before the wintertime." I smiled at the look on Maggie's face as I set my bags down. "You see, Mag, it's all about ecology. I buy new jeans in the fall, wear them all winter, then I turn them into cut-offs, wear them all summer, and then I give them to Goodwill. It goes full circle."

"You're insane."

I shrugged and headed for the kitchen.

"Where are you going now!" she screeched like a hundred banshees unleashed from hell.

"I'm going to go make some coffee," I said.

"Coffee? No, no! We don't have time for you to drink any coffee! No, we have to go now, right now, nothing that might make you feel any better about this whole thing, nothing that might make you feel like you still have any semblance of a normal routine, or any freewill whatsoever. We have to go, and we have to go now so that we can sit around in the airport so long that the print on those uncomfortable chairs is tattooed to our asses. You can drink the rank-assed shit they serve lukewarm and that costs eleven dollars a cup at the airport."

All right, I admit it. That isn't exactly what she said, but she might as well have.

Maggie had me drive to the airport as she read to me from a book about the Island of Death. She always has me drive; I think it's a holdover from when John was still alive. He apparently was one of those guys who thought his dick would fall right off if he had to be a passenger. Of course to tell the truth I've always had to drive in any relationship I've ever been in, so I'm thinking he and I would have gotten along just fine—provided we never had to drive anywhere together.

". . . speculation that the island was cursed started when the local mainlanders told investigators of the Hidden Island Hotel massacre that it was the revenge of the great God Caca Poopoo (all right, that isn't the real name, but I told you, I'm not too good with names, that's Maggie's department). The mainlanders said that legend had it that the island had been consecrated to Caca Poopoo with blood sacrifices . . ."

Now I'm feeling really good about going because we've got even more violent death, and to tell the truth I've never had to relive a ritual sacrifice and wasn't looking forward to doing so, but all I say is a very flippant "Yea!"

"The first of the mutilated vacationers was found on the front veranda. His eyes had been gouged from his head and were hanging free against his cheek . . . Do you think you'll be able to get any energy from the original victims since that building has been partially dismantled and rebuilt?"

"Oh, gee! I certainly hope so. It's always been my great wish to know what it would be like to have my eyes gouged from my head and left to dangle like misplaced earrings," I muttered.

"You'll probably want to steer around as many sites as possible. Not get on too many in a day's time," Maggie said thoughtfully.

"Is there anyplace on the entire island that hasn't been the site of some horrible mutilation?" I asked.

"Not too many," Maggie said. "Still, if we make a map for you to carry, you can know when you're coming up on one."

I just nodded because I knew she was trying to help, but the truth was that there would be no way of insuring that I wouldn't be walking into an energy center. Oh, if I'm very careful I can feel energy and steer around it, the problem is that I forget to be careful and so would you. It's like when a kid first gets on a bike and they're so careful because they know they can get hurt, then when they don't get hurt they forget to be careful and that's when they get hurt.

Maggie wasn't thinking because as she well knows, being a forensic pathologist, you don't always find the body at the site of the murder. Also there were times when the energy of the place where a chase or torture took place left a much stronger imprint on the fabric of time than the actual murder did. Lots of times when the actual death occurred the person wasn't even conscious anymore. There had been a couple of times when I'd stood nearly on top of a dead body and gotten nothing at all because nothing violent took place in the spot where they found the body.

The only way I can think of to explain what I "see" is that a violent crime leaves energy, a signature of sorts. A dying person's final emotions are extremely strong. They leave behind a "picture" that people like me can "see." Not that I've ever met any other people like me, or that I know why I'm this way.

You know the movie where the kid says, "I see dead people"? Well, I *don't* see dead people. What I see are events that took place, the last things a person saw as they were dying. I usually see their murderer, or the brick wall their car ran into. But other things besides actual death can leave a signature on a place, for instance a bad beating, a rape or constant despair.

I can't go into a nursing home, a hospital, or a mortuary without becoming physically ill from trying to keep out all the visions and voices that flood my mind. So most times I just don't go.

That's why I always cringe when people say I talk to the spirit world, or that I see ghosts. See, most of the people I see *aren't dead*. Most of the people I see are alive. They aren't the victims; *they're the murderers.*

Like I said, I don't know why I'm this way, but I've been this way as long as I can remember. I believe it's part of the reason my parents were so quick to write me off when I finally told them I was gay.

That and the fact that I'd never managed to make up my mind what I wanted to be when I grew up. I'd taken two years of pre-med, decided that was going to take too long and switched to law. I only lasted there for three months. Turns out you have to sell your soul to Satan to become a lawyer. Then I tried psychology, which I managed to gag down for a whole year before I realized that it was a huge load of crap.

So I think that between the "weird psychic thing" and the "never going to be anything" thing, my middle-aged, well-to-do, highly social-climbing parents just had a complete meltdown when they found out I was queer, too. It was just the icing on the cake. I think they were ready to be done with me anyway, and being queer was a highly respected reason to write a kid off in the Old South circles they run in.

Mostly I don't care, but every once in a while I get to missing them. You know, the screaming, the yelling, the being made to feel as if you're two foot tall, ugly, fat, and worthless. Anyway, I'll call them, and the conversation will go something like this.

"Hello, Mom, this is Lilly."—My real name's Lilly Rose. Now wouldn't you change your name, too? Especially if you were a

five-foot-nine-inch-tall, sports playing, butch dyke?—*"How are you doing? How's Dad? How's Peter?"* Peter's my very deeply closeted, I've got a wife and two kids so I can't possibly be gay, brother, who also isn't speaking to me these days.

"I'm fine, your dad's fine. Peter and his family are fine. Are you still gay?"

"Are you still a tight-assed bitch?"

She hangs up on me then, and next year I call them again, just to make sure everything's still the same. It's somehow comforting to know everything is status quo.

This is of course the biggest reason why I didn't tell Maggie to go fuck herself when she did this horrible thing to me. I've got no family, no real career, I can't keep a lover for more than a week, and most of my other friends are just great as long as I'm helping them out and until I actually need something from them.

Maggie accepts me, and all that I am. Oh, she bitches about the way I dress, my smoking and bed hopping, but at the end of a really bad day when the whole rest of the world has shit on me and ground it in, I know that Maggie will be there with a comforting word, a pat on the back, and some really bad coffee.

Damn, what that woman does to coffee shouldn't be legal.

We get to the airport by eight o'clock, and even with all the new bullshit, we're still processed and sitting around waiting by ten, drinking the horrible swill that passes for coffee in these places. Of course Maggie's going on and on about how it's the best coffee she's ever had, and I can't be sure if she's doing this because her coffee is soooo bad that this really does taste good to her, or if she's mostly doing it to keep me from spitting it in her face. Like maybe it's just yet another of her attempts to make me think that things aren't really as bad as I think they are.

". . . Anyway, when Knight bought the island it says he immediately began to have paranoid delusions of being watched . . ."

"And yet he remodeled the hotel and moved his family in," I interrupted Maggie.

"Yes," Maggie nodded. "Of course you know how people get after the fact. *Aunt Flossy had a feeling of impending doom. Why just last week she canceled the paper and her dentist appointment. She must have known she was going to die.* Someone might have once caught him looking over his shoulder and later came to that conclusion, or maybe just maybe he was feeling the death of those other people. Maybe he was seeing it sort of like you do . . ."

"And maybe the signatures of the murders slowly drove him crazy until he wound up imitating them." It wasn't hard for me to figure out where Maggie was going. For all the ways that we are so obviously different, we think a lot alike. Besides, we'd known each other long enough that we often finished each other's sentences. "Or maybe he knew all along what had happened there and he was twisted and planned to murder his family and kill himself all along. Maybe he was some mad serial killer and there are bodies buried all over the island." Now it just sounds ludicrous even to me, but at the time, believe it or not, I wasn't kidding. That's how freaked out I was getting about the whole thing. The closer we got to actually being on the island, the more freaked out I got. I guess it was after hearing Maggie laugh and going over what I had just said and how ridiculous it sounded that I decided maybe I ought to be popping Valiums instead of drinking coffee.

I realized I needed to calm way the fuck down. I took a deep breath and reminded myself that the visions couldn't actually hurt me. I had ibuprofen for the headaches, and if I just stayed alert, tried to walk around the hot spots, I'd be OK. I focused on the million dollars, and that seemed to help a lot. I focused on the idea that millions of people were going to see my parents' gay, dropout, disinherited daughter on a rank-assed reality TV show, with her middle-aged lover, and I felt even better. I must have smiled.

"What's so funny?" Maggie asked.

"I just got a vision of one of my parents' friends calling to tell them that I'm on TV, what I'm on and with who. Damn! I wish I could be a fly on the wall when that happens."

"Flight fifty-three to Cancun has been delayed," the voice from above said. "The new departure time will be twelve fifteen."

I turned to Maggie and gave her a dirty look. She smiled helplessly and shrugged. "It's not my fault."

I had a feeling I was going to be hearing that a lot in the next week.

The flight was fairly uneventful, and I might have actually gotten some sleep if Maggie had shut up for even ten minutes, which of course she didn't do. I wondered how I was supposed to keep all the facts about Knight Island separate from the very elaborate, yet still mostly boring—in my opinion—cover story Maggie had woven for us. I could just see myself slipping up and saying something totally twisted like, "Maggie and I met in nineteen sixty-three, shortly before they found the first mutilated corpse."

Maggie kept insisting we had worked on our cover story together, but that was a load of horse crap. I may have been half drunk but I still remember that night.

She'd tossed out all my ideas as being too tawdry or too complicated. I had wanted something really interesting, like I was tending bar and she was a stripper and I had to beat a rude customer off of her, and she was captured forever by my raw animal sexuality. Maggie insisted that no one would believe that she would do something that lewd. I asked if I could be the stripper and she could be the bartender then, and she said that wasn't any better. My suggestion that we'd met at a nudist colony she totally scrapped.

Maggie insisted we keep our story as simple and close to reality as possible. "They've done a background check on us both, so they know all about us . . ."

"Well, not all," I had said making a face.

"Which is why we have to get our story straight and make it sound right," Maggie insisted. I think I was on my fifth or sixth beer that night, so I rolled my eyes, belched, and said, "They know that you write books about paranormal activity and such, and if they've read your book, they're going to figure out that I'm the 'medium' that you used, since you used my 'real' name. That was fucking brilliant by the way. Have I ever told you that?"

"About a million times. It seemed like a great idea at the time since no one you know knows that's your name, but of course in retrospect their background check no doubt uncovered that . . . Listen, it's not a problem, I'm going to ask that they not disclose what we do on the air or to the other contestants . . ."

"And we all know that TV execs, like lawyers, are people of high integrity. Everyone already knows that you're a weirdo writer chick, but so far the whole world doesn't know I'm a fucking psychic nut job, and for some reason I'd like to keep it that way. I can just see the little bar under my picture every time the camera's on me, *Vivian Storm AKA Lilly Rose Psychic Detective,* or some damn thing."

"Quit being so negative. Think about getting away from all this cold and bad weather . . ."

"Maggie, it's the end of July in South Carolina," I said in disbelief.

She smiled. "It can sometimes be cold. Think about being in Cancun, the beautiful tropical breezes, scantily dressed women parading up and down white sand beaches . . ."

"While we're stuck on the dreaded Island of Death." I downed the rest of the beer I was holding. "Here's a happy thought. Maybe they haven't finished their little background check. Maybe they'll figure out who we are and we won't be going at all."

"In the computer age a background check takes about five minutes. They know who and what we are, and they still chose us."

"Or maybe it's the reason they chose us from all of the thousands of applicants. Maybe they picked us because it couldn't hurt to have the woman who wrote a best-selling novel about spooks and her psychic girlfriend on their reality horror show."

"Maybe." She shrugged. She wasn't actually listening to me. All her focus was on going to the island. "So, at any rate we have to have our story straight . . ."

"Or not so straight as the case may be," I teased. Maggie gave me a dirty look. I think she realized then that I was more interested in drinking another beer than working on our cover story.

"Could we get serious for a minute?"

I nodded and then asked a question that said no. "So, Maggie, are you the top or the bottom?"

At any rate I *was* mostly drunk and not paying attention the night Maggie decided where our love had first bloomed and what sort of a relationship we had, so maybe it was a good thing she had gone over it again in the plane, even if it was mixed with all the facts about the cursed Island of Death, and it was probably really good that she reminded me again as we were walking out of the plane.

"Now remember, Viv. We met at a crime scene; you're a sketch artist who occasionally works with the police. My husband had just died. The kids were both gone. I was feeling abandoned in the world, lonely and vulnerable . . ."

"Wait a minute." I stopped in mid aisle and grabbed her so that she had to stop, too. This of course caused people to bitch, as they had to work their way around us. "Our cover story is that I took advantage of you in a moment of weakness?"

"No, no! You helped me through a really hard time, one thing led to another, and before either of us knew what had happened we had fallen in love. I'm guessing I'm just one of those bisexuals that falls in love with the person, not their gender. We've been together three years, my daughter approves, but my son really doesn't, and his wife is completely upset about the whole thing. We still keep separate residences because of these conflicts, but hope to live together soon."

I grinned and started walking again. "So . . . do we do it a lot?"

Maggie sighed, "Would it make you happy to say so?"

"Yes, yes it would. If I'm going to be banging an older broad with a homophobic son who runs her life, I at the very least want to be getting it a lot."

"Very well then, we go at it like rabbits . . ."

"Whoa! Rabbits do it in about three seconds. Have you got a lot to learn about lesbian sex! A quickie lasts forty-five minutes."

"You're kidding," Maggie said.

I shook my head no.

"Then if we're doing it a lot, how do we ever get anything else done?"

I just smiled and shrugged.

There was a guy in formal limo driver attire standing with a sign that said Vivian Storm and Margaret Holmes. He was a nice-looking Hispanic man, short with an easy smile and dark brown eyes, and when I saw him and the camera crew behind him my blood ran cold because I knew there was no turning back.

It was a suite in the rather lavish hotel Whatsit the network had booked us into. The producer Raymond Kennedy—who I called Dead President Guy—was there, and so was "The Relative." *His* name was Franklin Knight, but until I could remember his name I just called him "The Relative," because that's what he was—one of the heirs to the Garret Knight estate. Which of course put him right away on Maggie's shit list, because he was one of the assholes who wanted her to spend a small fortune to research the island.

I knew as I was shaking the guy's hand and Kennedy was introducing him just what this meant. He knew who Maggie was. When he gave me that knowing smile, the one that people always give me when they learn of my "abilities"—you know, the "humor the flake because she might be dangerous" look—I knew that he knew exactly who I was, too.

I immediately found the need to get back at Maggie, so when Kennedy said as he was taking a seat in one of the huge armchairs, "So, how long did you say you'd been together?" I answered, "Three glorious years," and sat next to Maggie damn near in her lap as she was sitting down on the couch. I wrapped my arms around her neck and planted a big wet one on her cheek. Maggie flinched and turned bright red. I smiled at Kennedy and then looked at Knight and winked. "She keeps me busy, if ya know what I mean. Ain't that just the way it is with the quiet ones? They surprise you in the sack every time."

Kennedy smiled that "oh we've picked a winner" smile, and you could almost hear the cash register bells going off in his head. He set the briefcase he'd had in his hand in his lap and opened it, and then he took out a paper and pretended to read it. I knew damn good and well that he had way too much invested in this project not to have had all that shit memorized by now.

"And you work in a bar, Ms. Storm?" he asked.

"Yes, and I work with the police department as a sketch artist. Every once in a while I do a portrait, but mostly Maggie supports me."

Maggie had her hand down by my leg out of sight of the two men, and she pinched the living shit out of me. I'm guessing she'd wished she hadn't when I jumped up rubbing the wound and yelled, "What did you do that for!"

Kennedy was a very happy little producer, no doubt sure that we'd help make his show a hit.

"So, have either of you watched *Chicken Out* before?" he asked.

I never had. Maggie had told me all about it, but I declined her offer to watch them on tape. I mean if you were me, would you want to watch anything that had to do with dead people?

"I have, but Vivian won't watch the show," Maggie said honestly.

"Why not?" Kennedy asked.

I shrugged and didn't say a word. I figured he knew.

He looked a little perplexed by my sudden silence, so I pretended to be looking down Maggie's shirt and was smiling lecherously. It was fun to watch her squirm.

He cleared his throat. "All right, then let me tell you a little something about *Chicken Out.*"

"Shoot," I said, turning to give him my full attention.

"We've done three other shows. Each one in some supposedly haunted place. The Tower of London, Winchester Mansion, and the château in New Orleans"—you know the one that's supposed to be haunted where the famous voodoo queen lived—I can't remember either her name or the château's name, was her name Marie La Beau? It doesn't matter—anyway, he says, "The object of the game is to outstay the other couples . . ."

"Why couples?" I asked.

"What?"

"Why couples? Why not singles, or brothers and sisters, or mothers and sons? Why couples?" Maggie gave me a look that said she'd wondered the same thing.

"A psychiatrist suggested that people would be more willing to fight their personal fears if they were with a loved one . . ."

"And a parent is too protective of a child, a sibling too protective of a younger sibling. You aren't protective enough of a friend, and they might not give you the moral support you need." That was Maggie thinking out loud which she did almost as much as I did. "There is a dynamic between people who are intimate."

"They make a better show," I said with my usual cynicism. They did it because it made a better show, no deeper reason. This whole thing was about ratings. What was going to get them the best ratings, and nothing else mattered. Maggie was right. There was a certain dynamic between people who screwed, and it was different in every couple. A dozen scenarios played out in my head using my friends that were couples as examples thrown into our situation. They would fight, they'd screw, and they'd gang up on other couples. Everything I could think of made for great TV.

"Well, that is what it's all about, Ms. Storm," he said. I didn't tell him he could call me Vivian, which seemed to annoy him, so I was happy. "In the past it's just been a waiting game to see who could stay in the haunted place the longest. We had all the footage, and then we cut and pasted it and turned it into sixteen shows. This time we're going to be doing something a little different. First there will be no camera crew on the island. Cameras have been set up all over the island and throughout the house and outbuildings. They are battery run and motion activated. There is no satellite feed. We won't see the tapes until you're all off the island and we can retrieve them from the cameras. You'll be on your own with no contact with the rest of the world. There will be the eight contestants, four couples . . ." Apparently he thought we couldn't do the math. ". . . two cooks who will prepare all your meals, make sure necessary toiletries are restocked, the generator is refueled and things like that. And Mr. Knight will be there to answer any questions you might have about the place."

I was pretty sure that Maggie knew more about the damn island than Knight, and that his main job was going to be to try to scare the hell out of the rest of us.

"You will be given no linens. You will have to pick your sleeping quarters from the rooms and beds available. Except for your meals and the stocking of the bathrooms, you will be left to fend for yourselves with the gear you've carried with you . . ."

"There will be eleven of us. Just like there were eleven people at each of the other massacres." That was Maggie again. I guessed maybe Kennedy wouldn't be so quick to debase our math skills in the future. "That's why there will be no camera crew. You want there to be exactly as many of us as there were of them."

"Precisely," he said.

"That's sort of creepy," I said.

"Well, that *is* the idea, Ms. Storm. Not thinking of chickening out already, are you?" He was smiling a condescending smile.

"I'm not afraid of the dead," I said.

"I shouldn't think you would be." That was Knight, and he was giving me "the look" again. I decided I was going to find a reason to kick his ass just as soon as we got to the dreaded Island of Death. He was making fun of me. I could read it in his features, hear it in his voice, he thought I was a fake, a phony at best. At worst he thought I was some hapless flake.

Maggie patted my back in a calming way, which shows how well she knows me. She looked at Kennedy. "I'm assuming you both know about my book and about Vivian's gift."

Kennedy nodded. "Well of course."

"I don't see any reason for the other contestants, or the general public for that matter, to know. Do you?"

"Neither myself or Mr. Knight will tell the other contestants; it might give them an edge, but it will be part of the show. It's just too big a bonus."

I sighed, resolved. We'd already signed the fucking contract—the one that I had begged Maggie to reconsider when I read it. I'd had just enough law school to know when I saw an ironclad contract, the kind you should never sign. Ones with clauses like, *neither my heirs nor I will hold the producers of the Chicken Out show or LYNX Network responsible in case of my injury, death or dismemberment.*

The whole world was going to know that I was a "flake," because no one ever believed that my "gift" was real until they saw for themselves, and the truth was I didn't blame them.

I got up and started pacing back and forth. "Well, this is fucking beautiful," I mumbled.

"There are two other slight changes from our normal routine," he said in a voice that said *shut up so I can finish what I want to say.* "You will leave for the island tomorrow. On the boat going to the island you will meet the rest of the cast. There will be three cameramen on board to film that. You will spend five days on the island, and whatever couple is still there on August twelfth will win the million dollars."

"Wait a minute," I said, stopping my pacing and looking at him. "What if there is more than one couple still on the island?"

"Then the million dollars will be split evenly among all the remaining contestants."

And that would be the clause in the contract about us agreeing that we understood that the rules of *Chicken Out* were determined by the producer.

So now I was going to the Island of Death, the home of the curse of the great God Caca Poopoo, and there was a very good chance that I wasn't even going to make a half a million bucks. This was starting to really suck.

"I really don't think you have to worry too much about more than one couple staying. I have to say that I'd be very surprised if any of you make it to the twelfth. In fact, I'm just hoping we get enough footage for our sixteen shows. Now, if either of you decides to leave, the other is ineligible. The only way around this is if one of you is dead."

I laughed then because he just sounded ludicrous. He was trying to scare us—me and Maggie! It was ridiculous, and I had the need to tell him so. "Let me tell you something, Dead President Guy." Maggie cringed at the tone of my voice and my use of my made-up name for him. "I have witnessed first hand a hundred brutal crimes. Maggie's a forensic pathologist, for Christ's sake. Do you really think you're going to scare us off with innuendos and a few parlor tricks?"

He ignored me as if I'd said nothing and turned all his attention on Maggie. "The house is fully equipped with all the latest ghost-busting equipment. Radical splitometors and laser transit-whatsits and frankincense and myrrh. All at your disposal. Of course any one of the contestants can use the equipment, however I doubt any of them will want to, much less be able to follow the rather simple instructions."

He was telling us that they were all stupider than at least Maggie was, which made me wonder what he was telling them about us.

"There will be four small motorized boats at the docks. At any time that you wish to leave, you can. Until then you will be completely and totally cut off from the mainland, no cell phones, no radios, no TV . . ."

"Not a single luxury," I sang and even the cameramen gave me a dirty look, I just shrugged.

Dead President Guy mostly ignored me. "As I said, the cameras are not linked to us here. Once you are there you will have to survive on your own wits, alone with no help from the outside world. Of course, any time you want to leave all you have to do is get in your boat and head for shore. You can see the mainland from the island, so it's a no-brainer."

"You're just going to put us there and let us go?" I was skeptical. "No direction, no contact? No trying to scare the shit out of us?"

"It's really not necessary on Knight's Island," he said with a smile. "This show will literally shoot itself."

"What if we all sit around for a week playing pinochle and eating peanut butter and jelly sandwiches?"

He smiled again. I did not like this guy's smile. "I don't think I have to worry about that."

He talked for another hour, and I'm sure some of it was important, but I wasn't really listening. I just wanted to get to the island and have the whole ordeal over with. As he, the camera crew and Knight—I never did figure out why it was necessary for him to be in on this meeting—were leaving, I walked to the window and looked down. I could just make out some scantily dressed women frolicking in the surf some three stories below me. As soon as those idiots in the monkey suits left I was going to go down there and see if I could catch me a little action.

"And remember, you aren't allowed to leave this room till we come for you tomorrow morning," Kennedy said and the door closed behind him.

I looked at Maggie. "Fuck that," I said and headed for the door.

I could see the protest forming on Maggie's lips as I opened the door and found two big-assed guards standing there. They glared at me, and I glared right back and closed the door.

"Well shit." I flopped onto the couch and looked dejected. "This whole thing reeks, Maggie. I could be home tending bar, hanging out. We've got a softball game this weekend. Everyone was pissed because that sissy Jack can't pitch worth a shit in those damn fake fingernails, and they know we'll lose the game. We should have been able to stomp those Big Ole Queens' butts."

"Do you really think you should be calling them that?" Maggie asked going over the map of the house Kennedy had given her.

"That's the name of their friggin' team, Maggie, not a derogatory statement."

"These are the spots the camera doesn't hit," Maggie said, handing me the map.

I almost looked at it. "Yeah, so?"

"So, he said he was telling us where they were because he knows that people can get nuts if they think they're being watched all the time."

"Yeah, so?" I said again. I was feeling really restless, almost claustrophobic. I didn't like being told I couldn't leave my room.

"So, do you notice anything funny?" she asked me.

I looked at it quickly and then handed it back to her with a shrug.

She sighed. "You could at least try to act interested. All these spots are cold spots. With all the murder and mayhem that's taken place in this house none of these spots, not a single one, is a hot spot."

"So?"

"So he's herding us into areas where there is less residual bad energy. Why do you suppose that is?"

"Maybe it's as simple as he doesn't care if we're off camera if we aren't in a spooky spot." I shrugged. I didn't know why she was making such a big deal out of it. I handed her the map back and walked over to my fanny pack—the dyke's best friend—and started digging around for my cigarettes.

"This is a no smoking room," Maggie said.

"So I'll smoke on the veranda," I said, pointing in its direction. I couldn't find the open pack I'd put there at the airport. I thought maybe I'd left it somewhere, so I walked over to my backpack that I'd carefully packed a whole carton in. The fact that they were gone, too, along with Maggie's silence, let me know just exactly what had happened. "God damn it, Maggie!"

"Now, Viv, you said you wanted to quit."

"I do, Maggie, but not *now!* Not when we're going to the wretched Island of Death with a bunch of strangers to poke and prod the energy of mutilation victims. Not with Dead President Guy locking us in our rooms where I can look at all the candy but I can't have any!"

I flopped hard in a chair and glared at her. "Isn't it enough that you've drug me along with you to hell without you taking my fucking smokes!"

"I'm sorry," she said.

But she wasn't. I went to the door and opened it again. I looked at the guards and smiled my best smile, even though they were glaring at me. "Are either of you guys married?"

"I am," the guy on the right said.

"Your old lady drive you fucking nuts?"

He smiled. "Sometimes."

"Good. Then strike a blow against household tyranny. Be a buddy and go get me a carton of smokes."

He looked at the other guy, who nodded that he thought it

would be all right, and I gave the guy twenty dollars.

"What brand?" he asked.

"Something smelly and horribly carcinogenic in a white wrapper, no filter," I said, turning to glare at Maggie who was ignoring me.

Ah, the boat ride! Beautiful white beaches, bright blue water, and seven people that I wouldn't have chosen to be in the same room with, let alone stuck on an island with.

Maggie and I had talked about it the night before; Kennedy was trying to re-create a horror movie feeling. Eleven people stranded on a cursed island with no contact with the outside world. An atmosphere created to terrify. I think Agatha Christie wrote the book.

There was the blond-haired, blue-eyed, perfect-teeth, perfect-hair couple with the combined common sense of an electric toothbrush. They were from that rare group of people that have never had any real shit fall on their heads. They got everything they ever wanted—including each other—and so they spent all their spare time doing things that were "dangerous and daring." In the first five minutes we knew them they told us about their skiing, skydiving, and white-water rafting trips. For fun I think they ate crushed glass and worked out three times a week. I called them Ken and Barbie, and still couldn't tell you what their real names were.

There was the strip-club bouncer, John Baker, and his girlfriend, a want-to-be model named Harmony Tune. I was thinking her name was just as made up as mine, and the only modeling she was doing was nude. She had the IQ of your regular garden-variety turnip, and wore at least a dee-cup bra—and I don't care what Maggie said, her boobs were real. John didn't talk much, and when he did it was to tell us all how unafraid he was and how he hoped we all knew what it was like to be losers. I called them Mug and Jugs.

Then there were the Wymans. I remembered their name right off because I remember just looking at them and thinking, "Oh, why, man?" They were covered in talismans and crystals, and each was a good twenty pounds overweight; if they bathed once a week that was a lot. I could tell they had cats way before they showed us the pictures of their twelve "babies" because they smelled of cat piss and everything they owned was covered in a layer of cat hair—including the clothes they were wearing. They made my skin crawl. I don't like filth. They kept calling on the mystical power of the goddess to protect them, all of us, in fact, which I thought was sort of nice considering we were all trying to win the same million dollars. Of course they said their true purpose was to try and put the restless spirits to sleep.

Male Wyman—At least I think it was the male. It was hard to tell them apart from behind—got into a discussion with Maggie in a hushed whisper, which I was sure pissed the cameramen off royally. Wyman kept looking up at me and giving me an awed look, and I realized that Maggie and I had already been made.

Damn photos on book jackets, hers of course, mine wasn't on there, but once they'd figured Maggie out it was a given who I was if they'd read her book. No doubt he had, and he already knew who and what I was. Which did nothing to endear him to me. He was exactly the sort of people that made people like me look bad. Idiots who ran around pretending to wield a power they couldn't even begin to understand.

"Well, there it is. The Island of Blood, the natives called it. We all know it as Knight's Island," the Relative was saying as the boat slowed coming to the tattered dock.

I looked up. The island was badly overgrown, but even through the jungle growth I could see the huge house staring at us from broken windows.

"Home to two brutal massacres separated by twenty years.

Forty years ago the first murders took place. Twenty years ago my late and troubled great-uncle repeated the pattern of death and destruction. It is said that the ghosts of all the dead still haunt this island." He looked right at me, as he said it just as the boat docked, "Let's all see what the dead have to say, shall we, Ms. Storm?"

As I was getting off the boat I punched that bastard right in the face.

CHAPTER FIVE:
MAGGIE

Whether it was the ultra-feminine scream or the belly-flop splash that alerted me to the disaster, I cannot say. My conversation with the rather repulsive Mr. Ned Wyman had left me cold and angry inside, to have been "spotted" like that barely into our adventure. I had hoped to keep my career, and thus Vivian's gift, a secret. If the rest of them knew, they were likely to get right in my way, and ruin my chances of getting any real research done. Not to mention how mad Vivian got when people knew.

Fat chance of keeping the secret now, I'd fumed to myself. The urge to plant one of my fists in Ned's flubbery lips—or tell him a new way to wear those crystals—was strong. So rather than give in to a base urge, I stepped away and looked out over the ocean. That was when all hell broke loose to my back. I turned in time to see Vivian advancing onto the dock, living up to her last name, and the rest of the guests rushing to the side of the vessel and pointing to the water.

Naturally, I had to go see for myself what had happened. Knight was in the chest-deep water, sputtering and shaking his head. His nose was bleeding, turning the white silk suit he wore crimson.

Oh, thank you, Vivian, I thought. *Add insult to injury.* Or vice versa was more likely in this case. I snatched up my rucksack and charged down the plank to catch up with her. Not easy since she has the long stride of a giraffe, and I look something like a hedgehog trying to keep up, but I did manage to snag her arm.

She jerked around, a cobra ready to strike until she saw that it was me. The startled outrage gave way to a genuinely wicked smile.

"What was that all about?" I demanded.

"Nothing," she said and shrugged. "He . . . made a pass at me."

"Oh, I really believe that," I said.

"Okay, so the bastard was getting on my nerves," Vivian shot back. "He deserved it."

Somehow, I couldn't help but agree, but with all that had happened in the last twenty-four hours, I wasn't about to let this pass. I took a deep breath, trying to restore the last vestige of my own calm. "I can't take you anywhere, can I?"

Vivian blinked, then laughed. "No, *Mom*," she said. "Guess you can't."

"You are incorrigible!" I said, letting my anger swell. "You went out of your way to embarrass me back there in the hotel. You broke every rule just to spite me, and now you could very well get us thrown out of this contest."

"Like that would be the end of the world?" Vivian said. "I'm not here because I want to be, remember?"

"Look, you know how important this is to me."

"Yeah, yeah," Vivian said. "So important, you drag my ass here without my permission and drop me on a fuckin' island that is already giving me the creeps . . ." She trailed off and glanced over my shoulder back toward the boat. I turned, curious to see what had her attention. They had hauled Knight out of the water and were throwing a blanket about his shoulders. "She hit me!" he spluttered. "I can't believe she hit me!" Several of the Mexican crew were tossing luggage on the creaking boards of the dock. Not one of the men on the boat showed any inclination to step onto land. In fact, there was something frenzied about the way they were unloading the rest of the passengers and the two servants. The latter pair cast about with unease.

"Something is not right here," Vivian said.

I held back a remark about understatements. Besides, Ned and his wife Astaria started in our direction now. They passed us, wearing Cheshire smiles, and I bit my tongue and looked away.

"He knows who we are, doesn't he?" Vivian said.

I sighed again. "Yes."

"Well, that's just fucking great," Vivian said, "your cover is as good as blown. First Knight and the producer, and now those two fruitcakes, why don't we just erect a billboard with your bio and picture while we're at it, and tell everyone I'm a freak?"

"Maybe not," I said, trying not to grind my teeth in frustration. "He said he wouldn't tell . . ."

"Right, and pigs *do* fly . . ."

"Hey, be careful!" That was Harmony Tune. She was trying to grapple for a duffle bag that one of the Mexicans was about to pitch toward the dock. "I'll carry that myself!" she said.

The man either didn't understand her or was good at pretending that he didn't understand. With a shrug, he threw the duffle over the rail, and Harmony tried in vain to catch it, and missed. She squeaked in outrage. It landed with a heavy clank, followed by what sounded like a whirring vibration. Harmony's eyes went bug wide. Her face flushed a bright shade of pink that blushed right to the roots.

"Hot damn, she's got the right equipment," Vivian said.

I came very close to reaching over and slapping her for being impertinent. Then again, knowing Vivian, she might actually like that, and it would have only given her another opportunity to embarrass me. Besides, Harmony was sobbing like a three-year-old whose pet butterfly had fled. Even her boyfriend looked a little uneasy. He coaxed her onto the dock, making consoling noises.

"Come on," I said. "Let's go claim a room."

"Sure—as long as it's back in that hotel in Cancun . . ."

She had hardly said it, though, when the boat's motor revved and it shot away from the dock. The last thing we saw was the cameraman leaning over the rail, shooting our reactions as he rode across the waves back to the mainland.

The hotel was not in the best of conditions. The cooks kept trading looks and occasionally whispering to one another in Spanish. I had tried to follow some of the conversation—I spoke Spanish—but they were keeping their voices low. About all I could make out were references to Xipe Totec, whom the Aztecs had called The Flayed Lord, a god who demanded the sacrifices of blood, skin and hearts, and something about Knight.

As to Knight, he entered the hotel and stood in the lobby, a pool of water forming at his feet. The blanket about his shoulders made him look like some mad inventor. He cast his gaze on the rest of us as we entered. He tossed a surly look at Vivian as she finally walked in and moved to stand by me.

"She hit me," he said peevishly pointing at Vivian.

"We know," Harmony said and rolled her eyes.

Knight took a deep breath, unable to hide his outrage as he looked at all of us once more. Wiping the stream of blood on the blanket, he straightened himself up and pretended to be dignified again.

"This was Casa Knight," he said. "You'll find that the rooms on the second floor are in reasonable condition, but for safety's sake, test the floors before you claim one. Wouldn't want any of you to meet with an . . . unwanted accident before things get underway." I noticed that his glance slid over Vivian as though he hoped she *would* meet with some sort of accident.

"Depends on what you mean by *unwanted*," Vivian said.

I pursed my lips and resisted the urge to tell her to can it.

"Well, of course, I mean it would be tragic if someone fell through the floor or tripped on the old stairs," he said in a rueful manner. "Just be careful."

"Fat lot he cares," Vivian muttered to me. "After all, they made us sign those waivers that won't let us sue his fancy ass off."

"Now, you all know the rules," Knight continued as he regained some of his composure. "Go forth and find your rooms. The staff will start preparing the evening meal."

He looked pointedly at the cooks who traded looks, then hurried away. I swear, I have never seen two people who could look so unhappy to be where they were at the moment—well, aside from Vivian who was pitching glances every which way.

Harmony and John went first, lugging their heavy duffle bags. The Wymans were standing together, holding hands, and I swear I heard them chanting softly under their mutual breaths. As for Mr. and Mrs. Maxwell—I heard Vivian refer to them as Ken and Barbie, but their real names were Winston and Jolene, and they both had European accents—they hauled out of the main room to find a place to exercise before the meal.

That left Vivian and myself facing Knight, whose smile would have made me nervous were it not for the water damage that had turned his hair askew, and undone his comb-over. He was clearly balding on top.

"Well, Ms. Storm?" Knight said.

"It's got . . . charm," she said, glancing around. "Come on, Maggie, let's see if they have a queen-sized bed . . ."

I stared hard at her for a moment. She knew perfectly well there were no beds, but there was an antsiness to her nature that made me follow her lead and head for the stairs. Besides, I could see Ned was watching me, and his looks were more unnerving than Knight's sick smile.

It took Vivian nearly twenty minutes to pick a room. Not that she was happy with any of them, and I can't say as I blame her. Clearly, the deserted areas were in need of cleaning. And then there were the cameras set up here and there. One got used to the click and whir of them when one worked in a police station, since there were security cameras in certain places. Vivian could not resist tossing the finger at each one as we passed it. I suspect the producers are going to be doing a lot of pixilating on this show. At least she wasn't mooning them.

Yet.

We were in the last hall when Vivian stepped up to an open door and then backed into me so fast I thought she was being attacked. I managed to catch my balance, though not before crossing half the corridor in a drunken dance.

"Don't follow me so close next time," Vivian growled.

"I won't," I said. Her face was whiter than the chalky adobe plaster that coated the inner walls. Slipping past her, I glanced into the room she had been so eager to flee. The walls were stained dark with great gouts, and though the color had faded to a thin gray-brown, I knew it had to be blood.

"Yeah, this is one of the hot spots," I said, wishing I had taken time to find out where the spectrometers and other equipment were being kept. There had to be a ton of spectral energy in this room.

"Too hot," Vivian said. She was already halfway down the hall. "Damn, doesn't anyone ever clean this place?"

"No one—except the workmen who got the kitchen and

bathrooms working and installed the cameras—has been here since . . ."

"I know, I know." Vivian stopped in the hall, hands on hips, a lanky fire-haired Amazon in shorts. "Well, this is about the best one I see," she said, and gestured to a doorway at the right end of the hall. "But I'll be damned if I'm going in there first."

Shuffling through my rucksack, I hauled out the maps. "Well, that corner doesn't seem to be connected to any of the deaths," I said.

Vivian grunted and held her place. I walked down the hall and stopped in the doorway, peering through.

The room was actually quite sunny, and a bit cleaner than most. No furniture, though. Just a balcony that overlooked the beach on down the way. And some once-white lattice panels that looked like they might have been winter shutters for the windows and doors. They leaned against the wall, bearing a patina of dust like everything else.

I walked on into the room, and the walls suddenly moved, undulating in masses of gold, blue and red. Startled, I froze, thinking that perhaps the old building was about to shift. One never knew. Tropical heat and storms could have weakened the structure.

"What the . . . ?" Vivian had stayed out in the corridor, and seeing my sudden stop, she froze, too.

I slowly turned so I could see better. Took me half a moment to realize what the moving mass was, and I laughed with relief.

"What?" Vivian said, still not coming in.

"Geckos," I said. "They're just geckos."

"Do they have germs?" she asked.

"Only if they bite you."

"Fuck, they bite?"

"Well, the big ones do," I said. "And bark."

"Swell," she groused. "Barking, germy lizards, and dead

people, and . . . get them out of the room! I am not sleeping in a room full of barking, germy lizards!"

"Oh, come on, Viv, these are just little ones," I said. Though in truth, I had never seen such a large colony of them. They were beautiful. As I watched, they migrated for every imaginable opening and vanished, leaving the plain walls in their wake. "And anyway, geckos eat spiders and roaches . . ."

"Oh, God, there are roaches in here?"

"Vivian, we're close to the equator. There are roaches and spiders the size of . . ."

"I don't need to know that," Vivian said, waving her hands and glancing back and forth. "But if the geckos eat them, that's okay. I just don't want to know about it."

"Okay," I said and set my bags down. "This is it, then."

"Yeah," she said, venturing in slowly. "This is it. Don't suppose those natives have a dust pan and a broom, do you?"

I rolled my eyes.

Vivian insisted on sweeping the place, so I sat out on the balcony to stay out of her way and got my bearings, comparing my notes to the landscape. If I was reading everything right, we were in the wing that the Knight family had not used because it was where the original hotel murders occurred. That meant there would likely be a lot more spirit activity to deal with.

Vivian had calmed down, and I suspected it was the chore of cleaning our little space that kept her from fretting. I knew she was feeling things. Now and again, she would stop and glance over her shoulder as though something were there. Then she'd take a deep breath and dive back into the domestic chores. She should have gotten herself a job as a housekeeper. I know a number of wealthy homeowners who would be pleased to have her in once a month. But knowing Vivian, she'd get caught smoking in the bathroom or helping herself to the bar or their daughter.

At one point I got tired of the dust she was stirring up and went downstairs to sit on the veranda, or what was left of it.

I went back to the room just as she was finishing up and the sun was angling toward the horizon. My stomach was reminding me that we had not eaten since before boarding the boat. Since Vivian and I knew how to pack light, we had already carted our luggage up earlier. The Maxwells decided to do everyone else the courtesy—for exercise, they claimed. Vivian muttered that they probably went through everyone's luggage to see if they could sabotage anything. I reminded her that her clothes already looked like they had been sabotaged. She snorted and went back to her sweeping.

But now she was through, and the room had a certain order in the way she had placed the sleeping bags and set up candles. I came back inside and noticed she had managed to set us in the center of the room.

"Any reason?" I asked.

"If anything comes crawling at me, I want to see it first," she said. "Besides, this also lets us see the door and the balcony at the same time."

"I like the candles," I said.

"Yeah, well . . . All this work has made me hungry and thirsty. Do you suppose they have anything on the order of a meal ready?"

I shrugged. "Only one way to find out."

It was getting dark outside. The air had that tropical musky odor, palm and sand, and warm winds, and brine laced with a hint of local flowers. I could have stood there and enjoyed the scent, but Vivian was right. Food was a mere memory in my stomach. Besides, I wanted to see how the rest of the guest had fared.

We took flashlights so we could find our way. While there were candles and occasional lights in all the areas where cameras had been set up, there was an eerie darkness in the sections that had been left bare of video eyes. With the occasional pieces of broken furniture, flashlights were a necessity.

Again, Vivian would glance suddenly around as though something had her attention. "I hate this place," she muttered, and to prove her dislike, she walked up to one of the cameras and this time she did moon it.

I suspect there is going to be a lot of editing of tape before this is over.

At any rate, we found our way back down to the area Knight had designated as the "dining room." Ned and Astaria were already there, and Mrs. Maxwell had stationed her sleek, muscular frame in the opposite end of the room. Of Harmony and her hunk, there was no sign.

Knight was absent as well.

At the sight of Vivian and me, Mrs. Maxwell—Jolene—waved. I tried not to notice that Ned and Astaria were watching me with that smug expression of theirs. If two people ever looked like escapees from Lewis Carroll, it was that pair. I could almost imagine them on mushrooms with hookahs.

"So," I said cheerfully to Jolene in hopes that the Wymans would keep their distance. "Did you find a suitable room?"

"Oh, yes," she said, and I narrowed her accent down to Swedish. "Winston selected such a nice room with a large space for our equipment."

"Your equipment?" Vivian interrupted.

"Jah, we brought our gym with us," Jolene said. "We make videos, you know."

"Adult?" Vivian asked, and I wanted to kick her. Jolene merely blinked.

"Exercise," she said. "We have a show, Winston and I. We

thought it would be nice to make a tropical exercise video while we were here."

Hmmmmm, there had been nothing said by Knight and Kennedy that the Maxwells were in "the business." I saw Vivian quirk an eyebrow as though this had registered with her as well.

"Wonder where the chow is," Vivian said and looked around. "You'd think they'd at least have a bar. This was once a hotel."

Jolene shrugged. "I have not seen any of the servants."

Servants? "You mean the cooks?" I asked.

"Whatever," she said in a tired manner. "I must go see what is keeping Winston."

She pushed past us and made for the hall. Vivian and I traded looks.

"Let's go find the kitchen," Vivian said and, glanced around. "The Wymans are giving you creepy looks again."

I frowned, wishing that I wasn't such a law-abiding person who believed strongly in the sanctity of life. If I were ever to go nuts and go on a killing spree, the Wymans would certainly have been first on my list of victims. I followed Vivian into the hallway behind the dining area. The odor of food was strong. Something was burning.

Before I could comment on that, one of the cooks came charging at us, screaming in Spanish. I caught only a word or two because he was babbling insanely. We had to step out of his way.

"He said angel of death," I muttered.

"What?" Vivian quickened her pace. The two of us were practically running toward the kitchen. We ran in, skidding to a halt.

The room was filled with the odor of burnt enchiladas. I could smell the beans and the corn, the onions and meat.

But the smell was not what drew either my attention or Vivian's. We were both staring at the man bent forward, his face buried in what must have been an enchilada pie. It was smoking where it had laid on the griddle too long.

And the long handle of a Ginsu kitchen knife was protruding from between his shoulder blades.

Chapter Six:
Vivian

"So, I guess this means dinner's going to be a little late," I said to Maggie as I looked at the cook lying facedown in the enchiladas.

Maggie grabbed a towel off the counter, walked around and took hold of the knife.

"Well?" I asked, knowing full well what she was doing because my first instinct had also been to wonder if it was a fake, something done just to scare the hell out of us.

"It's real." She dropped the towel and moved her fingers to the man's throat. "And he's dead." She started spouting some medical garbage then. It sounded sort of like this, "The knife went between his number this and something that rib and struck his main ventricular bleedy thing, causing him to bleed out almost immediately." She looked thoughtful. "Of course I'd have to do an autopsy to be sure."

"So much for your whole 'the dead can't hurt us' theory," I whispered.

"Vivian, you know a ghost didn't do this," Maggie said in a scolding tone.

"Gee, really, Maggie? Good thing yer a scientist, or we never would have figured that out," I spat back sarcastically. "There's a fucking killer, a living, breathing murderer on this island with us."

I heard a commotion at my back and turned to see the entire rest of the "cast" standing there, no doubt thinking what I'd be thinking if I'd caught them leaned over a body with a knife in it's back.

"What in God's good name!" Ken shouted.

Just then Knight was drug in by the remaining cook. Knight was out of breath and as white as a sheet, although it would be hard to know whether that was because of the news of the death or the spectacular bleeding nose I'd given him earlier in the day, which I don't care what Maggie says, he had comin'.

"Oh my God," Knight said he looked at Maggie. "Is he . . ."

"Yes, he is," Maggie said.

"Who, why?" Ms. Wyman said. "Juan was such a gentle soul."

All right, his name wasn't Juan, but he reminded me of the guy from the coffee commercials.

"You knew him?" Maggie asked suspiciously.

"I'd just met him, but," she turned to look at me. "You know how it is when you have the power . . . You just *know*."

"Actually, I wouldn't have a fucking clue." I ignored her and turned my attention to Maggie. "So . . . do you suppose it would be all right to take him out of the enchiladas?"

Maggie looked up and spotted the camera in the room, then nodded, no doubt deciding that the crime scene had been well documented. I moved around and helped Maggie move the corpse off of and away from the stove and our ruined dinner. I looked at her and she read my mind.

"Put him on his stomach."

We did, and when we stood up I noticed that Jugs was crying and clinging to Mug—who just looked put out. The Wymans were chanting. Ken and Barbie where consoling each other as Knight looked ready to puke, and the remaining cook looked like he was ready to swim off the island that very minute if he had to.

"How long you suppose he's been dead?" I asked Maggie.

Maggie looked at the burn on the side of the guy's face and

back at the smoldering enchiladas—it was a real shame they got ruined. They smelled really good—"Not more than thirty minutes. Was there any sign of a struggle?" she asked, looking at me with meaning. I hadn't found the hot spot yet, so I knew he hadn't been killed at the stove. He had been killed somewhere else and put there, which pissed me off no end because it meant someone had purposely ruined dinner. I looked around quickly and found drops of blood on the floor that looked as if they'd been smeared. I followed this trail—with my eyes—to a puddle of blood in the corner. Around it were the same smears. I realized that this spot was almost totally, if not completely, out of camera range.

"Over there," I said, pointing. Maggie gave me a look. Seeing that I was in no hurry to move, she also knew I was purposely blocking. I had been ever since we'd landed on the island. It was the only way I was going to be able to stay on this island for seven days without going ape-shit crazy. Even with the blocking I could feel the energy pulling at the corners of my mind. I was in no hurry to drop that guard now.

I realized then that everyone but Knight was looking at Maggie and me as if we were from another planet. I wondered if I'd gotten enchilada sauce or blood on my shirt, and I looked down to see as Maggie said, "Ah . . . I'm a forensic pathologist, and Vivian is a police sketch artist, so . . . Well, we're as used to this sort of thing as you can ever actually be."

"One of you is a murderer," John said.

I started to protest. "Now hold up there, Mug, we just found the body . . ."

"I didn't mean you and the other dyke. I meant all of you."

"Yeah, well where the fuck were you?" I asked hotly. Homophobic prick! If he wasn't bigger and stronger than me I would have punched him like I did Knight. Now who says I have no sense of self-preservation?

Maggie ignored us both, instead asking the other cook something in Spanish. He spouted for nearly five minutes. When he was done Maggie nodded and got that thoughtful look she always got when she was on some case.

"Well?" I asked impatiently.

"Huh?"

"What did the little Spanish man say?" I asked.

"Oh . . . Jesus (no, his name wasn't actually Jesus, either, but that was the only other male Spanish name I knew) had started the meal when the generator went out. The generator is in a separate building that is apparently quite a ways away, so he left Juan in charge and went to see what was wrong with the generator. When he got there the generator had been turned off. So he restarted it and was on his way back when he got very tired so he sat down, he took a drink because his nerves were very on edge and he assumes he dozed off. But he couldn't have been gone more than forty-five minutes." Again she gave me that expectant look, at which point I gave her a *you've got to be kidding* look and tossed my head in the direction of the others.

"I can feel the negative energy in this corner," Female Wyman said, stepping over to the corner.

"Go figure," I said flippantly, "negative energy in a bloody corner." I sighed in a resolved way. What did it really matter what these bunch of coconuts thought of me? When this aired at home—and I had no doubt that they would air it in spite of the fact that their little show had cost a man his life—there was going to be that little bar every time my picture came on which would say *psychic hooha* or some damn thing.

I gave Maggie a dirty look. "All right, here goes." I dropped my shields and walked toward the corner. I didn't have to get all the way there. The cook had put up a fight, but against who? He was screaming something I couldn't understand, and all he was seeing was some shimmering outline. A human form concealed in . . . what? I couldn't be sure I was seeing anything at all. The form before me was twisted and distorted and seemed to change from one moment to the next. I knew what this meant, because it had happened to me before. The victim wasn't sure of what his attacker was or what he was looking at, so his mind was trying to fill in the gaps. What I was seeing hadn't been what Juan had seen with his eyes, but what he had seen with his mind. Then I felt his arm twist up and behind his back; he was forced against the wall and the knife drove into his heart and it exploded. Maggie was right. Death had come quickly.

I drug myself back to the living and found Maggie hanging on to my elbow.

"Viv?" she asked gently.

"He didn't see the killer," I said. "I saw shimmering images, nothing really solid, nothing I could pin a name on. The killer was strong."

Mug laughed then. "What sort of crap is this?"

I ignored him for the moment, too dazed to even get angry, and unfortunately too dazed to lift my shields. Maggie was helping to move me to a stool when I stepped on another hot spot—an older one, but one so brutal that it burned twice as brightly as the one before. I felt the victim, a young man with everything to live for, who knew he was about to die. I felt his terror as the madman with the pistol approached. He raised the arm and fired a dart of some kind—a tranquilizer of sorts. I felt as the fight left the body and sleep crept upon him only to awaken strapped to the huge butcher table where he had been slowly and painfully killed as the madman said over and over again, "All must pay, all who enter must pay."

When I woke up I was saying, "All who enter must pay." I found myself in a cold spot in the front room. Maggie was by my side and the others were just standing around gawking—except the cook, who was gone. I could see the fucking camera.

It's red light was showing that it was on, and if I'd had the strength or the fortitude I would have gotten up and thrown something at it.

This was it. I'd be labeled the biggest weenie in the world on national television. I'd never get laid again. Maybe I could move and change my name . . . again.

"You scared the living hell out of Jesus. He ran out of here screaming," Maggie said. "Are you all right?"

"What a stupid fucking question!" I spat back as I sat up. My head spun, and I had to lean forward and put my head in my hands.

"So . . . what did you see?" Maggie asked excitedly.

I sighed. I realized this was precisely why she had wanted to come to the Dreaded Island of Death, why she wanted me here, but I thought we had a more pressing matter at hand. "Maggie, someone's dead. We have to do something."

"I've got an idea. Why don't you split-tails head for the mainland and go tell the cops?" Mug said.

The game. This bastard still wanted to play the game.

"Hey, dumb fuck, someone's dead, and one of you killed him . . ." I started.

"I want to go. I just want to go!" Jugs cried.

"You ain't going nowhere, sugar. We're in this for the long haul."

"But, John . . ."

"No buts," Mug said.

"Someone has to go to the mainland and inform the authorities," Ken said.

"Then you go, Nazi boy, cause it ain't gonna be us," Mug said.

"We would willingly forfeit our right to the prize and leave, but our power is needed here to quiet the restless spirits," Male Wyman said.

"You couldn't hold a fart!" I bellowed. "We'll go, we'll be the first to 'Chicken Out.' Screw the game, people. Dead people can't spend money . . ."

"No we won't," Maggie said sternly. "We aren't going anywhere."

"Maggie . . . are you fucking nuts? Imaginary things that go bump in the night are one thing. But what we're up against here is a flesh and blood killer . . ."

"What about what happened to you? What about what you saw, or failed to see?" Male Wyman demanded.

"I ain't communicating with the restless dead. I'm seeing trace energy . . ." It was clear by the looks on both Wymans' faces that I was wasting logic on them. "At any rate I was all for dealing with the dead, but I ain't into staying on the island with some living psycho killer."

"Did you see a flesh and blood killer, Ms. Storm?" Female Wyman asked.

"No, but . . ."

"The dead are taking their revenge on the living, and the only way to stop them is to put these spirits to sleep once and for all," Male Wyman said, and I think the fucking idiot was for real.

"We aren't going, Vivian," Maggie said sternly. "There is a million dollars at stake."

"I'm the one who needs the money, Maggie, not you. What about your kids, Maggie?"

"What about them?" She winked at me then. I had no idea at all what she was playing at, or why she would choose to stay on the island knowing there was a killer at large. "Knight is the only one with nothing to lose. He's the one who should go to the mainland."

It was agreed that Knight would go, but it was almost dark, he was a weenie, and we all wound up going down to the dock where the four little boats were supposed to be parked.

"What the fuck!" I said, running up to the edge of the water. There was just enough daylight left that I could make out three of the boats sitting on the bottom. The fourth was gone.

"Well, at least now we know who our murderer was. Jesus must have killed Juan. He came down here, fled in the one boat and sank the others so that we couldn't follow him to the mainland," Knight said.

I wanted off that island right then and there. I'm not a cringing coward, far from it. But I was sure that Jesus wasn't our killer, which meant someone was going to an awful lot of trouble to make it look like he was. A killer who premeditated a crime to this extent was too crazy to screw with.

Too many things didn't add up for me, but then I had a little more information than the rest of them. If Jesus was the killer, why wouldn't Juan have been able to identify his killer? Maggie must have known that, too, so I was wondering why on earth Maggie had seemed to suddenly lose the last shred of her brain. Was she being affected by some curse of the island, or did it have something to do with the onset of menopause? Could you blame menopause for crazy behavior the way I blame my PMS for every stupid thing I do and say?

I knew Maggie's kids were counting on me to protect her, and if I could get one of those boats up and running, I was getting her off the island if I had to carry her crazy ass kicking and screaming.

I kicked off my shoes and dove into the water. I swam over to the boats and then dove under. I felt more than saw that each boat had a hole in the bottom of it big enough to stuff a cat through, and the spark plug had been broken off in every motor. To me this was more proof that Jesus was not our perp, because unless I'd been out for hours—and I was sure I hadn't been because I never had been out for more than a few minutes before—there was just no way he had enough time to go running in supposed terror from the house and then take a hammer or a rock or whatever and do the damage to these boats. But if he hadn't run off, where was the fourth boat? I broke the surface of the water gasping for air.

I was wondering if we could get a boat to the surface, even with a hole in it. The boats were big and filled with water. They would be heavy even with the buoyancy of the water, but there was a hole and that should let the water run out. We could get a boat to the surface and patch it and use the spark plug from the generator to get a motor running—after we got it dried out of course.

It was dark, so it would be the next day before we could even think about it. I dove under again, hoping I could see a little better, but between the encroaching dark and the salt water stinging my eyes I couldn't see anything.

I came to the surface again to hear Maggie screaming, "Vivian, what on earth are you doing?"

I walked out of the water and said to no one in particular, "The boats have all been scuttled."

"Well, that's it then. We're all stuck." Knight was doing a good job of sounding scared shitless, and I wondered if somehow this—all of it—wasn't just part of some very elaborate gag.

"Well what now?" Barbie asked.

"I guess we get something to eat, choose up sides, and go to bed," Maggie said.

"I . . . I couldn't eat," Jugs said with a cry.

Between you and me I really wasn't all that hungry either right then, but I knew I'd better eat something if I was going to take a bunch of ibuprofen—which I was going to have to do to fight the headache which was already coming on fast. I felt like a drowned rat.

Without a word we started back for the mansion as one group. Maggie moved up beside me. "I'll guide you around the hot spots," she whispered, and I nodded. "By the way, it's a psychotic killer."

"Huh?" I asked, now totally confused.

"A psycho killer would be someone who kills psychos. What you meant to say was a psychotic killer."

"We're stuck on a haunted island with a *psychotic* killer, and you find it necessary to correct my English," I said in a whispered hiss.

Maggie smiled and shrugged.

I had my blocks running on high, but still had trouble in a couple of spots out front of the house even with Maggie's guided tour around the hot spots, which must have looked funny to those following us. But they followed in our footsteps anyway.

"I think we should all stay in groups. No one should be alone," Maggie said.

"But . . . Jesus was the murderer, and he's gone," Knight said.

I wasn't about to tell any of them what I thought, because I was sure one of them was the murderer, and if they were it was better they thought I was as stupid as Knight. Unless of course Knight was actually the murderer, in which case he was one hell of an actor.

"In case he comes back," Maggie said. "Vivian, why don't we go upstairs and get you cleaned up and into some dry clothes? When we're done we can all think of what to do about Juan's body and dinner."

The TV crew had actually made the kitchen and two bathrooms functional. Barely. The shower looked gacky and was rust- and sludge-stained. I stood outside it looking in, dripping on the floor. Maggie was standing in the closed doorway.

"So, what do you think?" Maggie asked.

"That you're crazy for wanting to stay here," I hissed. "Not that it really matters now. You know of course that there's no way that Jesus had time to trash those boats out and make his getaway. Besides which, while I don't understand why we didn't hear whoever was trashing the boats in the first place, I'm thinking someone was bound to hear the motor start and take off. This means the murderer is still on the island."

"Yes, but maybe it's not one of them at all," Maggie was downright excited. "You said you couldn't get a fix on the killer as Juan saw him. Maybe the killer is spectral energy. Maybe the dead *can* affect the living."

"And that would be a good thing!" I shrieked. "You've gone insane, Maggie. Besides, I hate to tell you this, but once again I have to remind you that there aren't any boogers out there. Just energy. Juan didn't know who his killer was, he couldn't see him—for some reason that I'm sure is more of science than science fiction—so his mind was making up possible solutions."

"Oh." Maggie sounded more than mildly disappointed.

"You'd better quit worrying about your pet project, Meg, and start thinking about this." I lowered my voice even more than it had been. "We're stuck on a deserted island with a killer."

I heard a whirl and a click then, and looked up to see a camera was in the bathroom. While the toilet seemed to be a blind spot, the shower wasn't.

"Fucking beautiful." I pointed to the camera, and Maggie looked at it with immediate irritation.

"Well, I don't know why *you're* so upset," Maggie said. "Of all the women in this house I'm the only one whose body should never be seen by the living unclothed."

"You're being a little hard on yourself there, Maggie. You certainly have a better body than Female Wyman."

Maggie made a face then. "Yes, but I'm assuming she doesn't actually bathe. Now come on. Hurry up, get a shower and change so we can keep an eye on them. I want to find the equipment. Maybe the spectral energy is causing people to go crazy."

"Key-rist, Maggie! Would you let it go? Who cares about any of that shit now?" I started to undress and realized I was more embarrassed to be undressing in front of Maggie than I was the camera. I took her shoulders and turned her around before I undressed, which made her laugh. With great trepidation I stepped into the shower—which seemed to be both cockroach and gecko free. I washed the salt water from my eyes and my body. "Maggie, we have to find some way off this fucking island or find a way to contact the mainland so they can come and get us."

"If Jesus didn't take the fourth boat, who did?" Maggie asked conversationally. I turned the water off and took the towel she offered me over her shoulder. I flashed my tits for the camera and smiled.

"The real killer . . ." I suddenly realized what Maggie was getting at. "Which means it's probably here hidden someplace. We'll go look for it first thing in the morning." I took my clothes from Maggie and put them on. She had laughed that I wouldn't stick them on the floor, but she could laugh all she wanted, I still wasn't doing it. I noticed then that Maggie had grabbed her camera when we were in the room. I didn't have to ask why.

"So what's the motive?" Maggie asked me as we started downstairs.

"A million dollars," I said, and "duh" was implied.

"But why kill one of the cooks?"

I shrugged. It was a damn good question. I'd wondered that myself. Really the only thing that *did* make sense was that he'd had a fight with Jesus and Jesus had killed him. And if Jesus didn't kill him, and if the real killer had the boat hidden somewhere on the island, then where the hell was Jesus?

A light bulb went off over my head and I nearly yelled, "He

caught the guy trashing the boats or hiding the other one."

Maggie nodded. "I'm still worried about why no one heard the damage being done to the boats or the other one getting away."

"They have oars," I said, now on a roll. "He could have moved it with the oars and no one was likely to hear. Everyone was pretty preoccupied with setting up their rooms. Checking the place out. You can't see the docks from the house. All we have to do is figure out who wasn't in the house for an extended period of time during the day."

"All right, but here's a better question. If the killer wants the money, then why sink the boats? Wouldn't he want us to leave?"

A cold chill went up my back, and I stopped in mid-stride, as we were about to start down the staircase. Maggie looked at me, no doubt thinking that I was having a vision, which I wasn't. "What if money isn't the motivator?"

Maggie didn't have to ask what I meant. I watched as the dawning came over her face, and she said in a hushed tone, "What if he's a psycho who wants to relive the killings of the past?"

"Then he wouldn't want us to be able to get away."

In the kitchen Maggie snapped a bunch of shots of the blood on the floor and in the corner, and of Juan's back at the point of entry. Then we had to move the corpse and clean the blood from the floor and wall. When I say "we" I mean mostly Maggie, because I spent most of my time dancing around hot spots and basically getting in the way more than helping. Maggie insisted we gather what evidence could be found before we totally screwed up the crime scene. She wanted to look at everyone's hands and scrape under their nails, but no one was having any of that.

Barbie suggested that perhaps Jesus had actually gone for

help, and that we shouldn't move anything. From the looks on everyone else's faces it was obvious that they didn't share her naive optimism. Maggie suggested that if we didn't clean up the mess and move the corpse we were going to be dealing with blowflies and maggots in the only kitchen we had. She bagged all her evidence in some Ziploc bags she found. She looked at the side-by-side refrigerator, and I knew what the bitch was thinking.

"No, absolutely not," I said shaking my head.

Maggie nodded. "Probably too small, anyway." She took out her trusty map of the island. "There is an old walk-in refrigerator in the same building that they put the generator in. It doesn't actually work, but it should keep the body cooler and at least it will keep the flies and other nasties out."

Ken and John carted the body and Maggie's samples out to the old freezer as Maggie cleaned the blood and yuk up off the floor. I couldn't help her without freaking out, and the others seemed more than happy to sit and watch her do it.

"You see this pattern in the blood, Vivian?"

I nodded, "Looks like he tried to wipe it up."

"I don't think so. See the tracks going out the back door?"

I nodded, "He's wearing some sort of robe, something that's dragging on the ground and smearing the blood."

"And wiping out his foot prints," Maggie said.

My guess is the two women were way too busy pretending to be devastated to actually help Maggie, and the Wyman's figured they were helping by standing close to the stove where the body had been found and calling upon the goddess to send the spirits of the restless dead on their way.

When Maggie had finished she flung the refrigerator door open wide. "Well, who wants to cook? I've done my part."

I cringed when Female Wyman volunteered. "Wash your hands," I ordered. I was sitting at the counter on a stool, which was probably the least violated spot in the kitchen.

Maggie sat down on a stool beside me, looked up and smiled before she said to Female Wyman, "Vivian's a little bit of a clean freak."

"And yet I'm so hungry I was about to eat those enchiladas old Juan fell facedown in," I said conversationally.

"How . . . how can you just be so flip about a man's death?" Barbie asked.

"It's how I cope, I guess," I said with a shrug.

"When you have the power that she has, you'd have to be able to distance yourself," Male Wyman said. I gave him a dirty look, and he cringed. He was a weasel, and to tell the truth I was sure that if someone was just in this for the killin' it was him and his creepy-ass wife.

"Just what are you?" Barbie asked, and her tone was accusing.

Knight seemed to ignore her question as he asked his own. "Why did you say *All who enter must pay?*" I could tell from the look on his face that something I had done had made him a believer, because his whole manner toward me had changed.

"Because that's what the murderer kept saying to the boy," I said.

"What did you see in here, was it Adam's murder?"

I shrugged, "Was he a young man, probably in his twenties, who was basically dissected on that table?" I asked, pointing.

Female Wyman groaned and moved quickly away from the table, which she had been preparing to set the cooking supplies upon. I was wondering how if she was so in tune with the other realm she didn't know that was a bad spot.

"Yes," Knight said, obviously shaken. "At least they guessed that was where he died. That's not where they found his body . . ."

"It was found strung back together like a scarecrow and hang-

ing from a tree just outside the back door," Maggie finished for
him, proving at least to me that she really did know as much
about the house as Knight did.

"Carved into his flesh were the words *All who enter must pay*,"
Knight said.

I'm thinking if the boats had been there, both Harmony and
Barbie would have been in them and gone, with or without
their men. Unless of course they were just really great actresses
and one of them was the killer.

"What are you?" Barbie asked again.

"I'm a fucking psychic, all right! The dead leave me messages
and I read them," I spat out. I expected someone to laugh, but
no one did.

Mug and Ken walked in, and without a word went to wash
their hands. I realized I was watching every move Female Wyman made, and it certainly wasn't because of the view, that
would have taken my attention over to Barbie and Harmony.
No, I was overlooking all the really great tail in the room and
focusing on this woman I wouldn't have screwed with her
husband's dick, because it had suddenly dawned on me that if
she was the killer, what was to keep her from poisoning us?

"Oh, this is going to be a really fun week," I muttered under
my breath.

Our meal was barely edible. I would have thought that a fat
woman with a fat husband would have been a really great
cook, but she wasn't. I was just happy I didn't find a cat hair
or I know I would have hurled.

Back in our room that night all I really wanted to do was
sleep. But Maggie had a million questions, and the first thing
she did as soon as I sat down on my sleeping bag—after carefully checking it for creepy crawlies—was to light all the candles
in the room and hand me my damn sketch pad and a pencil. I

automatically started drawing. Not our current murderer, because I had no idea what he looked like, but the one I had seen in the second vision.

I sketched as I answered Maggie's questions into the tape recorder she held just inches from my mouth. Which was irritating all by itself, because it was close enough that I could hear the little tape real going round and around.

"You didn't see what the murderer looked like?"

"No. I told you the image shifted. Juan wasn't sure what he was seeing. One minute it looked like a ninja, the next like Death. He was afraid, and he wasn't sure what was coming after him. He was very superstitious, and he was scared to begin with, so when he couldn't make out his killer his overtaxed imagination started filling in the gaps. He kept saying something."

"What?" Maggie asked.

"I don't know." I was a little pissed at her then, because the drawing was becoming all consuming at that point, and I really just wanted to draw. "Tell you what. You be the freaking psychic, and I'll be the scientist, and while you're at it, you can feel your body being slashed apart and take my fucking headaches, too."

She handed me a couple of ibuprofen and my canteen, and I gratefully took them.

"So what did he say?" Maggie asked as soon as I had finished.

"I don't know . . . *The elephant has my mama* I think."

"The last words a dying man said were, *the elephant has my mama?*"

"Sorry, Maggie." I shrugged. I don't know what she wanted from me. It wasn't like I wrote copy for the dead.

Maggie looked thoughtful, then said, "He was speaking Spanish. He barely spoke any English, and he was obviously terrified." She paused a moment, then continued, "Did he actually say 'the,' can you remember?"

"It makes no sense at all without the *the*," I said.

"Try to remember exactly what he said, Vivian," Maggie pleaded.

"He said el . . . elf . . . elfan . . . tas . . . my . . . Mama."

"You're sure it was mama?"

I thought harder. "Mada, yes I think it was mada."

Maggie started mumbling, then she stopped and looked up at me. "El fantasma me mata?" she said.

"Yes!" I said excitedly. "What's it mean?"

"The ghost is killing me. So it *is* spectral energy."

I growled at this. "You are insane. I told you. He didn't know *what* was attacking him."

"So tell me about the second vision. The old energy."

I told her what I'd seen and felt, though I would have rather not. I finished telling her the whole vision in the graphic details she wanted even as I finished drawing the madman. I turned the picture for Maggie to see. "Here's Mr. Knight."

"No, no it isn't," she said, looking troubled.

I looked at the picture. It was one of my better sketches. "But . . . this is the murderer."

"Then the murderer *wasn't* Garret Knight."

CHAPTER SEVEN:
MAGGIE

The whisper of a sorrowful sigh woke me from a sound sleep. I opened my eyes, remaining on my pallet for a moment before turning my head to glance toward Vivian. Under the protection of the mosquito netting we had draped over us against a possible invasion of the pesky blighters, she was scrunched about her pillow as though it were a lover and she looked dead to the world. Only the rise and fall of her shoulders assured me that she was still among the living.

Puzzled, I sat up, glancing around our room. Vivian had put a barricade of broken furniture and the lattice panels over the closed door—in case someone tried to get in during the night, she claimed. I doubted seriously that it would stop someone getting in, but at least the noise they'd make trying to get through would give us some warning. Tiny wisps of moonlight were slipping through the broken slats of balcony door we had been forced to prop up to cover that opening. The mosquito netting made it fuzzy and surreal. I stayed there, listening to the distant call of night birds, the irritating ratchet of crickets, and the occasional scuttle of a gecko traversing the walls in search of a meal. And just when I had convinced myself that nothing was amiss and started to lie down, I heard the sigh again.

It was hollow and filled the room, echoing faintly.

What the . . .

Carefully, I pushed back my blankets and slipped on my shoes. We slept fully dressed, ready for action, as Vivian put it.

Crawling quietly out from under the netting, flashlight in hand, I walked around the room scanning the shadows with light . . .

Another sigh—or was it a sob—whispered from one of the corners. I turned quickly and let the beam of my flashlight play over the shadows there. Nothing. Grumbling under my breath, I walked over to the corner, convinced there had to be an explanation. There were not supposed to be any hot spots in this room. Vivian had assured me of that, and there were none on my maps.

The corner contained some rotten remains of furnishings. Vivian had cleaned the room, but she had left the ruins of old furniture in place. I scanned the light up and down, leaning closer, peering at the corner. A gulping sob emanated from the area over my head. I gasped, stepped back and threw the beam of light up there, but I misjudged the distance and clipped one of the old rails of what might have once been a bed. It shifted with a clatter.

Vivian shot upright as though stung, and with a shout, she seized up her own flashlight, wielding it like a club. Her startled expression as she whipped around in my direction turned to an angry frown.

"Damn it, Maggie, what the hell are you doing?" Vivian snarled.

"I heard something—or someone," I said. "It sounded like it was over here."

She turned on her flashlight and let the light play over me and the corner. "I don't see anything," she said. "Just you and broken furniture and peeling paint . . . and a gecko."

I turned just as one of the lizards went scuttling out of the corner and ran for another opening in the wall up high, a crack where the plaster had torn away. I shook my head.

"I bet what you heard was the gecko," she said and crawled

back into her pallet, turning off her flashlight and lying down again.

"Geckos bark," I said, "but they don't sigh or sob."

I imagine Vivian was rolling her eyes. But she had already turned her back to me and was snuggling her pillow again.

"Yeah, right, you were probably having bad dreams because of Mrs. Wyman's cooking. I knew we should have sent out for pizza . . . in fact, maybe that's what happened to the extra boat."

"Is that supposed to be funny?" I asked.

"No," Vivian said. "Good night, Maggie."

Well, I thought. I let my flashlight linger on the corner again. The sound had stopped. Frowning, I crossed the room and crawled back under the netting, determined to get some sleep.

Just hoping I wouldn't have my usual dreams.

In spite of a rotten night's sleep, I was the first to rise. I suspect it was because of the thumping music of native drums that filled my ears. Wrong jungle, I thought as I groggily sat up.

Vivian was still asleep. The world had that ash-gray look that preludes dawn. Some of the geckos were scampering merrily across the walls and floors. I glowered at them, wondering where one got a cup of coffee in this hotel.

Pulling my shoes on again, I pushed my hair out of my eyes and went over to the balcony. The door scraped ominously as I shifted it out of the way.

"Whaaaaaa!" Vivian pushed her face out of her pillow, one hand reaching for her flashlight, and I was grateful to be out of striking range when she banged it on the floor as though flailing at an attacker.

"Sorry," I muttered, and slipped out onto the balcony.

The music was louder. It had a sort of jungle beat, and it emanated from below and to my right. Leaning carefully, I was treated with a view of a large patio courtyard filled with trees and weeds and dead potted plants that acted as a natural divider between the next wing. A small window of an opening in the greenery revealed a woman's posterior of a pasty coral shade that looked remarkably like naked flesh. Squinting—I didn't have my glasses on—I realized it *was* naked flesh, dancing to some sort of weird new-age music.

"Why, Maggie, didn't know you liked bare ass . . ."

I jumped back from the rail. Vivian was there, leering at me. "I was just trying to figure out who it was," I said defensively.

She leaned and looked. "Ewwww!" she said. "It's the Wymans. Looks like some sort of greet the sun ritual. And if I'm not mistaken, I smell burnt rope on the breeze."

I looked again. "How can you tell it's the Wymans? I can't see much more than a behind."

"Both Barbie and Holly have fine, tight asses, nothing like that, and neither of them strike me as the sort who would have pimples on their butts." She made a face and said, "Must be the female of the species."

"Are you sure?"

"Don't see a pecker. Then again, as big as his gut is I suppose his dick could be hidden up under the roll of his belly."

I shuddered at the very thought and quickly stepped back into the room. This was not something I wanted to witness without coffee. For that matter, I doubted I wanted to witness it *with* coffee.

Vivian followed me back inside. "So, did you keep hearing your noise last night?"

"I went back to sleep," I said, moving stuff around to look for my notepads.

"Good. I'm going back to sleep now."

"What about getting an early start?" I asked.

Vivian frowned. "Not without coffee."

"I was thinking of that myself," I said.

We found our way back to the kitchen without trouble. Sunlight was starting to stream in through broken windows. As we passed the cameras, Vivian once more gave into base urges to throw birds and make faces at each lens she passed. I will admit this morning I was tempted to join her, but my thoughts were on the kitchen itself, the scene of last night's murder, and another murder twenty years ago.

Winston and Jolene were already there when we arrived. They were mixing some sort of sludge of fruit and mystery powders.

"Oh, just in time," Winston said, and I pegged his accent as more British than his wife's, even though like her, he was Scandinavian right down to his toes. "I just made a large batch of my Morning Special. Here, have some."

He thrust a plastic cup into my hands filled with the pureed mixture.

"Looks like something that would give a cat the runs," Vivian said to me in a low voice as she leaned over and looked into the cup. "Are we ever going to get any real food in this place?"

I sort of agreed. It had a peculiar sweet odor, but when I sipped a little, it tasted all right, if a little bland. "What all is in it?" I asked.

"Papaya, mango, honeydew melon, and our secret Power Powder mix which is a blend of all the vitamins and minerals your body will ever need," he said cheerfully. "It will clean all of the impurities right out of your body."

"Told you it would give a cat the runs," Vivian said, and waved away the plastic cupful he offered her. "I need coffee. Real coffee. Too bad Juan is gone. Bet he made a great cup of Colombian." She grinned at her own joke.

"Caffeine is bad for the body," Jolene said with a toss of her head. "You would do well to break yourself of the demon brew while you are still young."

"Caffeine is the *only* thing good for this body," Vivian said. "Ah, there's a coffeepot." She dodged several hot spots to race to the counter.

She waved away my offer to make coffee and set about making it herself. Soon enough, the smell was filling the kitchen. The rest of the immediate area, too, because I heard voices as I was downing my first cup.

"Coffee! Now you're talking," said John, practically hauling Harmony in his wake. She looked more than a little frazzled. "Just what you need, Babycakes."

Harmony came around beside me to look for a cup and help herself. I couldn't help notice the dark rings under her eyes.

"Did you sleep all right?" I asked.

She looked at me, almost hesitant at first. Then sighed. "I thought I heard someone crying last night," she said.

"Crying?" I repeated.

"She was dreaming," John said, pushing his way between us and fixing me with a glower that would have set ice on fire. "Don't be giving her ideas, okay? She's spooked enough as it is. No way I'm letting you scare her into leaving."

"It's very unlikely anyone is leaving until we figure out what happened to the fourth boat," I said.

He sneered and herded Harmony away. I saw her look at me with the slightest plea before he ushered her out of the kitchen.

"I heard someone crying, too," Jolene volunteered. "Winston thought it was a howler monkey, but it sounded just like it was in the room with us. Of course, that was after I thought I heard someone sighing. I suppose it was the wind playing through the ruins of this ghastly place. Do you suppose it is just that our imaginations are getting the better of us already? Or maybe they have planted audio equipment to make sounds at certain times. Since they don't know what's going on here . . . Well, if equipment in the house has been programmed to make certain noises at certain times, it's not going to stop just because someone has been murdered here."

"Possibly," I said. "We have the right atmosphere to create mass hysteria without any help."

"Isn't that the whole point of the game?" Winston asked. "To create an atmosphere that causes us to want to leave so that only one couple can win the money?"

"True," I said. Vivian was at the outer door of the kitchen, eyes roving warily over the scene as she sucked down her coffee. I wondered if she was seeing spooks. "Only one way to find out," I added.

Winston nodded in agreement. At that moment, Jolene gestured for him to follow her. "Come, dear, we must get to work."

"Yes, my flower," he replied. They slipped out of the kitchen together.

Cautiously, Vivian came over to me, taking an indirect path through the kitchen. "You know, I think we ought to go look for that fourth boat," she said.

"I was rather hoping to find out where they had stashed the sensing equipment," I said.

"Maggie, this is no time to play ghost busters," Vivian said. "We really ought to find that boat and see if we can get off this island. After all, we need to get the police here to investigate Juan's death."

"Juan?" I said, glancing at her.

"The dead cook," she said.

"Eduardo, Vivian. Can't you say anyone's name right?"

She sneered, and I frowned.

"I was rather hoping to take a look at the sensing equipment," I added.

"Maggie, the stakes in the game have changed."

"I know. Forgive me for being so selfish, but I really need to get material for my book, and . . ."

"Oh yes, Mr. Knight, we always greet Father Sun with open arms," a female voice announced.

I froze like a rabbit in the headlights as Ned and Astaria, with Knight trapped between them, came into the kitchen.

"How, uh, interesting," Knight said, though it was clear from his expression that he thought otherwise. In fact, as soon as he saw me and Vivian in the kitchen, his face took on a look of relief. "Is that coffee I smell?" he said eagerly.

"I'm gonna go look for the boat," Vivian said, and suddenly vanished out the door before I could join her.

Oh, great, I thought. *Leave me with the Boobie Twins.*

I would get her for that somehow. But for the moment, I decided I had to get out of the kitchen. Knight practically rushed over to my side and helped himself to the coffee. "This smells wonderful," he said as he poured a cup. "Just what I needed."

"Oh, you'll need more than coffee," Astaria said as she made for the counter. "I'll fix you one of my omelets. Anyone know where the eggs are?"

Ned was closing in from the other side, and I started to feel like a trapped rabbit. Knight and I looked at one another as though desperate for a solution . . .

"Actually, I've eaten," I said. "I was just on my way to see if I could find the sensing equipment and . . ."

"Actually, I never eat breakfast," Knight said, taking my arm, "but I will be more than happy to show you the equipment, Ms. Holmes. Come on."

Like a pair of greyhounds, we sprinted between Ned and Astaria and raced for the door.

"That was a serious mistake," Knight said as we followed

several twists and turns in the corridors. The place was such a maze, I only hoped he knew where we were going. "I didn't want to be alone after Eduardo was found dead last night, but I never dreamed those two could be so . . ."

"Weird?" I supplied.

"Worse," Knight said. "They sleep naked. The woman, she sits on her cot like a Buddha and moans some sort of mantra while he goes around with a candle and . . . plays with himself."

Well, I thought, there goes Vivian's theory about him not being able to find his penis.

"They insisted I should take off my clothes . . . but I didn't," Knight continued. "It was hard enough with *them* taking off *their* clothes . . . I spent most of the night with my head buried under the blankets because they decided to make love . . ."

He shuddered.

"I can imagine," I said. "Except, knowing their religious beliefs, I gather she was emulating the goddess instead of a male god. And perhaps the lovemaking was part of the ritual. Perhaps they were practicing some ancient fertility rite . . ."

"All I know is they kept grunting like pigs, and I kept waiting for the cot to break the way it squeaked and groaned . . . and then there was all the sobbing."

"Sobbing?" I said and stopped him. "You heard sobbing last night?"

Knight pulled back. "Well, yes. But I thought it was them . . ."

I frowned. "Everyone reported hearing sobbing and crying and sighing last night. Even I heard it."

"Well, they *were* sort of loud," Knight said and started on. "So, where is your lady . . . husband . . . what do you usually call your mate?"

"Partner," I said. "Vivian's out looking for the boat."

"The boat?" he said.

"The missing boat."

"Well, that's a waste of time," he insisted. "Obviously, Miguel took it and fled after he killed Eduardo."

"We're not so sure," I said.

Knight shook his head. "No, you're wrong. I suspected there was something funny about Miguel the day we got here. He was awfully eager to get Eduardo alone."

"But if Miguel had killed Eduardo," I said, "why bother to wait till they got to the island where he was bound to look like the only suspect? There's no reason for any of us to kill Eduardo, he wasn't even eligible for the million dollars. They were in the kitchen together practically from the moment we arrived, he's the obvious suspect so again, why kill him here?"

"They're a superstitious lot, perhaps he sacrificed him to their god," Knight said.

"Maybe."

Knight looked uncomfortable. "If it wasn't Miguel, then that means it's one of you. If it wasn't Miguel, then why did he take off? It certainly looks to me like he's the killer."

I stopped him again. "I am a forensic pathologist," I reminded him. "I've been over hundreds of murder scenes, and if there is one thing that I've learned it's that the real murderer is rarely ever obvious."

"Be that as it may," Knight said, and his face returned to its guarded expression, the one he wore when we first set out on this trip. "I am still willing to bet that Miguel killed Eduardo. I heard them fighting after we got here."

"Over what?"

"Don't know," Knight said. "I don't speak Spanish, but it was obvious from their tone of voice and from the wild waving of arms that they were disagreeing on something. Now do you want to see the equipment or not, Ms. Holmes?"

I sighed. It occurred to me that the argument might have been over nothing more important than what they were cooking for dinner. After all, Miguel had been sent to fetch something for the meal that probably should have already been brought to the kitchen. But Knight was apparently unwilling to listen. And I *did* want to see the equipment.

He started on again, stopping at last before a large metal door with a key-coded padlock. He stood between me and the keypad as he punched in four numbers. While I could not see the numbers, I could tell that he touched a diagonal pattern from lower left to upper right then dropped to lower right before he reached for the star key. Seven-five-three-nine, I thought. How simple could you get? A buzzer sounded, and he turned the handle, opening the door.

So here was another chamber that had been well prepared. It looked like it might have been a vault at one time, for the walls were heavy metal. There was an air vent up above, but no windows and lots of wires feeding into a conduit that would have led to a power source. Knight reached in and flipped a switch, and fluorescents spread their bluish light over everything.

It was a room of equipment to die for. Spectrometers, heat sensors, computers, printers, all the snazzy stuff that I could only dream of owning. I would have to sell my house, both my children, and probably my soul before I could have afforded such stuff. Even the labs I had worked in when I was a full-time forensic pathologist were nowhere near as modern. I moved into the room and stared in breathless wonder.

Knight had moved in ahead of me, but he stopped rather abruptly.

"What's wrong?" I asked.

He turned and looked at me, his face going pale. "Uh . . . I'll be back. Close the door when you leave."

He sprinted from the chamber as though he had seen a ghost. I frowned and looked back.

Well, there was something over in the corner that resembled

a figure under a cloth. I edged over to lift the edge, always mindful that even a sealed room could contain vermin, and was greeted with the sight of what looked like a satellite dish. Shrugging, I covered it. What the hell was that for? Must have been a backup. But that didn't make any sense. Kennedy had said they weren't watching us, and if they were, surely they would have sent in police by now.

As I looked at it, I could see that it had been moved. There were scrape marks on the floor. But that could have happened when the crew brought it in. Kennedy had assured them they were alone, cut off, that there was no live feed. So why would there be a satellite here at all? I decided it was something the workmen must have used as they were installing the cameras and getting everything else up and running. God alone knew what tricks and surprises they had set up to try and scare us.

As I glanced around, I saw that the vault also contained a series of recording machines that were working in full swing. I walked around and found a row of tiny TV screens hooked to computer feeds. This was state of the art. No tapes needed with all the digital feeds. As I moved from tiny screen to tiny screen, I could see the various parts of the house and the hotel and the areas around the island. It occurred to me then that all someone had to do was sit here and monitor all this, and they would know everything that was happening—where every person on the island was.

I was contemplating this when I heard a faint whine. Turning, I saw that a camera was mounted in the back corner of the room. It gently arched back and forth, surveying all that it could see. Eagerly, I turned back to the screens, trying to determine which feed it was hooked to, interested to see if I looked as bad on camera as I suspected.

But for all my searching, I could not find a single screen portraying this room.

I looked back at the camera and frowned. Maybe I had better find Vivian and tell her about this. Now that I had the code, I could get in whenever I wanted to. I abandoned the room, shutting the door behind me. It closed with an ominous thunk. I hurried out of the corridor, seeing an exit, and wanting a little air as my brain thundered over the oddity I had just discovered.

So who was monitoring that room . . . and from where?

CHAPTER EIGHT:
VIVIAN

I figured Maggie deserved to deal with the Wymans on her own after telling everyone that we thought the fourth boat was still somewhere on the island, which basically screamed, *We don't think Jesus did it! We think one of you is the killer.* I swear, it was as if she *wanted* to fall victim to the psychotic killer we were sharing this little piece of hell with. Perhaps then she could check out all her ghost theories without all the bothersome being alive stuff.

She gets so tied up with her work . . . I mean here we were stranded on a deserted island with a killer and no way to get hold of the mainland, and Maggie's more worried about finding material for her book than she is looking for a way off this island of death.

I wanted to go look for the boat that could save us all while she wanted to go in search of equipment she could set up to monitor the so-called "ghost activity" in the house. And yet most people who know us back home would say that she's the practical one.

I just don't get it.

I was walking along with my only real direction being to step around the hot spots on Maggie's little map—which I had decided that I would go nowhere without. Then I slowed down and started to try to find our killer's trail.

I'm thinking I'm probably doing things about right. I put myself in the killer's head. I kill Juan and then what? Do I run down to scuttle the boats and row the fourth away, or have I already done that and now all I have to do is get away, clean up and stash my disguise?

I found myself starting to look for tracks in the little areas of dirt and leaf litter that peeked through beneath the vegetation. Tracks that looked like they'd been made by someone wearing a long skirt or robe. I'm thinking it's a sure bet that the Wymans have some sort of ceremonial robes in their bag of tricks. I didn't find any tracks that looked anything like the pattern in the blood from the night before, but I found about everyone else's footprints. Rope sandals in two sizes which no doubt belonged to the Wymans, which made my mind go *Aha!* A man's big boot print, which I guessed to be Mug's. A shoe too small to fit anyone but Jugs—they say nothing grows well in the shade—lots of sneaker prints that could have belonged to any of the rest of us—or even the crew that set up the generator and the kitchen, fixed the bathrooms, or set up the cameras.

I started to go in search of the killer's disguise. He might have stashed it out here somewhere. Then I realized what I was doing. I was supposed to be looking for the boat, and instead I was looking for clues, which wasn't a whole lot better than Maggie wanting to play with Spectorwhatsits, and look for ghosts.

I figure that the killer scuttled the boats probably shortly after we landed. It would make sense. After all, that was when the rest of us had been preoccupied with getting our shit brought in and finding someplace to sleep. At that point none of us would have been suspicious enough to notice any noise. There hadn't been a reason to be suspicious, because at that point there weren't any dead bodies in the kitchen and it was daylight so no one was worried about ghosts yet.

As I started back around the house and toward the dock I realized something else. Between a slight rise in the land, a row of palms, and dense jungle underbrush, not only could you not *see* the dock from the house, but you probably wouldn't have been able to *hear* anything unless it was really loud. Knocking holes in the bottom of the boats would have made a dull, thudding sound.

When I got to the docks I started to take off all my clothes and go in to have a better look at the boats, and then realized I was getting off track again. If I couldn't find the other boat, then I'd see if there was any raising one of them. I flipped a coin and started my search on the east side of the dock. I quickly ran out of beach and was scampering over huge rocks covered with jungle. It was really beautiful. The surf crashing into the rocks on my right, the jungle to my left, and me scampering over the rocks like some young bronze goddess. I only wished there was some good-looking women there to impress with how really butch I was—what good shape I was in.

Screw it. Since no one was watching I decided to take a break and have a cigarette. I sat down on a rock hanging over the ocean, took the pack out of my pocket, extracted a cigarette and lit it. I took a long drag, and that was when I heard it. I turned and looked to where I had heard the noise and there was a camera. I looked away and smiled, glad that my most excellent butchness was not going to be lost to the masses. I started talking, don't ask me why, I thought it was a good idea at the time, I guess.

"It seems that I alone among all these idiots understand the importance of survival. Ghosts. Ha! I'm not afraid of ghosts. But there is a real killer here, a real killer with real weapons and a whole boatful of motives, for I do not believe for even one moment that Jesus killed Juan . . ." Oh yes, I went on like that for several minutes, sounding more and more idiotic as my speech progressed. I'm a fair actress, but that day I was just acting like an idiot. It was one of those times when your brain is telling you that you should shut up because you sound like a moron, but you just keep talking because you're trying to make yourself sound like less of an idiot. I fell silent as I finished my cigarette, knowing that they would no doubt choose this little piece of tape to air to the millions of people who were going to watch this program. So I field stripped my cigarette, got off my ass, found a coconut and wasted the next fifteen minutes trying to knock the cage and the camera it held out of the tree. Realizing I was never going to be successful, and knowing that with this last little bit of tape there was no way I was ever going to get laid again, my search of the coast for the missing boat was somewhat less urgent. I was beginning to welcome death.

When I had walked far enough that I was sure the boat would be too far away to do our killer any good I turned around and walked back, then started walking to the west. The beach ended sooner here. I thought about getting in and swimming but decided that might not be a good idea so I climbed up the rocks to the top of the cliff—wasn't really much of a cliff, maybe only a twenty foot drop. Below, huge rocks dimpled the shoreline making an abundance of boat-sized hiding places. This is where I would have hidden the boat, and I damned the coin for sending me in the wrong direction. The jungle at the top of the cliff was dense, damp, and moldy smelling. I wished several times that I had a machete as I pushed and pulled myself between vines and trees and bushes. I wished there had been a vantage point from which I could see into all those little hidden coves, but there just wasn't. So I decided to climb a palm tree.

I'd seen it on TV before and decided it must not be all that hard. I took off my belt, took the strap off my canteen and tied them together. Then I wrapped them around the trunk, made a circle, tied the other end and . . . Well, it's a lot harder than it looks, and of course there was a camera, which I'm sure caught the hugeness of my ass as I tried time and time again. Finally I got the rhythm of it figured out and I managed to make it about half way up a very bent palm tree. Fortunately it gave me a very good view of the coast below. Unfortunately there was no boat. I climbed down the tree feeling puzzled and pulled the map from my pocket. I immediately slapped myself in my forehead with the palm of my hand—just because it always feels so good when you quit.

Damn it! Knight's Island is a little piss-ant sized thing, only about a hundred acres in size, and the mansion sits smack in the middle. That means that if the killer knew the island the boat could be on any side of the island and the killer would still have access. If I hadn't doubled back I would have already made it all the way around the island; as it was, I still had half the island to walk around and I was almost out of water and feeling a little tired and hungry so I decided to cut across the island to the house, then take off again after I'd refueled, so to speak.

I put on my belt, fixed the strap back on my canteen and headed back toward the house. That's when it happened. The king, queen, and little princess of all roaches flew out of the jungle and attacked me. And yes I did, I screamed like a little sissy girl. Being thus humiliated there was nothing I could do but hunt the bastard down and kill it—which I did with a stick.

Hell has no fury like a butch-dyke forced into a situation where she acts like a screaming fem.

My kill lay there like some reject from the paleoanthropopic period. I made chopsticks from a piece of bamboo and picked it up (well I sure as hell wasn't going to touch it) and started back toward the hotel. Naturally, I forgot to watch the map and where I was going and didn't have my shields up, so of course I wound up hitting one hell of a hot spot. The victim was a young woman, part of the staff, she wondered briefly as she fled in terror if she had finished polishing the silver. She was being hunted, and she had stopped here. She looked around for him—I got a glimpse of the killer's face, a man of about twenty with pure evil looking out of his eyes—She was wondering if he'd think to look for her here, if he was still after her, if there was a chance for escape. And then from seemingly nowhere an arrow and a thudding sound as it hit her chest. She wasn't dead, and the killer walked up looking into her face as she lay on the ground and he laughed. The most wicked sound I have ever heard. He took hold of the arrow, and he began to play with the shaft, moving it gently around, poking and prodding so that there was intense pain till the very moment she died.

When I came back I was on the jungle floor. I quickly jumped up, pulled my T-shirt out of my pants and up over my head and pulled my shorts down to make sure my body hadn't been subjected to the unwanted attentions of giant cockroaches. Finding myself clean I put myself back together and started looking for my "kill." I found him still lying on one of my makeshift chopsticks. I found the other and picked him back up. I leaned against a tree, looking at him and had a moment's satisfaction thinking that perhaps some psychic bug would come to the spot where I'd killed him and see the horror of his death and have to deal with a bug headache at least as bad as the one I suddenly had.

With my free hand I skillfully extracted the map from my pocket and opened it with the help of my teeth. I soon realized that it would have done me no good at all to have been looking at Maggie's map, because I was now utterly and completely lost. I folded the map back up . . . All right, wadded it back up and put it into my pocket.

If I was even close to knowing where I was, the hot spot I had just located wasn't on the map. No doubt because—as I had told Maggie in the first place—bodies didn't always wind up where they got killed.

My head was pounding and I just wanted to get back to the hotel and my ibuprofen stash. I was sure of one thing. I had turned away from the coast, so as long as I kept going in the direction I was going, there was a very good chance that I was going to run into the hotel. Maybe. I couldn't be sure that I hadn't gotten turned around when I'd had my vision.

I strained to see if I could hear the ocean, but instead I heard the same crappy music I'd heard that morning when I'd seen the abomination that was Female Wyman's ass. The mere thought of it made me reconsider my sexual orientation. I went toward the music and realized that it was slightly different hideously crappy music.

I climbed a set of stairs up to a veranda on the east side of the hotel, and there lay Barb wearing nothing but expensive sun glasses, sunning herself on a blanket.

First I decided I was very comfortable with my sexual orientation after all, then I looked around to make sure no one else was around, and then I took a few minutes to just enjoy the view. Assuming that she didn't know I was there.

"You like what you see?"

I damn near jumped out of my skin as I said, "Yep," in a drool-implied voice.

She took off her dark glasses, got up on one elbow and gave me possibly the most practiced come-hither look I have ever seen. "I like what I see, too. I swing both ways, you know."

"No, I didn't." There I stood with my cockroach kill clasped between homemade chopsticks in my hand, covered in jungle dirt, sweat and grime, and I'm thinking she's either full of shit or she's got some really twisted ideas about what's sexy.

I'm about to throw my kill down and jump her bones when Ken comes out, robe in hand, and it's obvious that he's pissed. He starts yelling at her in some foreign language and throws the robe over her. Which I just thought was really rude of him.

After all I obviously wasn't done looking.

She says something back to him, which doesn't sound very apologetic.

He glares at me. I grip my kill tighter and head for the side door of the house. As I'm about to go through it I turn to look at Barb and she smiles at me.

I get up to our room and lay my kill down on the floor—on Maggie's side of the room. I find the ibuprofen, swallow about four of them with all the water that's left in my canteen and then I light a cigarette. My head is whirling. Between the vision and not finding the boat and seeing both Female Wyman and Barb naked in the same day, I think I'm having a little lesbian meltdown. I needed a shower, but if I'd tried to take one then I'd have wound up masturbating with or without the damned camera—and that would have just been too embarrassing. So instead I went about the task for which I'd brought my kill back to the room. I took a long drag as I looked for a gecko. I found a good-sized one pretty quick, but he got away. Fortunately, while he was getting away another one ran right into me. I grabbed its tail, and before he could bite me I blew smoke in his face. I did this two or three times and he seemed to first get more pissed off and then calm down. I sat on the floor next to the cockroach and picked it up with the chopsticks. I put the dazed gecko down, keeping a wary grip on his tail, dragging him backwards when he tried to bite me. Then I moved the roach toward him. I'm figuring if I can make it hate the roach it will be a much more efficient roach killer.

I started verbally taunting him first. "Na na na, you're a stupid ugly gecko, you can't catch me I laugh at your . . ."

The gecko snapped a piece right out of the roach.

"Wow! You're a vicious little bastard," I say in delight.

I rub the roach in his face. "See, I'm not hurt, you're a

weenie, a big weenie and . . ." That little bastard did not like to be teased.

So I'm sitting there minding my own business trying to train my little gecko friend when Maggie walks in all in a snit.

"Where the hell have you been? And what the hell are you doing!"

I quickly shoved the roach and sticks under Maggie's bedroll and let my new friend go, hoping she hadn't actually seen. I turned around with my cigarette clutched in my teeth, smiled and shrugged. "Nothing," I said in that tone of voice that is almost an admission of guilt.

Maggie frowned. "Vivian, I asked you not to smoke in the room."

I sighed with relief, and rather than argue with her got up and walked to the balcony without saying any of the things I was thinking about second-hand smoke not probably being a real big problem in a room with what amounted to a ten-by-ten-foot hole in the wall. Or the great logic it took to be worried about second-hand smoke, but seemingly not worried at all about being trapped on a deserted island with a crazed killer.

"I half thought you'd been killed. Where the hell have you been all day?"

I smiled then. She was mad at me because I'd scared her. She was mad at me because since I wasn't actually dead or injured and bleeding at the bottom of a cliff somewhere there was no excuse for me to have worried her.

"I went to look for the boat."

"And?"

"I made it halfway around the island and didn't see it. I need to make a swing around the other side . . ."

"It's too late for that. It's already three, you'd never get done before it got dark."

I nodded. That made sense. "I stepped on a really nasty piece of vision out there."

"Yes, well you can tell me about that later. Right now I need you to help me hook the transendentalrometer, the gogliafran and the sriptorectalthing wump up in that room you didn't want to go into last night."

That just wasn't right. She was hardly interested at all in my really graphic horrible vision. I was disappointed, and I was filthy, so I whined. Yes, I whined—and in front of the cameras, too. You really do forget the sonsabitches are there after a while. "I'm dirty, I'm tired, I'm hungry, I have a headache and I just want to get a bath and something to eat."

"Yet just a minute ago you were all ready to walk around the second half of the island," Maggie pointed out. "Now come on, you've got to see this anyway."

As we walked down the stairs and through the endless corridors I found myself wondering how the hell she could remember where it was.

"I've told you . . . there aren't any ghosts, Maggie. I swear all this stupid shit and . . ."

"I would think that someone who sees the things that you see would be a little bit more open-minded. I have had equipment hooked up in rooms while you had a vision, and the temperature *does* drop," she said. "I know what I saw."

"Yeah, I know. There was light in the bulbs." I sighed. I was never going to win this argument. I don't know why I kept trying. "So . . . you suppose if one of them had been a real dim wit he would have stuck a candle in their head instead?"

"That's not funny, Vivian," Maggie said. When she used that tone of voice with me *I* felt the temperature drop in the room.

"Sorry," I said.

She nodded and went on as if I'd said nothing tasteless. She's used to my bad jokes and black sense of humor.

"I saw the code, but I kept wondering why they locked the

equipment up in there with the monitors."

"The monitors?" I asked.

"Yes, that's right. There is a vault. I guess it was the old resort vault. Anyway, they set up monitors there, and here's the thing—why are there monitors if no one's watching us?"

"You think there's someone else on the island?"

"Or everyone isn't who they seem to be. Knight had the code to the lock, maybe he was supposed to watch us. See where we were, what we were doing, and try to scare us into leaving."

"Well, that is what we assumed his job was," I said. I felt like I ought to be dropping breadcrumbs or something so that we could find our way back.

"Except now he acts more afraid than the rest of us," Maggie said.

"Well, someone's really dead now, and I don't think any of us counted on that."

"There was something else that puzzled me. Why put the equipment we'd need to ghost hunt in the room with the monitors?"

"Maybe to keep it from the elements or the vermin," I said. "They've got cockroaches the size of small cars here. Which is just one of the many reasons that you now owe me forever."

She nodded. "I guess that makes sense, but whenever we wanted to get the equipment we would immediately know that someone, probably Knight, could sneak down here and watch us whenever he wanted."

"Maybe they want us to know. You have to admit that of all the things, besides the corpse in the enchiladas, what's the scariest?"

"The idea that someone might be watching us in the hope of terrifying us," Maggie nodded, seeming to like that bit of logic. "Now, the generator feeds the lines in the vault, which powers the monitors, though there is a huge bank of batteries in there so I'm guessing they could run quite a while by themselves," she said thoughtfully then just shrugged. "There are several hot lines in the kitchen which I think is closer to the room. But it's still a long way, so we're going to need quite a bit of extension cord to run the equipment . . ."

"What about the Relative?" I asked excitedly, totally destroying her train of thought.

"Who?"

"The Relative guy."

"Really, Vivian, couldn't you just call him by his name? What about him?" she asked in that pissy tone, which nearly screamed, *Don't interrupt me!*

"If he was watching all of us, he could have known that Jesus left for the shed, and that would have given him time to kill Juan. If he was watching, he would have known when the best time to scuttle the boats was. If his job's to scare us, well the murder did a pretty damn good job."

"I'm sure killing people wouldn't have been part of his job description, Viv," Maggie said totally disregarding my idea.

Which made me say in a pissy tone which nearly screamed, *Don't rain on my parade* . . . "Yeah, well, what if the island's driving him crazy? Some people are natural actors. They can make damn near anything sound and look sincere . . ."

"Like you, dear," Maggie teased.

"Yes, exactly like me," I said, then realized that she wasn't necessarily saying that this was one of my most endearing qualities. It didn't matter; I was on a roll. "Who says Dead President Guy's hands are clean? Maybe he paid the Relative to come here with us and kill us for ratings."

"Now you're just being ridiculous."

"I hate that!" I spat back as Maggie worked on the code for the vault door.

"What?"

"*That,* that snippy little superior lilt your voice gets when you think you've caught me being a huge dumb-ass," I said.

The door opened and Maggie ran in to pull out the equipment she had no doubt scoped out earlier. I just stood there staring mesmerized, as it hypnotically swung to and fro. It wasn't moving much—just enough.

"I'm sorry, but I'd believe the network was in on this before I could accept the idea that cowering, cringing, glass-jawed Knight could be a cold-blooded killer. That's odd, the satellite dish is gone."

"I agree," I said.

"That it's odd that the satellite dish is gone?"

"No, that Knight isn't the killer."

"Good, what made you change your mind?"

"Because he's hanging by his neck from the ceiling, and his color doesn't look good."

CHAPTER NINE:
MAGGIE

"Vivian, can't you be serious for even one minute?"

Okay, so I will admit that I felt more than a little exasperated at that moment, and being in such a state of mind will clutter my common sense and narrow my focus. I turned swiftly and roughly pushed the dangling pair of legs out of my way so I could see her face.

"This is not a time to be cracking wise about . . ." I started to tell her.

The legs swung back and kicked me in the shoulder, nearly knocking me off my feet. My mouth opened, and I had every intention of spitting a curse or two at my attacker when it hit me—figuratively this time—that Vivian was staring at me with a rare look of horror, and that I was shoving legs in well-pressed pants and expensive Italian shoes aside as though they were a shower curtain. I stopped and looked up.

"Oh, Jesus, what is *he* doing up there?"

It was Knight, all right, and as Vivian had so aptly put it, his color was not good. His tongue was sticking out, and the leg of his trousers was damp with piss. I detected a hint of fecal matter, too. The body in the course of strangulation evacuates everything: mucus, saliva, urine and feces. In spite of what the movies show, hanging has never been a clean or romantic way to die.

"Well," Vivian said as though calculating every word. "I would say he had a little help."

Selina Rosen and Laura J. Underwood

I looked back at her. She wore an expression that was a cross between wanting to laugh and not daring to laugh.

"A little help?" I said. "The question would be who, since hanging a man even of Knight's size would take a certain amount of strength. Now, if he was alive at the time he was hanged, then he would have done a lot of kicking and struggling, and would have knocked things over, but it doesn't look like anything here has been disturbed since I left. Of course, if he was strangled and then strung up, he would have been heavier—deadweight is always harder to handle, you know. So he must have been killed elsewhere and dragged back here . . ."

Vivian's expression lost all hint of amusement. One of her eyebrows had practically crawled up into her hairline.

"Uh . . . right," she said and slowly backed toward the door, looking suspiciously at the coded lock. "You know, Maggie . . ."

"Know what?" I asked.

"Nothing." She said it too fast to suit me. "Uh . . . maybe I better go see where the others are . . ."

"Yes, that's a good idea," I said. "The sooner we find out where everyone is, the sooner we can . . . wait." I turned and pointed to the rows of digital monitors. "We can look here and see where everyone is . . ."

Vivian seemed awfully reluctant to come over to the console. "Come on," I said.

She took a deep breath and stepped over to one end, keeping some distance between us. Ignoring her, I started scanning the monitors. I found Ned and Astaria first, much to my chagrin. They were sitting together in one of the chambers, and it looked like they were chanting. Or playing footsie. I didn't want to guess. There was still no sign of Miguel. Harmony and John, and Jolene and her husband were missing too. I moved down the rows of monitors and finally found Harmony. She seemed to be sleeping in her room.

114

"Well, almost everyone is accounted for," I said.

"Who's missing?" Vivian asked. She stayed on the other side of the console, looking at Knight.

"John," I said. "And Jolene and her husband . . . and Miguel." Miguel who everyone but us assumed had taken the boat. "By the way, did you have any luck looking for the boat?"

Vivian had glanced at the floor as though something had her attention, so my question startled her. "I told you no. I'll check the other side of the island tomorrow," she said.

"Well, what have you been doing all morning?" I asked.

"You know what I was doing, I was looking for the boat . . ." Vivian said.

"This is getting us no where. I need to examine that body."

"Why?"

"Well, he's got a cord around his neck," I said. "It would be nice to know what kind it is."

"Looks like a power cord." Vivian knelt down then.

"But where did it come from?" I said. "That's what we have to find . . . what are you doing?"

"Nothing," Vivian said, but I would have sworn she pocketed something. She got back on her feet and stepped off to one side. "Just looking for clues and . . ."

She got that look on her face. The one she gets when she is "seeing" things. She must have found the hot spot. Her breath came in short gasps and she quickly backed away, staggering like a drunk. "No, no," she said softly. "It can't be . . . it can't be . . . why . . . why . . . please, no . . . ?"

"Can't be what? Vivian?"

I dashed around the end of the console just as she dropped to her knees. Kneeling beside her and putting an arm around her waist, I managed to get her back up on her feet. She was like a sack of potatoes, and being she was taller than me, I was not having an easy time, but I got her over to a chair.

Slowly, her color returned to normal.

"Are you all right?" I asked.

"Maggie?" She looked a little puzzled to see me.

"You saw something," I said.

She shrugged. "I'm not sure." The glazed expression turned guarded. "I think we better tell the others that Knight is dead."

I nodded. Sooner or later, they would have to find out anyway.

Normally, I can read Vivian like a book because she does little to hide her feelings about anything. I, on the other hand, will admit to being more guarded. Comes with the territory. A professional forensics pathologist cannot afford to be open . . . messes with the head. Besides, one has to remain distant to keep from getting caught up in the tragedy of the victim.

Vivian, on the other hand, was usually uninhibited when it came to making observations—or at least bad jokes—about the world. This was not like her. She had nothing to say as we traversed the halls, seeking the rest of the participants in this strange ordeal.

I was not so keen on finding Ned and Astaria first, but they are as unavoidable as the flu in a room of school children. More so, I was under the impression that they were looking for us—or me. Ned took one look at me and said, "Is something the matter, Ms. Holmes? You look like you have seen a ghost."

I started to say that was Vivian's department, when Jolene and Winston marched into the room. She practically came over and put an arm around Vivian's shoulder like they were old pals. "Dahling," she said in a syrupy way. "You look terrible. Are you feeling all right?"

Winston looked more than a bit disturbed by this, and I could not help but wonder what might have happened to cause this. What had Vivian been up to when she said she was looking for the boat?

"I'm fine," Vivian said and slipped out of the grasp. "We . . . found another body, that's all."

"Another body?" Astaria said. "Oh, dear, I just KNEW something was wrong. I felt a change in the spiritual energy here. Who was it? Poor Harmony?"

"Actually, it's Knight," I said carefully, watching to see the reactions on their faces.

Shock. Pure shock. "Oh, my God," Jolene said and put fingers to her lips. "He was murdered? How?"

"Hanged," Vivian said. "In a locked room, no less. Talk about a mystery."

"You consulted his spirit, of course?" Astaria said, honing in on Vivian like a big bee drawn to honey.

"Uh, no," Vivian said. "Doesn't work that way . . . I told you . . ."

There was a thunder of feet and more people arrived. Harmony and John came at a near run and arrived out of breath, Harmony looking as though she had seen a ghost herself. "What's this I hear? Knight is dead?" John said in an angry voice.

"Yeah, Knight is dead," Vivian said, and I looked at him.

"How did you know?" I asked.

"Well, you're all standing here talking about murder and hanging and locked rooms," John said. "I could hear you all rattling on about it as I was coming up the hall. And besides, Harmony heard you and your dyke lover as you were coming here."

"Oh," I said and frowned. Here I had thought this might be a clue . . . I shrugged.

"And anyway, if the room was locked, how did the two of you get in to find him?"

Vivian shot me a glance.

"Well, I know the combination," I said. "Knight took me to

the room earlier to show me the equipment, and I watched him use the lock . . ."

The gravity of my own words dawned on me then. I knew the combination. I was with Knight.

"Look here," I said firmly. "Knight took me to the room, then for some reason, he left abruptly. I went looking for Vivian, and we went back to the room together . . ."

Their faces went blank. I felt like I was a child again, staring at rows of heads on a table—flaccid, expressionless stares.

"Okay, so perhaps I had opportunity, but I certainly don't have a motive," I said.

Well, as I thought about it, I did have a motive, but I was not about to tell this lot that I had been trying to get here for months, and that Knight and his family had refused to allow me to come at nearly every turn. And it hit me then that one could accuse me of plotting his death solely out of revenge for his refusal.

"Look, we need help getting him down and putting him in the icehouse with the other corpse," Vivian said. "Any volunteers?"

There were hesitations, then finally John and Winston nodded.

"Lead the way," John said, looking at me suspiciously. I took a deep breath and started following the twisting paths back to the room where the recording equipment was. And I was not pleased to note that everyone came along for the ride. En masse we moved through the halls, rather like a funeral party on its way to a burial—or a parade of witnesses going to the executioner's block. Silent as the grave . . .

I planned to sleep with one eye open that night, for sure.

CHAPTER TEN:
VIVIAN

I got stuck on body detail with Mug and Ken.

You ever try to untie a dead guy from a ceiling fan and gently lower him to the floor—all while some menopausal forensic pathologist is telling you not to drop it?

Here's a clue, just drop it, because I don't care how big you are or how hard you try, it's going to drop like a turd out of a horse's ass anyway.

He had been hung with one of the extension cords from the vault where we'd found him. The killer had wrapped it around his neck really tightly. When Maggie had been trying to remove the cord, and I'd yelled out, "Would you look how well that mother is hung!" nobody laughed. I was very disappointed.

Maggie took pictures again and samples, and I was thinking what I know everyone else was thinking—that Maggie's got to be our number one suspect. I'm also wondering what I'm going to do with the cell phone I found on the floor and pocketed earlier.

I wanted to see if it was still working. I thought temporarily about just whipping it out and trying it right then and there, but at that point I didn't trust any of them, not even Maggie, maybe especially not Maggie. If it worked I could call the mainland, and we could all get the hell off the island. But one of them was a coldblooded killer, and if I took that phone out of my pocket, he or she might just go berserk, pull a gun, and start shooting people. After all, if the killer could get a cell phone onto the island, why couldn't they have smuggled on a gun as well? I was going to have to wait till I was alone and then check the phone out.

I wound up with an arm. Ken had the other arm, and Mug had the feet. I had thought he was getting the worst part of the job, then I realized that even on a little wizened guy like Knight most of the weight was in the top part. Besides, his head just sort of hung there staring at me accusingly, so I wanted to yell out, "Hey! I didn't know the crazy bitch was a murderer! Don't you judge me!"

I started to bitch about trading places with Mug, but then I caught a whiff of shit and decided that Mug definitely had the worst end of the job. I ignored Knight's staring.

We started talking—as I guess all people do when they're carrying a corpse through an old hotel which was supposed to be haunted, and they're trying to win a million dollars by not chickening out.

Huh?

"It would help if the stiff was a little stiffer," I said as I almost lost my grip. I remembered what Maggie had said about deadweight.

"Maybe if you and your old lady hadn't killed him . . ." Ken started. He kept cutting me dirty looks, and I didn't have to wonder why he was quick to point a finger at me.

"We found him; we didn't kill him. Besides, you know for a fact that I was walking around outside all day. You met me when I got back."

"You might have been walking around to throw us of the track while she killed him."

"Maggie?" I laughed very convincingly, and added, feeling smug with my performance, "Maggie isn't strong enough to haul a full grown man up to the ceiling by his neck." Though my own thoughts were that Maggie had spent most of her life solving crimes—murders. She knew all about leverage and all about murder. She could have devised a way to do it and to have been out of the room when Juan had bit the big one, too. Maggie was too smart. In order to solve murders you had to be able to see what I saw or think like a criminal.

Maggie'd had a real bone to pick with Knight. Though none of them knew it, I did. Maggie had wanted to come to the island to do research; he'd blocked her. She'd had to deal with heavy losses the last few years, and then there was the whole menopause thing. She might have had a hot flash and just lost it.

"But *you* are," Mug pointed out.

"I am what?" I asked.

"Strong enough to hang a grown man," Mug said.

"I was walking around on the island . . ."

"We don't actually know that. You might have just walked around the house in time to gawk at my wife's naked body," Ken said accusingly.

"You did hit him in the face hard enough to knock him off the boat," Mug pointed out helpfully.

"Why would Maggie or I kill either Juan or the Relative?"

"Same reason every one of you are suspects," Mug started. "The money."

"Fuck that! Why kill either of them? Neither of them were even eligible for the money. Do I look fucking stupid?" I demanded.

Mug looked me up and down and then said, "Yes."

In that moment I almost liked him. After all, being a smart-ass was something I could actually respect.

"Why for that matter would any of us have any reason? Where the hell are you going?" he asked as I started to drag them to the right.

"Around a hot spot," I explained. They both sighed that *We forgot we were with the crazy psychic chick* sigh, and I damn near dropped Knight just for the hell of it.

"So far you and your bitch have found both bodies," Mug pointed out.

"So far . . . that implies there will be more," I said, giving him an accusatory look. "Actually if you remember correctly, Jesus found the first body."

"Who the fuck is Jesus?" Mug asked.

"I think she means the cook," Ken said. "I'm thinking that with Knight dead, he's no longer a suspect, and you and your woman are the only ones telling us what happened."

"Yeah, how do we know that you aren't just feeding us a line of crap?" Mug asked.

It was a good question, and one that I'd asked myself earlier when Maggie was very carefully gathering evidence. She could gather only things that would clear her and implicate someone else, if she were the killer.

I didn't want to believe my best friend was a murderer, but had to admit that it didn't look good for her. Where had she been yesterday while I'd been mucking out our room? And I'd been gone all day that day. She had more than enough time to do whatever she wanted, and she'd admitted that she'd had Knight take her down there. What had she done for the rest of the day?

Of course, I was an even better suspect. I'd been gone all day, and except for that short time that I'd been seen by Barbie, Ken and Maggie, and at breakfast—or what I like to call *reasons-to-go-on-a-diet*—I'd been out running all over the island completely out of sight of everyone but the cameras. I was big enough to haul the body to the ceiling; I'd already hit Knight. I guess except for the fact that I knew I didn't do it—and in spite of what my friends think, I'm really not self-destructive—I'd be pointing a finger my way, too.

All right, maybe I'm a little self-destructive.

The answer came to me in a flash. If I had done it, I sure to hell wouldn't have made it so damn obvious that I had—and neither would Maggie. I probably would have sighed with relief at that point if I wasn't afraid I'd get a big whiff of shit.

"Listen, you couple of dumb fucks. Maggie and I are probably the most educated idiots on this island. If we had done it, you surely to God wouldn't be thinking that we did, because we would have covered our tracks a hell of a lot better than this. For one thing, we wouldn't have been the first ones to find the bodies," I said, all logical-like. "Besides which we don't know that Jesus left the island. In fact if he is the killer and he's smart this would be just the way to put us off him and get us to going after each other."

"I don't think that Spic was that smart. However you and your old lady are way smart enough to use reverse logic," Mug said. I remember thinking at the time that I was surprised that a muscle head like him even knew what reverse logic was, and then I decided that Maggie had definitely done it, because she was just that smart.

"You just stay away from my wife," Ken said, totally out of context and while giving me yet another go-to-hell look.

Mug laughed then, "Dude, what's your problem? Hell, she can do my old lady if I get to watch."

I suddenly had a need to change the subject and had the perfect opportunity. "Hey! Haven't we been in this hall before?"

That's right. We had each decided that the other was leading and had gotten lost. We were carting a shit-stinking corpse all over the mansion.

We finally found our way out of the mansion and made for the old freezer. Going through doors with a corpse, by the way, is a real bitch.

When we finally got in the freezer, we all looked at each other and then dropped the body unceremoniously on the floor. I rubbed at my arms because they hurt, and I didn't care about looking butch at that moment. I heard the whirl of the camera and found it almost comforting. If one of these bastards was the killer, he'd at least have to kill me on camera.

Then I noticed something that was hard to ignore. "Hey guys, didn't you put Juan's body in here?"

"Who's Juan?" Mug asked.

"The other cook. Where's the fucking cook's body?" Ken yelled like a girl. He was either really scared or a damn good actor.

We did a quick search of the freezer. No body, and no bags with Maggie's carefully collected samples, either.

"Why would anyone take the body?" Ken asked in a hushed whisper at my shoulder. Apparently he had forgotten that he was mad at me and had decided that I was less dangerous than Mug—to which I immediately took offense. I've always considered myself to be actually rather intimidating.

"To get rid of the evidence," I said, and dumb-ass was implied.

I walked outside and started looking for tracks, but the best tracks I found were ours, and a trail that had obviously been rubbed out with a palm frond—that trail disappeared in the dense jungle.

"What about Knight?" Mug asked.

"He didn't do it; he's dead," Ken said.

"Not that, moron," Mug bit out. "What about Knight's body?"

"What about him?" I asked.

"Well . . . Do we just leave him here, knowing that someone will just come and steal his body? Do we take him back with us, post a guard . . . what?" Mug asked.

For a dumb guy he was sure saying a lot of things that made sense.

"Who would we trust to guard him? Who wants to be out here alone all night like a sitting duck waiting to be picked off by the killer? As for taking him back inside with us, I'm voting a big no on that one." I walked away from the freezer and started back to the house. "I say we leave him here. Face it, we're all going to be keeping a half an eye on the freezer now. The murderer would have to be nuts to try to take this corpse. Now if you'll excuse me I have to get a shower. For some reason carting around the shitty dead always makes me feel filthy."

Maggie and the other "womenfolk"—and, yes, I think Male Wyman did belong in that group—were in the kitchen when I walked in. I didn't know what they had been talking about, but they all turned their eyes toward me when I walked in.

"Vivian, the energy you felt in the vault, was it old or new?" Maggie asked.

"Christ on a crutch, Maggie!" I was pissed. I suddenly felt like my skin was crawling from the thought of all the filth I'd wallered in. I'd had not one but two visions that day, so my head felt like it was about to bust, and I was on a mission to get into the bathroom, lock the fucking door, and see if I could call the mainland with the phone. The last thing I wanted to do was sit and rehash a vision I'd had. Especially since I was sure that more than any of the other evidence, this vision implicated Maggie. I spit out a short, revised version. "He was grabbed from behind as he was coming out of the room, a piece of extension cord went around his neck, and he was dragged back in the room. He thrashed around till he was dead, and all he saw was the killer's masked face. The killer is wearing one of those black masks that you can see out of but not into, and an all-enveloping metallic silver cloak with a hood. He didn't say anything as he was fucking choking to death. Now if you'll excuse me, I want a shower."

I stomped off. What I hadn't told them was that Knight had his hand in the loops of the cord, and had been able to pull it away from his throat just long enough to croak out, "You!" and, "Why?" He had felt confused by the attack. He had felt that he was safe from this person, and now they had attacked him without provocation. In the moment that I'd had the vision, filled with the knowledge that Maggie had opened a coded lock to enter the room, I had been sure that the person he had trusted, the person who had killed him, was Maggie.

Like I keep trying to say, these images are vague. The dead very seldom jump up and point a finger and say, "Him! He's the one that killed me." It's death energy. Weird things go through people's minds when they're dying. Who would tell their mother? Who would take care of their cat? Did they kiss their kids that morning? Had they finished polishing the silver?

So if you think there are any answers in death that would just make you wrong.

One thing was for sure; the killer knew his shit. That silver get-up of his reflected light, and no doubt played hell with the cameras. It would make the killer seem at least partly invisible on film as the material was reflective. So, my hope that at least the guy that was probably going to kill all of us was going to be caught on tape and go down in a big way was probably not going to happen. He was in this get-up when he was committing the murders, and he intentionally wasn't speaking.

It was easy to see why the superstitious cook thought it was some sort of spook. But Knight had instantly known better. He had known who was behind that mask. But who was it? And how had Knight known without seeing or hearing his killer speak?

Knight hadn't spoken the killer's name—of course, because

that would have just made life too fucking easy.

I collected some clean clothes and my shampoo and towel from our room and headed for the bathroom. I locked the door for two reasons. First, I realized that being alone I was making myself an easy target for the killer, and second I wanted privacy while I checked out the phone. I carefully moved out of camera range.

It was dead of course, and when I flipped it over it was obvious why. The battery had been removed. I had picked it up and pocketed it so quickly I hadn't noticed.

It was worthless to me, and now I had put my fingerprints all over a piece of prime evidence. I crawled into the shower and turned the water on. I scrubbed at my skin till it was almost raw. Then I dressed and went back to the kitchen where it was obvious by everyone's mood that Mug and Ken had told them about the missing body.

The Wymans were sitting in a corner of the room in lotus position, clasping each other's hands and chanting. I rolled my eyes and walked up to stand behind Maggie on the stool she was sitting on, because I had decided while showering that she wasn't the murderer, and even if she was she was my friend and maybe I was a hell of a lot safer if she was the killer because I was sure she liked me enough not to actually kill me. I was just as sure that the killer meant to carry out the pattern of death on this island by killing every single one of us.

So maybe I was screwed no matter what.

"I was just saying that I think it would be safer for everyone if we all stayed together in the same room, if we stayed together all the time. Then no one will be able to do anyone any harm. Then we'll all know what everyone else is doing. It's just for five days, and then the boat will come to get us. If we all stay together, the killer won't be able to get the rest of us," Maggie said.

I nodded. That sounded like good, sound logic to me. "We could all move our things into the dining room. It's more than big enough. It's close to the kitchen and the downstairs bathroom, and . . ."

Mug glared at me and said, "Well, I'd expect you to agree with her. She's your girlfriend after all . . ."

"My partner, she's my *partner,* don't negate our relationship," I hissed back. Maggie cut me a funny look, no doubt wondering why I was being so vehement about a fake relationship, but I just hate it when straights act like gay people's relationships are so temporary. Even though most of mine have been.

"Your *partner* then," he snarled out. "The truth is that if we're all in the same room, it's only going to make us that much easier to kill. A few bullets, and . . ."

"The killer doesn't seem to be using bullets," Ken pointed out. "I think they're right. We'll all be safer if we're staying in the same room. If we're all together."

"Then we'll all be sleeping with the killer. One of you is the killer," Jugs said. She was clinging to Mug's arm tightly, and crying. She looked ready to break. No doubt if the boats had been usable she would have been the first to chicken out. That was if Mug would let her.

"You know what I think, Mug?" I started.

"My name is John," he said.

"Yeah, whatever. I think that if the boats hadn't been scuttled, Jugs . . ."

"Her name is Harmony," he said hotly.

"Yeah, whatever," I said. "My point is that she wouldn't have lasted the night unless you physically forced her, and with all of us wanting the money as badly as you do, we wouldn't have allowed you to force her to stay. So you would have been the first one to go chicken shit, and you would have lost. You're a big guy. You could have easily killed both these men. If you're the killer, it makes sense that you wouldn't want us staying in the same room, because it would stop you killing us all."

"You're just trying to pull everyone's attention away from you and your woman . . ."

"My *partner* . . ."

"Your fucking partner, then. She knew the combination to that room. Did any one else know it? No, no one . . ."

"The door was open when the killer struck . . ." I started.

"We only have your weird-assed word on that. I don't think it's a good idea to take the word of some dyke that talks to dead people. Who knows whether the door was open or not, and only she," he pointed at Maggie, "had the combination."

In the corner the Wymans had stopped chanting, and Male Wyman got to his feet, raising his hand. "I . . . Well, I had the combination. Knight took me down there yesterday to get an extension cord to run our CD player."

The dumb-ass didn't even know that he'd made himself a suspect. I was thinking that he just didn't care because he was the killer, or he was really so fucking stupid that he thought the dead were killing people.

Turned out to at least look like the latter, because the next thing the dumb fuck said was . . . "The killer is not of this realm. It isn't any of us, but only the bad energy which has gathered in this spot, and perhaps if we did all stay together our combined auras could ward off that evil."

I don't know if it was just the idea that we'd be sharing the room with the killer, or that we'd have to share space with the Wymans, but suddenly the whole staying together thing fell apart before our eyes. I don't think it helped matters that Barb had slowly crept up behind me and was playing with my ass, and it probably didn't help that I knew and didn't stop her, or that Ken saw and all but ran across the room to pull her away from me.

"I think perhaps we had better all stick to our own quarters, and our own mates," Ken said, glaring at me. I remember thinking that if he was the killer, I was toast. He continued his line of thought only after giving Maggie a, *can't you see what's going on right behind your back* look. Maggie was, of course, oblivious. "So far, both victims have been alone. If we stay in twos we should be safe enough . . ."

"What about the missing evidence?" Maggie asked. "If we separate, the killer may very well get rid of Knight and all that evidence as well."

"Your *butch*," Mug started, sliding me a glance to see if I was going to let that one slip by—I pretended not to notice, just to screw with his head—"suggested that since we'll all be looking for the killer to move the body it would be stupid for them to do so."

Maggie shot me an angry look, and I shrugged apologetically, knowing instantly why she was angry. Now everyone knew, and even if our murderer had been stupid enough to move the second body, they weren't likely to do it now. That meant that was one way we weren't going to catch them.

Outside night had fallen. Barb and Ken made dinner with us all looking on, making sure they didn't put anything in it that shouldn't have been there. It was probably very healthy because it tasted like cardboard and had the consistency of lumpy milk and lettuce. We ate in silence. Then chose up sides and went to bed. Once in our room I covered our door with the old latticework and furniture as I had the night before and covered up the door to the veranda as well with Maggie's help.

"So," Maggie said shooting me a look as I lit the candles. "You either no longer think I'm the murderer, or you're trusting me not to kill you."

"You've got to admit, Maggie," I said, more than a little ashamed. "It did look like you were the only one who could have done it . . ." I also explained to her about the vision. "By the time ole Mug suggested that a really smart person would use reverse logic, I was sure you'd done it again." I grabbed a cigarette out of my carton and lit it. "And don't you dare say shit about the fucking smoke. It's been a horrible day, and you should just think of it as mosquito repellent."

She nodded. "So what's with you and"—Maggie knew her name, but as I said I still don't remember it—"Barb?"

I told Maggie about my encounter with her earlier that afternoon, and what she'd been doing in the kitchen.

"What sort of a woman goes after another person's mate, especially when they are themselves attached?" Maggie asked thoughtfully.

"Hey, I'm the fucking bomb," I said with a laugh.

Maggie smiled then and shook her head. "If you say so, but I'm being serious."

"The same sort of person that thinks glacier climbing and bungee jumping are good times. They're both excitement junkies. Danger freaks," I said. "She wants to do me because it would be dangerous. We might get caught, by you, by him, or by someone else who would tell you or him. It makes it exciting. I've run into her type before . . . Hell, I've screwed her kind before."

"You're horrible."

"Yeah, because I have to tell you that I'm beginning to believe that none of us are going to make it off this island alive, and if I get a chance to get one more piece of ass before I go, I'm going for it," I said shaking my head emphatically.

"We aren't going to die because we're going to be smart." Maggie started pacing back and forth looking thoughtful. "Why kill Knight?"

I started jumping up and down. "Oh, oh, oh. Phone!" I said excitedly as if it answered everything.

"Phone?" Maggie stopped pacing and looked at me like I was crazy.

"Phone," I said as I reached down, pulled it out of my backpack and brought it to her. She took it from me and immediately tried to use it. "It doesn't work. Flip it over—the battery pack's gone."

"Where did you get this?"

I explained to her and apologized again for my lack of trust. "Don't you see? Knight was trying to use the phone. He was calling for help . . ."

"Why wait till today?"

Well, that was a good question. I hadn't really gotten that far in my logic. "And who was he calling, and if he did call yesterday why didn't the little boat cavalry ride in today?"

Maggie nodded. "I wish I had my lab. Better than that I wish that people would quit dying so that I could get a chance to set up the specrectaloptinator. They have one down there, you know. It gauges what zodiac sign a restless spirit is."

All right, you guessed it, that isn't what she said, but it's close enough to get the gist.

"I wish people would quit dying because if they don't, pretty soon there isn't going to be anyone left for them to kill but you and me."

"Yeah, that sucks." Maggie sat down on her sleeping bag and made a face. She stood up quickly and looked for a stick. She found one and picked up the edge of her sleeping bag. "What in hell's name is that?"

I cringed as I saw the half-eaten monster roach and the chopsticks. Then, as if to add insult to injury, my little gecko buddy came running over—and I swear he was wagging his tail. I reached down and picked up the roach with the chopsticks and held it out to him. He took it and ran off.

I looked up at Maggie and smiled helplessly. "I call him Jake."

CHAPTER ELEVEN:
MAGGIE

"You gave it a name?"

Vivian blinked at me. "Yeah."

"So which one did you name Jake?" I asked. "The gecko or the roach?"

"I didn't give the roach a fucking name," she said. "Jake's the gecko."

It was real hard not to roll my eyes. "And where did you get the roach?"

"Out in the jungle," Vivian said. "The little mother attacked me when I wasn't looking. Why didn't you warn me that roaches were predators?"

"Roaches are scavengers," I said. "Not predators. And anyway, why did you bring it back here?"

"So I could train old Jake there to kill roaches . . ."

I sighed and looked at the gecko peering at us from the corner. "Vivian, you don't have to train geckos to kill roaches. They eat roaches naturally."

"Yeah, well, I wanted to make sure he would do it on command . . ."

I opened my mouth, then closed it and shook my head. Then I started to laugh, because I suddenly had this absurd image of Vivian standing in the middle of the room, looking like the falconers of old, swinging the roach around on a string to convince the gecko to attack it.

"What?" Vivian said.

"Never mind."

"Never mind, nothing. You were laughing at me," she said.

"I was laughing at the thought of you training a gecko, that's all," I said. "What's with the chopsticks?" I picked them up.

"You think I was going to touch a roach with my bare hands?"

"Wouldn't that depend on who rolled it?" I asked.

"Oh, that's real funny," Vivian said. "You wouldn't know a roach if you saw one."

"Yes I would . . . I . . . experimented with pot . . . once . . . when I was in college. But it made me sick, so I never tried it again."

"Weenie," Vivian said.

"Look who's talking," I said. "Don't you lose dyke points if they find out you're afraid of roaches . . ."

"What would you know about dyke points?"

"You're always talking about dyke points."

Vivian sneered. "I'm surprised you listen to anything I say."

"So what else happened while you were out there looking for the boat?" I tossed the sticks aside. "Jake" disappeared with the whisk of a tail.

"Exactly what I told everyone downstairs," Vivian said. "Well, almost everything . . ."

"What?"

Vivian rummaged through her pack and pulled out her sketchpad and a couple of pencils. Erasers rumbled like a little avalanche of stones, and some of her sketches fluttered to the floor, but she was too involved with the pad and the one pencil she kept hold of to notice.

"I saw someone," she said. "Someone from the past . . ."

She began to sketch, and I sat back, waiting as patiently as I could. The pencil flicked this way and that. Vivian was almost in a trance as black lines of graphite took shape on the white surface. At last, she took a deep breath and stopped, studying her handiwork.

"I felt someone dying, a young woman who must have been part of the staff," she said softly. "She was running away from someone . . . and when she stopped and turned around I saw this man . . ."

I took the sketchbook and stared into a face that sent a shiver down my spine. Something about the eyes, which Vivian had captured so well, was enough to make my blood turn a little cold. I almost got the impression they were looking at me. It was enough to make me put the picture down and look away.

"So that's what he looked like," I said softly.

"Yeah, he was a crazy son of a bitch, too," Vivian said. "He tortured the woman before he put her out of her misery . . ."

I nodded and looked back at the sketch. There was something vaguely familiar about the face. Something I could not quite put my finger on. And yet . . .

Frowning, I pulled out my book on Knight's Island. There was a section with pictures of the victims of each massacre. Glancing at them, I tried to associate the face in the drawing, but to my astonishment, not one of the victims—including Garret Knight who supposedly committed all the murders in a moment of insanity—bore any resemblance to the killer.

"This is strange," I said.

"What?"

"Well . . . all along it's been assumed that a member of the family went insane and killed the rest, but . . . that man doesn't look like anyone in Knight's family." I started flipping into the rest of the book. The resort murders had been earlier, and there were photos of those victims as well. "Where's that other sketch you drew?" I said.

Vivian pushed a couple of drawings aside and turned up the one she had drawn our first night there. Again, I compared it to the book, but there was no one who looked like the thin young person who had slain the resort residents all those years before Knight's family died.

I picked up her drawing from the night before and put the sketches together, and took in a long shuddering breath.

"What?" Vivian asked as I laid the drawings down.

"It's the same man, twenty years older, but he was never supposed to be on the island," I said thoughtfully.

"What?"

"Look, your sketches are of the same man, just older, someone who was not known to be on the island at either time. See . . . there's no resemblance to any of the faces in the book."

"Maybe he's someone they didn't have a picture of?" Vivian suggested.

"No, everyone who was on the island in both cases is accounted for in the books. Remember, the second killer was assumed to have been Garret Knight, who then committed suicide, and the first killer was assumed to have been a member of the staff who worked at the resort the first time, who also committed suicide. But you have seen the killer at two different times in his life, and he's not in the book."

She looked at me, and I looked at her . . .

"Are you thinking what I think you're thinking?" Vivian asked with a frown.

"What if the killer who is causing all this trouble now is someone outside the party as we know it?" I asked. "Maybe there is someone else on this island that we don't know about . . ." My mind strayed back to that camera that watched the digital monitors in the locked room.

"Oh, great, Maggie," Vivian said and sneered at me. "That's going to make it real easy for me to sleep at night."

"You're not the only one," I said and looked at our entrance. "You don't suppose there's a way we could barricade the doorway a little better, do you?"

"Damn straight there is," Vivian said. She bounced to her feet, and I crawled up a little more slowly. As I watched, she began to create a barricade of old boards and shutters. "Come on," she called to me. "Look for ones with lots of old nails in them."

"You're not proposing that we nail them over the door, are you?" I asked. "Because we don't have a hammer . . ."

"We don't need a hammer, and we're not nailing them over the door because I want to be able to get out if I have to." Vivian lifted a couple of the shutters. "But if we lay enough of them across the path, the killer is bound to trip over them and stab himself on the nails."

Well, it did make sense to me. So I gathered some shutters and helped Vivian lay them about the floor rather like scattered pick-up sticks. Only when we were satisfied that the layer was deep enough that anyone coming through the door was likely to land on one or more boards and cause a commotion, did we retire.

But I will admit that I lay there for a while, listening to the distant surf, the strange bird calls, and the occasional creak of a board out in the corridors . . .

I was never a late sleeper, and when an early ray of sunlight found its way past the debris stacked against the balcony door, I woke up. Vivian was still out for the count as I padded around, getting my head and my spirits together. I wanted a cup of real coffee, not the stuff that Vivian had made for us the morning before. She always made her coffee too weak; it looked more like tea than coffee. I could kick myself for not bringing some of those coffee singles that are like teabags. They don't make the best coffee in the world, but caffeine is caffeine to an addict.

I wasn't getting caffeine. I wasn't leaving the room . . . not without Vivian.

Our trap remained undisturbed. I moved the less formidable stack of debris on the balcony door and walked out to see if the morning sun and some fresh air might reinstate my brain. The air was only slightly cooler than normal, which was still warmer than other places I had been. There was a thin tatter of mist creeping in and out of the trees. And it wasn't alone. A female figure moved with a hint of stealth in every step. She was coming straight at the part of the hotel Vivian and I called home. I walked over to the edge of the balcony for a better look.

Panther-like, the woman continued to creep out of the trees and along the edge of the building. For some reason, she was more focused on moving without making a sound. But she wasn't doing a very good job of blending with her surroundings, especially wearing the thin spandex leotard and tights that left nothing to the imagination. And as she got closer, I quickly pegged who it was.

"Morning, Jolene," I called down.

I thought she was going to leave her spandex behind. She nearly tripped over the broken tiles on the old veranda as she looked back and forth, then up.

"Oh . . . good morning, Ms. Holmes."

"Call me Maggie," I said. "Everyone else does."

Jolene smiled. "Is . . . Vivian awake yet?"

"Viv? Sleeps like the dead. She's not much of one for mornings."

As if to make a liar out of me, Vivian came stumbling out, stretching and yawning.

"Really?" Jolene said and smiled.

Vivian looked down at the woman, and I swear the most lascivious smile spread across her face.

"I thought perhaps you'd like to join me in a session of . . .

exercise?" Jolene said, and it was clear that I was not being invited.

I stuck my tongue in my cheek and looked straight at Vivian. Her face went a little red. "Uh . . . maybe later," she said.

"Ah." Jolene's face fell.

"What she means is, we already have plans for the morning," I said.

"We do?" Vivian said with a sidelong look at me.

"Sure, we're going to go look for the boat, remember?" I said pointedly. "It was what we discussed last night?"

"Oh, yeah . . . right." Vivian shrugged, and I could tell from the look she gave me that she knew we had not discussed looking for the boat last night. "I'll catch you later, Jolene." She winked for good measure. "Don't warm up without me, okay?"

Jolene's smile spread like a thin line of blood across her face. "I'll be waiting," she said. "Winston will be practicing yoga all afternoon, and I do get so bored waiting alone while he is off in his little transcendental world. Maybe we could exercise then, yah?"

She turned and sauntered away, hips swaying provocatively. Just a glance smoldering with desire flicked back over her shoulders before she slipped back into the trees.

"That was a proposition," I said.

"You're catching on," Vivian said. "We'll make a proper fem out of you yet . . ." She wandered back inside. "Hey, God dammit! I'll tear your tail out if you do that again!"

I stepped back into the room in time to see the flash of gecko blue-green disappearing under the shutters. "What?" I said.

"Damn little mother tried to bite my toe!" Vivian said.

"A predator is a predator," I said. "He's just reverting to nature. Your toes probably reminded him of grubs or something . . ."

"Oh, thank you very much," Vivian said and glanced at her

feet. "That's all I need—him thinking my toes are grubs. Wait, you mean they eat grubs, too?"

"If it's a bug, they eat it," I said. "Larva, pupa, doesn't matter what stage . . ."

"They eat pubic hair?"

"Pupa," I said. "The non-feeding stage of an insect between larva and adult—a cocoon . . ."

"I knew that," Vivian said. "Remind me to get the little mother another cockroach. I'd rather he ate things that could run instead of munching on things that resemble my toes."

I merely smiled. "Come on, let's get dressed, get something to eat, and go look for that boat."

"How come you know so much about bugs?" Vivian asked, and I gathered my pack to find something that remotely resembled clean clothes in this tropical climate.

"It's the latest technique for determining time of death in forensic pathology," I said. "Now let's get going, okay? I want to be out of here before Ned and Astaria start some new ritual to the sun . . ."

Vivian sneered and started searching for her day clothes.

It was like watching a dance to see Vivian trying to dodge hot spots and trees. In a way it reminded me of when Anne was a child and would accompany me on hikes in the woods. Children think the trail is nonexistent. So they run in and out of the ferns and pines, and usually end up cracking their noggins on low limbs or crawling through the poison oak.

Vivian's dance was not quite as freeform, though. She was very methodical, taking a step or two, pausing, sidestepping and so on. I wished I had some of that equipment that was in the vault; it would have been great to see just how hot those spots were. If the machines could detect anywhere near as well as Vivian could.

Our path took us around the end of the island that Vivian had not explored.

"It occurred to me that I took the long way around yesterday—that I should have gone the other way instead," Vivian said and stopped again. She frowned, stepped back and moved around the other side of a tree. We had agreed that it would be better to stay just inside the woods and off the beach. This way, we were less apt to be seen. "The map has this cove on down around the headlands, and if I were going to hide a boat, that would probably be the best place to keep it."

"Assuming the killer didn't mind walking a long ways, that makes sense," I said.

"Yeah, well the psycho probably didn't walk at first. Besides the island's just not all that big. You could walk around the whole island in less than a day's time."

I nodded.

"And they probably cut across the middle of the island to get back."

"And why didn't we cut across the middle of the island?" I asked.

"Are you that eager to run into this psycho mother?"

"Not really," I said and sighed. "I'm not the Warrior Princess type."

"Yeah, well neither am I," Vivian said. She stopped again and peered off at the waves that surged gently across the sands. I glanced up and spied one of the cameras angled down in our direction. It was not stationary, and scanned back and forth like a security camera in a bank. As I watched it shift and stare at us, I suddenly realized why Vivian liked to mug for them. There was a temptation to stick my tongue out at it, but with my luck, that would be the one shot Kennedy would keep in to show millions of viewers. My dignity was more important to me than that.

"Let's go this way," Vivian said and started deeper into the trees. I followed, still watching the camera. It moved, its one eye staring at me like a Cyclops, and kept pace with our movements. In fact, it continued to do so until a tree obscured us from its view.

The terrain roughened a bit, slowing our progress. Here the tall palms dug in roots around rocks and sandy soil, and little pin oaks and scrub cedar filled in what gaps they could claim. I slipped more than once. Vivian scampered up it much more efficiently.

"Come on, Maggie, am I going to have to carry you?"

"I'm coming," I said, hoping my panting was not as obvious as it sounded. Damn menopause. I was having a hot flash now, and sweat poured off my skin. But I was determined and reached the summit where Vivian stood waiting. She eyeballed me with a sardonic smile.

"You're not that old yet," she said.

"Old enough to knock you down," I said and leaned against a tree.

Vivian sneered and started on. Part of me wondered if she was taking this path just to taunt me. Or get back at me for the remark about her toes looking like grubs. They don't really, but geckos have weird eyesight.

The headlands broke before us, revealing the cove. I stopped at the edge of the drop that plunged gently into a crevice of sand and stone where a few trees managed to cling. There were nests in some of the rock faces, and a multitude of sea birds—terns, gulls, pelicans—wheeled and sang croaking and screeching songs. Below we could see the inlet where tide pools formed when the sea moved out. The tide was moving out now, leaving crabs and other crustaceans high and dry. Briefly, I wondered if suggesting a clambake or steaming crabs would be wise. The dry biscuits someone made for this morning were still lumps of lead in my stomach.

"No boat," Vivian said more to herself than me.

I pointed toward the heart of the inlet. There was an outcropping of rocks obscuring the view. "From the looks of the land, I bet there's more to this inlet than we can see from here. The tidal pools are high enough among the rocks that I'm willing to bet there's more cove just past that small bluff. If I was going to hide a boat, I'd want it tucked into a small space instead of out here in the open."

"You might be right," Vivian said and started following the bluff we were on in that general direction.

We worked our way through the trees, stopping now and again to make sure we were still on track. The land sloped gently toward the bluff. A mass of sea birds were darting in and out of the area, and from here, I could hear them squabbling. Fighting over territory, maybe?

Vivian was still ahead of me, and she reached the lower bluff before I did. She crawled close to the edge and peered around the end of the small bluff as I was reaching the bottom of the descent.

"Oh, puke!" she said and suddenly jerked back and looked away.

"What?"

She squelched her face into a deep frown and gestured. "Damn, I didn't need to see that."

I crawled over to the edge.

Past the bluff I could see where the cove ended. Water trickled down the ragged edges of the rocks and formed a falls, though it wasn't spectacular. Peaceful, maybe . . . except that the whole scene was marred by the remains of a pair of hanging corpses that were being savaged by the sea birds. *Ah, nature,* I thought and sat down. Those bodies were little more than mutilated meat on bones, and only the flapping apron that hung like a rag from one leg of one corpse gave me any clue as to who they might have been.

"Well, at least we know where Eduardo and Miguel are," I said.

There was no way I could convince Vivian to climb the tree and cut them down so I could examine them, and besides, they were more likely to end up in the water. Nor would it have been possible to do much more than say, "Yes, they are dead," without the right equipment. Nature had destroyed a lot of visible evidence. Getting them back to the freezer would not be a simple matter without assistance. When a body becomes that mutilated, it's hard to move without a gurney or a body bag.

Besides, we already knew how Eduardo had died.

And now we knew what happened to his corpse.

Miguel had made the mistake of running. He'd separated himself from the group and made it easy for the killer to pick him off. Since he obviously hadn't taken the boat, he would have made his way back to the mansion, where there was food, shelter, and other people. The murderer would have known that he hadn't gotten away and would be waiting for him. Then he killed him and brought both his and Eduardo's bodies here.

I guess it didn't really matter how Miguel had died at this point.

"Where's a camera when you need one?" I muttered as we made our way back to the hotel. This time, we cut across land at a quicker pace. It was past noon, and the air was warm. I just wanted a drink of water.

"We don't tell anyone," Vivian said as we reached sight of the hotel.

"Why not?" I asked.

"Look, Maggie, we're dealing with some sick fuck . . . I mean, he takes dead people out and hangs them in a tree and feeds them to the birds . . . There's no telling what a psycho like that would do."

"But it would be nice to know why he stole Eduardo's body out of the freezer. Why he brought them all the way across the island to destroy them. There has to be a reason for that . . . some part of the killer's psyche that demands he mutilate and destroy the evidence." I frowned.

"Nice, my ass," Vivian said. She stopped and rounded on me, forcing me to back up a few steps. "It's a psycho, Maggie. They don't need reasons. You've autopsied enough of their victims to know that. I've seen enough of their handiwork . . . lived enough of their victims' last moments. It's a no-brainer, *comprende?*"

I heaved a sigh. "Okay, we'll keep it to ourselves . . . but I rather suspect it won't stay a secret for long. Sooner or later, one of the others will find them."

"That's *their* problem," Vivian said and shook her head. "The last thing we need is to be the first ones to find yet another body. Besides, there goes the whole 'Jesus is still here killing us' theory, and I'm thinking that's about the only thing stopping us being lynched right now."

We reached the back veranda where Ned and Astaria Wyman last performed their ritual dancing. They were there now, as a matter of fact. Fortunately, they were fully clothed as we walked up on them. Astaria was drawing sand circles on the broken cobbles. Ned was watching.

"Trying to make a sandbox?" Vivian asked.

"Shhhhh," Ned said. "She has to concentrate while she consecrates the circle."

As much as I wanted to leave the area, I was bound by my innate curiosity. "What is she doing?" I asked softly.

"She's going to see if she can find the body that disappeared out of the freezer," he said. "She's hoping the spirits will tell her where they've taken it."

I suddenly remembered Vivian's remark about how Astaria would probably have trouble conjuring a fart, and I wanted to giggle. Instead, I bit my tongue and started on for the hotel. Vivian stayed but a moment then followed.

"Those two are certifiable," she muttered.

I nodded. We headed on toward the courtyard between the buildings and made our way across cracked cobbles. Something resembling a large cockroach darted across our path, swiftly followed by a black snake. I thought Vivian was going to freak, but she stopped and muttered, "Damn, I forgot Jake's roach."

We were almost at the doors when Jolene suddenly appeared in our path. She blocked the opening and smiled.

"I've been waiting for you," she said. "Ready for your exercise?"

Vivian looked at me and smiled. "Catch you later, honey," she said with a wink.

"Vivian, I . . ."

"Hey, I'll catch you later," she said pointedly.

"But we agreed . . ."

Vivian leaned over to me to whisper, "Look, I am horny and so is she, and why waste an opportunity, all right?"

With that, she turned, grabbed Jolene's hand and headed down the hall.

"Just like a *guy*," I said. "Always thinking with the little head."

The last thing I saw was Vivian throwing me a bird before she disappeared down the corridor.

I sighed and leaned against the wall. This was not good. We were supposed to stick together, and now I was alone. Of course, I could have gone to the locked room, closed myself in and played with the equipment there, but the killer knew the code, and I was not about to be there when he or she walked in. I could have walked out and watched Ned and Astaria and their ritual, but I just flat didn't like them. Apart from which, I was hungry now, and thirsty.

I made the kitchen my destination. No one was there as I scrounged and found some crackers. Then I snatched up one of the bottles of water that sat in cases in the corner. It was room temperature, but I didn't care as I unscrewed the cap and took a slug.

So many questions raced about in my head. I stared at the site of the first murder, then looked up at the angle of the camera.

Why so many dead spots in the rooms? I thought. Why so many corners not covered with cameras? It was as if the studio crew had purposely left places where the killer could hide and never be caught on those cameras.

But why would they do that?

Ned walked into the kitchen. He didn't see me at first, and I held my place, not wanting to draw his attention in my direction. But there were not a lot of places to hide, and he turned and spotted me.

"Oh . . . I was looking for salt," he said.

"Salt?" I asked.

"Yes, to help in the consecration of the circle of power my wife is drawing."

"Ah, yes," I said. "The salt is over there." I pointed toward one of the storage units.

He stepped over, opened it and looked in. A container of Morton's Iodized Salt greeted him. He snatched it up in one pudgy hand.

"I thought one used pure salt to consecrate a circle," I said.

"One uses what one has. My wife is a modern witch. She has learned to mix the old and the new."

"Ah, yes. New Age," I said.

He frowned. "For someone who is so smart, you don't seem to have a lot of respect for our beliefs. But then, some people who are not who they pretend to be ought not to be so critical of others . . ." He turned for the door, a storm cloud of an expression on his face.

Great, I had no idea what he meant by that, everyone already knew who Vivian and I were by then. About my books and Vivian's "gift." Maybe he had just figured out that Vivian and I weren't a couple. Maybe he was just being such a piss head because he knew I didn't like him and thought he and his wife were big, fat phonies. I decided I'd be better off going back to the room and barricading myself in. There was no telling how long it would take Vivian and Jolene to finish their tryst.

Then again, why was I getting so upset?

Let Vivian have her fun. She certainly wasn't "getting any" from me on this trip. Except for the fact that there was a crazed killer on the island and we were supposed to be watching each other's backs and she was more concerned with watching Jolene's backside.

Still clutching my crackers and water, I made my way back to the stairs that would lead up to our room to work on making some notes. I had just put one foot on the bottom stair when I heard a high-pitched scream. My heart stopped; it had come from the same direction Vivian and Jolene had taken. I turned and ran toward the sound as fast as I could, my heart fairly thundering in my chest as I made the last turn. I could see the open door at the end of the corridor, Winston and Jolene's room. Without stopping, I burst in.

Vivian and Jolene were trying to untangle themselves from what was clearly a compromising position. I think it's what they call a "69." At any rate, they were both as naked as the day they were born, struggling to get apart.

The screaming was coming from the corner, from Winston, to be precise. He had gone purple in the face, and shrieked like a woman scorned as he scrambled about the room, grabbing up broken boards.

"I'll kill you, you fucking bitch!" he screamed. "I'll kill both of you!"

CHAPTER TWELVE:
VIVIAN

I was just having myself a good time, doing some of my best work and minding my own business. Of course I was doing somebody's wife, and I knew Barb was most likely into getting caught, so I guess maybe I should have known she'd lied about Ken's yoga crap. And with all that had happened since we'd gotten to the island I should have been prepared for all hell to break loose . . .

But, I was just way too busy to worry about getting caught.

Ole Ken burst through that door with blood in his eyes and immediately started looking for something to kill me with. Maggie ain't far behind him, no doubt having heard him screaming in a way that would have put horror queen Jamie Lee Curtis to shame.

I'm trying to untangle myself from Barb, and I'm looking for my clothes—which are basically thrown everywhere—because the last thing I want to do is get in a fight bare-assed naked.

Of course he gets hold of a big board and comes after me as I'm trying to get my shorts on, which basically puts me into the position of just being a huge bare-assed target.

Luckily, Maggie had apparently picked up her own board somewhere, and she popped Ken in the head. He stumbled and almost fell.

I had my shorts on by then, so I sent a good roundhouse kick into his stomach. He hit the floor, and I jumped on him and tried to wrestle the board out of his hands. It wasn't as easy as you might think, even with the damage Maggie and I had done to him. He was in good shape, no doubt from eating all that healthy crap and working out constantly. I wound up putting my knee in his solar plexus, and he lost his grip on the board. I, of course, flipped across the floor ass over teakettle.

But then I jumped to my feet like some ninja and redeemed my butchness. I held the board like the bat I would have been holding if I'd stayed home and played my ball game instead of letting Maggie drag me to hell.

I looked at Ken and said probably the stupidest thing I have ever said in my life, "I don't want any trouble."

Maggie immediately made sure I knew just how stupid this was, when she said in a voice just above a mumble, "Then maybe you shouldn't have had sex with his wife."

Ken stumbled to his feet, and I couldn't be sure whether he was hurt bad enough not to try to kill me, or if he was mad enough that a little thing like pain wasn't going to stop him from stomping my butt, so I stayed in a defensive stance.

Barb was standing in a corner wrapped in a sheet, and looking far from guilty. She was *smiling,* and I knew I'd been used. I wish I could say I was surprised, or that I really cared, but the truth was that I wasn't and I didn't, not as long as I got me some—and I had.

"Dammit, Barb . . ." Of course Ken knew his wife's name, but me—big shrug guys—still can't remember it. Considering the fact I had sex with her, I guess I really should but I don't. "How could you do this, *again?*"

"Ken," not his name, "it doesn't have anything to do with you. You know that I love you. I just need a woman every once in a while."

"Do you realize you were on camera?" Maggie asked in a disapproving tone, pointing at it, and I had a momentary shiver of pure joy run up my spine as I thought of my parents.

151

Ken turned on Maggie, rubbing his head where she'd hit him, and looking at her in disbelief. "Is that all you have to say? Doesn't it bother you at all that she just cheated on you with my wife?"

"Ah . . ." Maggie had no doubt forgotten that she was supposed to be my partner. I almost laughed as I watched the look on her face turn from mild embarrassment to mock anger. She was a shitty actress. She turned to me as she talked to Ken, "Oh, I've gotten used to her infidelity. She has the absolute morals of a common alley cat. Always running around with her tail in the air, looking for any tramp who'll spread her legs for her."

"Hey! Don't call my wife names," Ken said turning on Maggie.

"Don't you yell at my old lady!" I screamed back at him, just because I thought it was damned rude of him to be yelling at Maggie. After all, Maggie hadn't done anything to him. Except of course hit him in the head with a board.

"Your old lady?" Maggie said, giving me an incredulous look, and just for a minute it looked like she was going to lose it and start laughing. Then—no doubt to keep from cracking up in front of Ken and Barb—she yelled, "I've just about had enough of your shit!" and stomped out of the room.

I grabbed the rest of my clothes, still keeping a wary eye on Ken, and went after Maggie yelling, "Ah, honey, ya know I love ya."

Maggie looked back over her shoulder at me, a half grin on her face, and shook her head, never stopping her forward momentum; I just grinned back helplessly and shrugged. We had almost made it to the stairs when here came the rest of the troops.

"What in hell's name is going on?" Mug yelled at us, successfully blocking our way.

"Is someone else dead?" Jugs asked from somewhere behind him.

"No," I said quickly, knowing they were talking about all the yelling and thinking they didn't need to know about what we'd found earlier that day.

"Nothing but our relationship!" Maggie cried out, cupped her face in her hands and scooted right through them and up the stairs. I started to run right after her, but Mug moved to block my way.

"What the hell's going on?" he demanded.

"Yes, what's going on?" Male Wyman asked, trying to sound as forceful as Mug, which just didn't work.

"I screwed Barb. All right?" I said, just wanting to get the hell away from them. After all, I still didn't quite have my shirt on. You know how a tank top will sometimes hang, leaving you exposed in one place or another? Well, that's where it was.

"Who the hell is Barb?" Mug demanded.

"You know, Ken's wife," I said, and tried to push past him.

"Ken?" he asked. I wondered when he'd made himself leader of the tribe.

"You know, I do say, old chap," I said mimicking his accent.

"You slept with . . ." and, yes, even that meathead Mug had her name right. "Cool!" he said with real admiration.

"Now can I go?" I asked.

"Yeah, let the ass-kissing commence," he said with real camaraderie in his voice as he stepped aside.

By the time I got back to our room I had my shirt on but still had my bra and underwear in my hand. Maggie was sitting on her bedroll, and she looked up at me smugly.

"Like the way I got away from the Wymans, the big idiot and his timid girlfriend?"

"Very impressive, and thanks for saving my ass back there,

too, by the way."

"Would have served you right if I'd let him beat you to a pulp. Your *old lady!* Really, Vivian, is it any wonder you keep cans of beer longer than you can keep a girlfriend?"

Jake trotted up to me expectantly. "Ah gee, buddy! I'm sorry, I forgot your roach." He looked dejected and trotted off to hide under some rubble.

"You have remorse for forgetting to bring a gecko a bug, but none for having ruined those people's marriage," Maggie said, giving me her famous patented *You're pond scum* look.

"Hey! You heard him. She's done this before," I defended as I walked over to my backpack and dug out my cigarettes. Something was missing. I could almost feel it, so I dug through the bag. Then I sighed and flopped on my butt on the floor. "Fuck!" I said as if it explained everything.

"What?" Maggie asked.

"The phone's missing."

Maggie's face scrunched up in thought, "Someone took it?"

"Well, it didn't get up and walk out of my bag," I said. "Unless one of the Wymans' spells worked, and now they've enlisted the forces of good to animate objects to scare off the evil spirits."

"With those two coconuts, anything is possible," Maggie said flippantly. "Recently Male Wyman has started being really snippy with me."

"Maybe he thinks you're the murderer," I suggested.

"Maybe, but I don't think so. It's something else."

"Why take the phone?" I asked.

"Obviously the blood still hasn't made it back up to your little one-tracked brain," Maggie said, and I was starting to get a little pissed about the judgmental tone of her voice. I was thinking Maggie had gotten it plenty when John had been alive, lots more than I ever had. I had to get mine when I could, and if Barb didn't care about cheating on her husband why should

I? Hell, I didn't even know the guy. Guess I didn't really know her, either, considering that even now I can't remember her real name. "You'd take the phone if you had the battery. Let's say Knight was on the phone when he surprised the killer . . ."

"Nope," I said shaking my head. "I told you how it went down. He surprised Knight, and Knight knew the killer. Knight thrashed around a lot. What if the phone belonged to the killer? No boats have showed up, and surely to God if Knight had the phone—since he's not the killer—he would have called for help."

"The killer loses his phone in the struggle. It hits the floor, and the battery pack comes off. It wasn't stolen and the phone planted at all. It was an accident," Maggie said thoughtfully. "He drops the phone in the struggle. You find the phone. He realizes he's lost his phone and he comes back to get it, but all he finds is the battery."

"So how did he know I had the phone?" I asked.

Maggie takes in a long shuddering breath. The kind you do when you just realize something you'd rather not know. Then she looked up at the camera in our room. "Because he's watching us. The camera in the vault—the one trained on all the others. There must be a way that he's viewing it—a closed circuit TV somewhere."

"That's how he knows exactly when and where to strike," I said. "We have to stop that shit, Maggie."

"How?"

"Take out that fucking camera. Get rid of the monitors in that vault so the killer can't watch us." I was whispering then and looking away from the camera.

Maggie shrugged that she couldn't hear me, and it was my turn to look at her like she was a moron. She nodded and crawled over to where I was on all fours so that I could whisper it in her ear, which I did, and she nodded.

"Oh, are you girls working things out?" Female Wyman said

from the door. Because of the covert thing we'd been engaged in, we both all but jumped out of our skin, and the fact that it was one of the Wymans just made it that much worse. After all, we had just very skillfully avoided capture. "I thought I'd help counsel you through this. I am a high priestess after all, and . . ."

"Oh my shitting God," I said jumping to my feet and going back to my pack to get the cigarette I'd gone after in the first place. I grabbed one, lit it, and took a long drag.

"There's no need to get angry, Ms. Storm, I'm just trying to help."

"We need your help like we need a good case of hemorrhoids," I mumbled and walked out onto the balcony.

"Would you like to talk about it?" Female Wyman asked Maggie in a comforting tone.

"We'll be fine," Maggie said with more charity than I would have thought even she could muster. "We've been through this before. It's what happens when you have a partner who can't keep her fly shut."

"We find it's just so much easier when one doesn't try to make boundaries on their love. I go, as my husband does, to wherever my heart takes me. Our union isn't built on ownership. Perhaps if you and I were to join in love and joy and share one another, the healing could begin, and . . ."

It was obviously my turn to save Maggie. I stormed back into the room. "Hey, bitch, just back the hell off," I said. Maggie looked like a deer caught in headlights. I put my hand down and helped her to her feet. "I'm so sorry, Baby, it won't happen again," I said.

"I forgive you," Maggie said quickly. She looked at Female Wyman. "We'll be fine now, thanks."

"If you need to talk . . ." She let out a yelp. She was wearing those damned Jesus sandals, and ole Jake had just chomped him a big piece of toe. "Filthy little reptile." She started to chase my little friend down, and I ran and jumped between her and him.

"He's one of the earth's creatures," I reminded her.

She left in a huff.

Maggie and I looked at each other and started to laugh.

"We have got to find him a really big roach," Maggie said.

I motioned for her to follow me, and we moved under the camera. "They already all think we did it. If they catch us knocking out the cameras, it's going to make us look all the more suspect," she said.

I nodded. She had a point. "Wait! We could go tell them all that we think that's how the killer is working and suggest that together we destroy the cameras, and whoever is against it will be our killer." I felt pretty smart.

"What then?" she asked. I shrugged. I hadn't thought any further than that. Maggie suddenly grinned.

"What?" I asked.

"I was just thinking that Female Wyman has forever ensured my heterosexuality."

I nodded. "Hell, damn near made me rethink my whole lifestyle," I said.

"So what now?" Maggie asked.

"Gather the troops?" I said.

"I guess. Do we tell them about the phone?" Maggie asked.

"I don't see why. I mean it's gone now. The killer knows we had it . . ."

"Damn!" Maggie interrupted.

"What?" I didn't like the way she said damn.

"Well, why does he have the phone?" She then proceeded to answer her own question. "He has the phone because he's not working alone. Remember what we talked about last night?"

"The possibility that there is someone else on the island?"

"Yes. Well, what if one of these guys is working with that guy?"

"Then they would feed the guy the information he needed, and they'd always have an alibi. So who has had an alibi for all three murders, and just exactly *what* do you think is going to pop out of my fly since I can't keep it shut?"

We found the Wymans, Ken and Barbie, and Mug and Jug in the kitchen fighting over who was going to cook dinner. Apparently Mug had just informed the Wymans and the buff couple of just what crappy cooks they were, and the Wymans were taking exception. Ken gave me a dirty look that I mostly ignored as it occurred to me, not without a great deal of disgust, that the kitchen would be a good place to find bugs. I grabbed a spatula while they were all arguing, and steering way clear of the two hot spots in the room, went in search of something icky to kill for Jake.

I could hear that Maggie's voice had joined the din but wasn't really listening enough to know whether she was trying to get them to shut up long enough to tell them about the cameras or she was just siding with Mug and Jug concerning the others' cooking abilities. Most probably they were screaming about mine and Barb's little indiscretion.

I didn't care. I was on the prowl, my every muscle in tune, all my attention turned toward the hunt. I was vaguely aware that the screaming had reached an almost deafening tone when I picked up a box of food and a huge roach ran out. I stepped on it, screaming triumphantly, "I got you, you big nasty bastard!" and scooped it up with the spatula. I realized that the room had gone suddenly very quiet and turned to see everyone, including Maggie, staring at me as if I'd gone round the bend. "I really hate roaches," I explained as I looked for and found a plastic bag into which to put my prize. I slid the roach carefully into the Ziploc bag and pocketed it. Then I looked at the spatula with disgust. "I don't think we should use this to cook with."

"I should think not," Female Wyman said making a face.

I put the spatula on top of the refrigerator, thinking that I could use it the next time I needed to get food for my little gecko buddy.

"And you screwed that!" Biff hissed accusingly toward his wife.

Barb smiled totally without remorse. "She's sort of earthy."

"Oh, yes, that's exactly the word I'd use to describe an obsessive-compulsive clean-freak whose entire wardrobe consists of cutoffs and tank tops," Maggie said hotly.

"Hey, I'm not a clean freak," I countered. "If I was a clean freak, would I have stuck a bug in my pocket?"

Maggie rolled her eyes. "You picked it up with a spatula and put it in a Ziploc bag first. I hardly think that makes you the Crocodile Hunter."

I noticed then that Mug and Jugs were cooking, and I have to admit I was relieved, but I still started watching them. I fought the urge to run back to our room and feed the bug to Jake while it was still fresh, after all, wasn't the bag guaranteed to lock in freshness? I focused on the conversation but stayed out of it. Maggie had been trying to turn the conversation toward the problem with the cameras and the idea that we were being watched, so she could naturally introduce our idea to destroy the monitoring equipment. Unfortunately, the conversation kept coming back to mine and Barb's infidelity.

I watched the Wymans. Maggie was right. He definitely had a stick up his butt about something. She did, too, but I figured I knew why she was pissed off. No one, especially fat, ugly, greasy people, likes to be rejected. Wyman was glaring at Maggie and occasionally at me. Gone were the idiot smile and near idol worship. He was mad about something. Something he thought

Maggie had done. But what?

He turned suddenly and glared wordlessly at me, as if trying to mark me with his evil eye. I stuck my tongue out at him, and I didn't have to guess at why he was angry anymore.

"You! You have purposely awakened the evil spirits of this place. It was your intent all along. You have countered every spell my dear lady wife and I have tried to do to cleanse this place." He turned to glare at Maggie once again. "And you! You don't give a damn about the dead or the trapped souls here. All you care about is your book, and your tinkering around has awakened the spirits and angered them, and . . ."

"You're completely out of your fucking new-aged mind!" I accused. "Watch my lips, you freaking moron. The dead are rotting in the ground—worm food and dust. The dead do not get pissed off, come back and kill people. *Peo-ple* kill people."

"You both know more than you're saying. You're keeping things from the rest of us." He was right, of course, but how did he know that? Was it a guess, or did he know because he was the murderer, because he had access to that cell phone and the monitor? I knew one thing for damn sure, he didn't know because of his and his wife's "awesome powers."

I remembered Female Wyman's clumsy attempt to entice Maggie into a sexual encounter and realized what it had really been. She had been making sure we were in our room, and she was making sure we stayed in our room for a set amount of time, but why?

I liked the idea that the Wymans were the killers, because it just might mean that there would be a justifiable reason to kill them. I wished I could talk to Maggie privately about what I had just figured out, but there was just no way out.

"The only person who knows more than the rest of us know is the person who has a monitor and is watching us constantly." That was Maggie.

All eyes turned to face her as she explained what we had figured out earlier, and our theory that there was someone else on the island, without telling them the second part of our theory—which was that one or more of them were working with the killer.

"That makes sense," Mug said as he flipped something, which I hopefully thought was meat. "I mean, I've been thinking, and well what if Jesus never left the island?"

Like I said before, the guy was way too smart for a dumb guy.

We, of course, knew that Jesus hadn't left the island because we'd found him hanging in a tree like some morbid bird feeder. However that didn't mean there wasn't someone else on the island.

"We need to go to the vault and destroy that camera and the monitors so that the killer can't watch us," Maggie said.

Wyman seemed, at least for the moment, to have forgotten how agitated he was at Maggie. Or perhaps this was just the information he thought she was hiding from him. "I agree it makes sense. If they're watching us that would explain how they're avoiding being caught. How they're sneaking up on their victims."

I guess I should have kept my mouth shut, but if I were a model of self-control I wouldn't have boinked Barbie. "Yeah, 'cause spooks are always using hi-tech equipment when they go after the living."

Maybe that was why he was so mad at me and Maggie. Maybe because he had finally realized that our murderer really wasn't some incorporeal being, but a flesh and blood killer, just like the rest of us—and especially Maggie and I who he thought should have been his natural allies—had said all along.

Of course I preferred he's so pissed off at us because he's the killer and he knows we're close to catching him. See, I so had my hopes set on killing him.

"I think we should go bust all of that shit up as soon as we finish eating," Mug said.

Everyone agreed, which sort of blew my and Maggie's whole *the killer will balk* theory. I said as much to her when after dinner we were all heading for the vault as a group, our flashlights in hand.

"Shhh!" Maggie said, poking me in the ribs with a sharp elbow.

I think we all knew we were screwed when we saw the vault door was closed and locked.

"Did anyone close that?" Ken asked. An echo of "no" went through the group.

"It doesn't matter. I know the code." Maggie waded through them to the vault door and entered the code, once, twice, three times, nothing. She sighed deeply, "The code's been changed."

"Maybe you're just getting it wrong," I said, a panicked tone entering my voice. There's something about the idea that a lunatic is watching you that just makes you lose any grip you might have had. I waded through them to her side. "Try it another way; maybe you've just got one number wrong."

"Or maybe you two are the killers," Biff said in a hiss. "She had the code and now she doesn't. Seems awful convenient to me."

"Just because I screwed your old lady doesn't mean I'm a murderer," I spat back. He glared at me, and I glared right back. In that moment I was way too freaked out to worry about the fact that this guy could kick my ass. If he wanted a fight I'd give him a fight.

"I've got the code right," Maggie said. She reached in her pocket and took out a piece of paper. "See? I wrote it down."

"Try it again," I ordered.

She did, but nothing happened.

"I know the code, too, maybe you're doing it wrong." Male Wyman moved to the door and tried the combination three times with no more luck than Maggie'd had.

"What now?" Jugs asked with a sob. "He's just going to watch us, watch us doing everything until it's convenient for him to kill us!"

No one said anything, and I knew why. We were all basically thinking the same thing—except of course Maggie, who said in the most tortured voice I'd ever heard from her lips, "Damn! Now I'm never going to get to use that equipment."

CHAPTER THIRTEEN: MAGGIE

I was seriously starting to dislike the killer at this point. He had no idea what a crimp this was going to make in my plans, not to mention my book.

"Why in the name of God did he have to go and change the lock?" I muttered half aloud.

That was when I realized everyone was looking at me rather oddly. Especially Vivian. I think she can get those eyebrows all the way up to her hairline with little effort.

"He?" John retorted. "What makes you think it was a he?" He looked clearly disturbed that I'd said that.

"Figure of speech," I said.

"Figure of speech, my ass," someone muttered from the back of the crowd. Sounded like Ned.

Vivian merely passed me and started punching buttons on the door.

"What are you doing?" I asked.

"Seeing if I can break the code," she said.

"Are you aware of how many combinations a ten-key lock can have?" I asked.

"Have no idea," Vivian said, and continued to punch away like a mad telephone operator.

"Well, considering that's a ten-key pad, I'd say . . . about ten thousand possible combinations . . ."

"Maybe I'll get lucky," Vivian said.

"And there's only about a sixty-two percent chance of you

actually finding that combination," I added.

Vivian stopped punching and turned to tower over me. "Hell, Maggie, why do you always have to be such a pompous spoil-sport?"

"So what do we do?" Harmony asked. "I mean, what if he's locked up in there . . . just watching everything we do?" She crossed her arms over her chest and shivered, glancing up at the ceiling.

The camera was angled at the door and at us of course. I glowered at it briefly and turned away.

"If he's in there he's got to come out sometime," Ned said. "He'll have to come out sooner or later, and we'll be waiting."

"He's not in there, dumb-ass," Vivian scoffed.

"How do you know that?"

I sighed deeply. "Because the door can only be locked from the outside," I said, and kept from finishing my sentence with "Dunderhead" only with a great effort.

"Hey, don't you worry, sweet cheeks," John said, and put a meaty arm around Harmony's shoulders, crushing her to his side. "I won't let nothing happen to you . . . and besides . . . having some creep watch us all the time sounds kinda kinky."

"Maybe we could break the cameras?" Jolene said.

"Those cameras are boxed up in Lexan," John said. "Even if you could get past those metal cages. Then there is the fact that the damned things are ten feet off the ground, and I haven't seen anything that looks even remotely like a ladder."

That was true. The camera crews probably took the ladders with them . . . or stowed them someplace secret.

There was a ladder in the room with the equipment . . .

Too bad there was no way we could get to it.

"This is ridiculous," Ned said.

Unfortunately, I was inclined to agree with him.

"Well, we're not going to accomplish anything standing here,"

Vivian said. "Let's get the hell away from this place."

Like a small army, we all marched back up the twist and turn of corridors. I kept my mouth shut. This was just too much to believe . . . the killer had changed the code.

Which meant the killer knew Vivian and I had been in that room. And likely knew that I had returned to scout out the monitors and see if I could figure out who was being watched. He knew there were things in that room that we could use to figure out who he was, and so he'd locked us out.

"So what now?" Winston asked, looking sharply at Vivian when she cast a leer in Jolene's direction. The woman was now wearing a skin-tight tank, no bra, and shorts.

Oh, please don't start that again, I thought. Of course knowing Vivian she probably felt like she hadn't finished it yet.

"We have got to find a way into that room," I said.

"Are you kidding?" John said. "That's steel-reinforced concrete."

"How do you know that?" Ned asked.

John grinned like a wolf. "I was in that room when we took Knight's body down, and I did construction work for a time." He curled an arm and punched up a bicep. "How do you think I got started on this good body, dude?"

"Steroids," Ned said.

I frowned and watched the exchange. Ned was being awfully bold all of a sudden. *The slug turns,* I thought. *Why?*

"I don't do steroids, jelly belly," John said.

"Hey, you take that back," Astaria interrupted. "He doesn't have a jelly belly."

"Yeah, and I bet every time the two of you get it on, it's like watching Jell-O gelatin fuck . . ."

"I'll show you how Jell-O fucks, lard brains." Ned doubled up his pudgy fist.

"Hey!" Vivian snapped. "I think that's enough of that. If you boys can't play nice, why don't you go look for the killer . . . separately, that is? It's a fucking vault. Doesn't take a genius or even a construction worker to figure out that it was built to keep you from getting in."

John and Ned both looked at Vivian as though she had grown three heads and all of them had mouths full of fangs.

"Come on," I quickly added. "All this fighting is not going to get us anywhere. We have a problem. We have a killer who can see us, but we have no idea who he or she is. We have three dead bodies that alternately appear and disappear at the killer's whim. But we're all still alive, and if we work together, we can stay alive."

"Work together how?" Jolene asked, slipping Vivian a secret smile, and I started wondering if it was possible to neuter her right there and then . . .

I took a deep breath instead. "We do not separate. No one gets left alone. Always, stay in couples."

"Do we get to choose whom we couple with?" Jolene asked.

Okay, that was it. I stepped over to Jolene and practically got in her face. "You stay away from her, you horny bitch," I said. "You stay with Winston, and by God, you might actually stay alive!"

If the words had any effect at all, it was to make Vivian splutter. I fixed her with a nasty glare. I'd had it with this crew. Growling under my breath, I started out of the room.

"Hey, sweetie, wait," I heard Vivian call. "Remember what you said . . . no one goes anywhere alone . . ."

I said nothing. I just kept going.

I wanted to think things out without the "children" to distract me.

Vivian didn't leave me alone. She followed, which was probably for the better because I was halfway to the room, and the corridor looked spooky with the shifting of the sunlight toward the west. And it occurred to me that being entirely alone might be the wrong move, considering the cameras and who was watching them, and of course I was the one who'd just more or less ordered everyone to stay together.

"There has got to be a way to disable those," I said pointing to a camera as Vivian caught up with me.

"What, and screw up our chance to be seen by millions of viewers all over America—the world—as we get slaughtered in our sleep?" Vivian said. "You know, Maggie, this really was a dumb-fuck idea."

"What, me leaving the room?"

"This whole caper," Vivian said, and dodged one of the hot spots in the hall like a rabbit.

"Right," I muttered. "Well, first things first. As far as I am concerned, I am not letting the killer in on another bit of information."

"So what are you proposing to do?"

We stepped into our room. I looked up at the camera in the corner. It was sweeping toward me like a curious eye. A gecko ran from the cage, startled by the motion.

"We need to disable that camera first," I said.

"How?" Vivian leaned against the wall, then pushed away from it and sneered as she brushed dried chips of paint off her shoulder. "I wasted half a morning trying to knock one of those mothers out of a palm tree when I went looking for the boat."

I stepped over to the pile of debris that we had pushed out of the way so we could leave the room that morning. Snatching up one of the broken boards from an old shutter, I walked over and stopped under the camera. Inside the safety of the Lexan, it shifted down in my direction. With a growl, I swung at it . . . and missed of course, since I'm only a little over half as tall as the ceilings are high.

"I think you're gonna need a longer board than that," Vivian said.

"So help me," I said.

I turned and spied her peeling out a pack of cigarettes and sticking one in her mouth. My glower of disapproval did nothing to stop her from lighting it and letting it dangle out of her mouth.

"I'm telling you, Maggie, it's not worth it," Vivian said, but she was a sport enough about it to grab up a slightly longer board. So there she stood, one hip cocked, her long frame reminding me of a pose right out of a Marlene Dietrich film. Cigarette still dangling from her lips, she took a feeble whack at the cage. The small effort did nothing more than shatter the end of the wood and send a shower of small splinters skittering everywhere. "Shit!" Vivian muttered and backed away to keep from getting the debris in her eyes. "Stupid fuck idea. I don't know why I let you talk me into these things, Maggie."

"You didn't even try to hit it," I said and scurried around looking for a longer, stouter board. "If we could pry that damned cage off, we could probably knock the Lexan loose."

"Don't bother," she said, shaking wood chips out of her hair. "I tried everything from stones to coconuts . . . Those cages won't budge."

"Then maybe we can go over the roof and find the connections. Those things have to have some sort of wiring . . ."

"No, all self-contained. All battery operated. Remember, that's what Dead President Guy told us. It makes sense. They couldn't afford to take a chance on the half-assed electricity from a generator. This way if one camera goes out they lose that camera, not the whole system," Vivian said and took a long drag on her cigarette. I walked over to the balcony door to get some fresh air. "There is no way to knock out the whole system, Maggie, that's why they did it this way."

I did not want to believe that.

"We can cover it with something, then," I said.

"Cover it with what?"

"Clothes . . . panties . . . I don't care."

"Oh, great, that would be cool. Stuffing the crotch of a pair of my panties up there for all of America to see," Vivian said.

"Like you didn't moon the camera half a dozen times already," I said, arching my eyebrows. Then as I remembered, "Vivian, you had sex with the cameras running, and now you're worried about someone seeing your underwear."

"Hey, it's a free world," Vivian said. "If I'm dying, I'm getting some, all right?"

"Fine, but we can cover it with something. And I think I know *just* the thing."

"What?"

As Vivian watched, I walked over to her pack and scrounged out the box of cigarettes. The last pack slid out. I frowned. "Have you smoked a whole box of these?"

"Hey, I started on those back on the mainland, remember?" she said. "And anyway, what good will using my last unopened pack of cigarettes do?"

"Give me a hand and I'll show you," I said.

I stepped over to the wall so that I was under the camera. Vivian looked at me like I had lost every ounce of common sense I possessed . . . then again she had been looking at me like that since we got here.

"Well, come on," I said. "Give me a boost."

"What?" Vivian glared at me.

"Boost me up to the camera," I said. "How else am I going to get up there?"

"How much do you weigh?"

"None of your business."

"It *is* my business if I'm gonna have to lift your ass up over my head," she said.

I frowned. "One fifty," I said.

"Becoming a little butterball, aren't you?" she said.

"I'm big boned," I retorted.

"In the head, maybe," Vivian said.

I raised the cigarettes in one hand as though about to crush the whole pack. "Say good-bye to the last pack," I said with a nasty sneer.

"Okay, okay," Vivian said, and settling her current cigarette into the safety of a rock she had apparently found to use for an ashtray, she hurried over to the wall. "Be gentle with those. Unless you want to know what I'm like having a nicotine fit . . ."

"No different from the way you are every day, I'm sure," I said.

She threw me a bird then aimed one at the camera for good measure. "Whoever you are, you sick psycho, I'm gonna blame you for my withdrawal symptoms . . ."

"Oh, that's very good," I said. "Piss them off."

"Shut up and climb," Vivian said, and she leaned over, making a stirrup with her hands.

Okay, I have seen this done in the movies. One partner lifts the other with practiced ease.

Vivian needed more practice. For that matter, so did I. When I was a child, I rode horses for fun, and I never had trouble getting into the saddle then. But there was no saddle . . . for that matter, no horse. Just Vivian, and she proved to be a less than adequate ladder.

The first try, I stuck the cigarette pack in my pocket, and with one hand on the wall and the other holding Vivian's shoulder, I gave a little push, hoping to assist my ascent.

Assist my ass, as Vivian would say. I never even got my knee straight before I lost balance and tumbled toward the wall . . . because Vivian, presented by my weight, lost her "stirrup." She staggered back from the sudden loss of weight, and I dropped like a stone, barking one of my knees on the wall.

"Ow!"

I ended up on my rear end.

"Shit," Vivian said, and shook her hands out. "What did you stomp my hands like that for?"

"I didn't stomp your hands," I snarled back, picking myself up gingerly and knocking the loose debris off my pants. Good thing I wasn't wearing shorts. Otherwise, I would have been bleeding.

"Yes you did," she said. "Are the cigarettes okay?"

I rolled my eyes. "Yes, they were in my pocket . . ."

I didn't add that they were in my hip pocket. "Come on, I have to get up there. Maybe we can build a ladder or a platform, or find a chair . . ."

"There isn't a chair tall enough even for me to reach it," Vivian said. "Here, I'll be the ladder as long as you don't stomp me again."

"I didn't stomp you," I said.

"Right," she said and put her hands against the wall, then jerked them back. "Wait a minute." She hopped over to the beds and scrounged up a towel.

"Hey, that's mine," I said.

"Those are my cigarettes," Vivian reminded me.

She placed the towel between the wall and her hands.

"This way, I won't get splinters," she added.

"And what am I supposed to do?"

"Come on, Maggie, didn't you ever build a human pyramid?"

"Yes, but I was a lot younger, a lot thinner, and there were more people to hold me up," I said.

"Look, I crouch a bit, and you can use my thighs for ladders and climb up on my shoulders . . . oh, and do me a favor."

"What?"

"Take off your shoes," she said. "Those Reebok hikers of yours will leave tread marks on me."

"If you wore real clothes," I said.

"These *are* my real clothes. Now come on before I change my mind . . ."

It was easier, I will admit. Well, except for the part where I tried to step up and hold onto Vivian, and for a moment, I was straddling her back and sliding toward the floor. Then I grabbed her shoulders and she yelled at me for "digging my claws" into her. I tried to let go, only to start to slide again, and then I snagged her shirt, and it gave more than I thought it would . . . flimsy stretch cotton . . . and Vivian started to howl that I was ruining the only good shirt she had left.

But I did it . . . finally. I climbed the quaking Everest sweat-slippery slope. I even got up on her shoulders. She quivered under me from the pressure and weight of having me on her back. I snagged hold of the cage and gave a small tug. No, it held as firm as stone.

"Would you PLEASE hurry," Vivian growled.

I stuffed the pack of cigarettes into the cage. It fit exactly between the Lexan and the metal cage, blocking the lens and the sensor that allowed it to detect motion and follow us around the room. I knew I had succeeded when the red light on the camera that showed it was filming went off. Pleased with myself, I started to step back and admire the work . . .

And promptly fell.

Vivian, however, must have felt the shift. With a mighty heave, she shoved off and backed away from the wall, so that when I dropped, I slid down her back as though I were mounted on a horse again. With a startled whoop, I threw arms around her neck. She gave a sort of "gak" and lurched, nearly unseating me from her back. She must have backpedaled halfway across the room before she fell, and we both landed in a heap on the bedclothes and backpacks.

For a moment, we just lay there like a pair of old sacks tossed off by a miller.

"Fuck, Maggie, I bet you don't weigh less than one-sixty-five," she said.

I gave in to the urge to snatch up my hiker's pillow and whap her on the head.

CHAPTER FOURTEEN:
VIVIAN

When Maggie slapped me upside the head with her pillow I was almost glad, I needed something to drive the horrible images from my mind.

There are certain angles from which you should never see your friends, and after our whole Lucy and Ethel disable the security camera skit, I had seen Maggie from all of those and two others most people don't know about. I lay on the bedroll feeling like a discarded tube sock—sweaty, filthy and used.

Jake ran up looking expectant and I thought a little sympathetic. I dug the roach in the bag from my pocket and dumped it on the floor in front of him. "Bone apple tit," I said.

Maggie laughed, and then said, "You know that's not how that's pronounced."

"You pronounce French your way and I'll pronounce it mine." Jake gobbled up the cockroach like the greedy little lizard that he was then lay down by my foot looking contented.

Maggie looked at him then back at me. "That is just getting too weird."

"He likes me. I don't see what's so weird about that," I said.

"He's a lizard, Vivian, he's got a brain not much larger than a gnat's . . ."

"Hey, don't dis my little buddy," I said. I got up, careful not to step on my "buddy," and went to find the cigarette I had put down earlier. I did, thankful for the more-cancer-causing-than-tobacco chemical they put on the paper that stops it from burning when you aren't puffing on it. I relit my cigarette. "I want to take a shower."

"Yes, it's always a good idea to get naked in a room by yourself and run water so you can't hear when the psycho killer walks up and disembowels you."

"That's why you're going with me. You stand guard while I shower, and then I'll stand guard while you shower."

Maggie didn't argue with me, so I'm thinking that she wanted a shower just as bad as I did.

After we'd showered and brushed our teeth we went back to our room, checked it and the veranda twice, then shut what was left of the door and started stacking the debris in front of it.

We blew out the candles, drew our flashlights close, and started talking in whispers. We had stopped the killer from watching us, but if we weren't careful he could still hear us, and that could be worse.

"So . . . who are you thinking it is?" I asked.

"It could be any of them if there is an accomplice. It might actually be none of them. It's a small island, but there is still lots of room for two or more people to hide, and maybe that's something we ought to consider . . ."

"It's Dead President Guy. It's all about the ratings. It's the only thing that makes sense."

"Christ, Vivian! That's the stupidest thing I've ever heard even you say. He'd get caught for sure. It's too obvious. The first thing people would ask is where he was when it happened."

She had a point, so I relented. "Then I think it's Wyman."

"Which one?"

"Both of them."

"Do you think that because they get on your last nerve, or do you have a real reason for thinking it's them?" she asked, and I could hear the smile in her voice.

"If they're the murderers, we can kill them," I answered.

Maggie sighed blissfully. "Oh, that is a pleasant thought," she said. "I'll hang onto it and it will help me in the dark days ahead."

I laughed. "Maybe we should kill them anyway. We can make it look like the psycho did it, and if it is them the killing should stop."

"What about Mug?" Maggie asked. And again, yes, Maggie knew everyone's names, what a show off.

"He's smarter than he pretends to be, and strong enough to hang bodies over cliffs and from extension cords."

"Which I don't think Male Wyman is."

"But if it's both of them." A thought struck me. "What if they aren't the stupid metaphysical butt itches they appear to be? The rules of *Chicken Shit* said none of us could know each other before, and they didn't tell us anything about the others. Everything we know about them, we know from talking to them. We're lying about what we are, what if they're lying, too? What if they aren't really a couple of goofballs? I mean look at them, who would ever think they were the murderers?"

"Well you do for one," Maggie said with a laugh.

"Work with me here, Maggie. She was purposely keeping you busy today. Why? So that he could shut up the vault and change the code. He admitted that he knew the original code, and wouldn't you need to know the code, know something about the lock to change it?"

"Isn't it more likely that Barbie was keeping *you* busy so that Ken could come and get the phone?"

"Can't you just wrap yourself around the idea that I'm a very desirable woman?"

"Not really."

"Back to the Wymans being the killers. Let's say they are like evil geniuses, and they have an in with Dead Kennedy guy. Maybe they are even like working for him—then they'd know all the codes and shit."

"That absurd scenario would work with any single person or couple here," Maggie pointed out. "Which brings us right back to square one. There is no way without a lab that even I can begin to figure out who the killer or killers are at this stage in the game."

"This isn't a game, Maggie. People are getting killed, the bodies are stacking up—or they would be if the killer would stop taking off with them—and you and I are here with no way to the mainland—and unarmed."

"Well I didn't say it was a *fun* game," Maggie said. "Maybe we should just try to get some sleep."

"Should we maybe sleep in shifts? You sleep and I'll keep watch and then I'll sleep and you can keep watch?" I asked.

Maggie thought about it for a minute. "I don't think that will be necessary. We've got so much stuff piled around the door they couldn't get in without waking us up and giving us plenty of time to get away, or at least arm ourselves."

Then there was a blood-curdling scream. We both jumped up, flashlights in hand and on. We shone the lights in each other's faces, no doubt to see if the other was as terrified as we were. I'm thinking I looked every bit as chicken shit as Maggie did, and if there had been a way off that island, I'm thinking there's no way we would have won that money.

"What do we do?" I asked, still in a whisper.

"We better check it out," Maggie said.

"I was afraid you were going to say that," I said with a sigh.

It took us at least two minutes to move the debris from the door. By then there had been a second even louder scream. We each grabbed a board for a weapon and headed in the direction of the screams.

"I think that was Ken," Maggie said in a whisper.

I thought she was right. After all, it was hard to forget a

scream like that. We were halfway down the stairs when my flashlight caught a glimpse of silver. I shoved Maggie back against the wall, turned my flashlight off, and took my best "trying to get a home run" stance. I swung into the shimmering silver image where I thought its midsection should be, and it started falling backwards. Unfortunately it managed to grab the front of my shirt and I fell, too.

The next thing I knew there was a bright light and a soothing voice was saying, "What the hell do you think you were doing? You nearly got yourself killed!"

All right, when my head cleared a bit I realized the light was coming from a flashlight being shone in my face, and the voice wasn't soothing at all. Maggie was in fact screaming at me.

"Did I get them?" I asked.

"They got away," Female Wyman said. "But I think they were limping; Wyman went after them."

Yea, I thought, *You would say that. I hit him and he took off because he's the killer.*

I started to sit up and Maggie pushed me back down. I realized there was a cold rag pressed up against my forehead. "Be still for a minute. You aren't bleeding, but you've got a huge knot on your head and I imagine you've got a mild concussion."

"But now we'll know who they are, because they'll be the person . . ."

"Who's as banged up as you are," Maggie said. And I was thinking if she was really my bitch she wouldn't be all pissed off that I had done something stupid, she'd be turned on because I'd saved her life, so I was thinking that she was just giving everything away.

Jugs ran in then with Mug not far behind her.

"I went after Ken," Mug said out of breath. "But I lost him, tripped over a tree stump and landed on my face. He got away."

"Ken?" Maggie asked. "Just what the hell has happened?"

"Barb's dead," Jugs said near hysterics. "Strangled with a wire—it was awful."

"We don't know if Ken saw her and freaked or if he killed her in the first place," Mug said.

"Vivian hit the killer here on the stairwell. I don't see how it could have been Ken if you were after him," Female Wyman said. "Wyman's gone after the killer."

Wyman came back into the room then, flashlight in hand, a huge bruise over his eye, and panting like he'd just run a hundred-yard dash.

"I tripped over a chair and lost them," he said, rubbing at his wound.

I sat up and screamed. "Well this is just great! Ken has run off and both you idiots have head wounds, so that doesn't narrow things down at all. The only good, easy, piece of ass on this island is dead, and I'm damn near out of cigarettes."

CHAPTER FIFTEEN:
MAGGIE

If Vivian had not already had a knot the size of Manhattan on her forehead, I would have been tempted to pop her again. Here we were, surrounded by possible killers, and all she could think about was cigarettes and sex . . . She was driving me nuts . . .

But I could not very well give into an urge like that, certainly not in front of all these people. So I took a deep breath and stood up to look at our suspects.

John (he whom Vivian insisted on calling Mug) was gingerly holding his injury. "Here, let me look at that," I said in my best professional voice.

"I'll be fine," he said and backed away, staggering just a step.

"You don't look fine," I retorted. "Now come here and let me . . ."

He jerked back as I reached for him, and for a brief moment I honestly thought he was going to hit me the way his fist balled up. But apparently he saw the "Oh, shit" look on my face. He took another step and put up his hands. "Hey, I don't need to be examined by someone who might be a killer."

"Okay," I said and turned to Ned. "How about you?"

Ned stepped over . . . or I should say, he limped over with this simpering look and leaned down. There was a knot the size of a hen's egg on his forehead, and the center of it was split and bleeding. I reached up to press fingers to the area around the wound.

"Ahhhhhhhhh!" He shrieked like a girl and stumbled back. "You're hurting me!"

"I haven't touched you yet!" I said.

"You're hurting me, you lying lezzie bitch! You're trying to squish my head open . . ."

I opened my mouth to tell him that I would certainly like to do just that, because I was sure his head was filled with nothing but pudding, but before I could utter a word, Astaria stepped over between us.

"I'll take care of him," she said with a dark look at me. *So*, I thought, *No one wants an expert to look at their wounds? Fine!* What else could I conclude but one of them knew I could tell the difference between a whack from a board and a ground hit.

"In that case, I will go look at the body," I said.

"Not without me," Vivian said, and this time I did nothing to stop her from rising. She swayed just a little then straightened up. Together, we started for Jolene and Winston's rooms. Wryly I noticed that everyone else was following, too. This could mean anything, I thought. The killer is one of them and wants to see what I conclude, or they were just all too scared to be alone at the moment.

Or they still thought I was the killer and wanted to see if I was going to tamper with the evidence . . .

I did wish I had my portable lab. I should have packed it, but at the time, all I was thinking was how little I wanted to carry, and how all the equipment I really wanted was already here.

I had assumed foolishly that I would have access to stuff here that I could use . . . like all the spirit-sensing equipment locked conveniently in that armored room.

Damn it all.

Jolene was sprawled naked, facedown across her cot, her legs spread wide, and clearly she had tried to struggle. Her hands were knotted about the cot rails so hard that when I knelt and tried to pull one free, it was locked in a death grip. Her face was turned away from me, so I shifted around to the far side of the cot to get a look. Her tongue was distended, her eyes were wide. Gingerly, I pushed her hair aside so I could get a better look at the work the garrote wire had done to her throat. Nasty things, wire garrotes. They cut the flesh like a razor. This one must have been particularly sharp because it had severed her larynx. In fact, as I tried to lift her head so I could get a better look at the damage, I discovered the wire had nearly cut it off. I heard several of the others gasp as her head shifted to an unnatural angle under my examination. I let go for fear I was going to suddenly find myself doing a Salome routine . . .

"Damn," I heard Vivian mutter.

I ignored them all and crouched down, running my flashlight over the area of the wound. A crisscross of a cut had opened the back of her neck to the bone. So the killer attacked her from behind, and perhaps she was asleep at the time . . . except . . . why would she have been clutching the sides of the cot? I looked more closely at her wrists. Deep gouges indicated her wrists had been bound. I followed the marks and discovered the knots had been around the rail. Glancing down, I spied severed strands of ropes under the end of the cot.

She was tied down? I frowned and shifted positions again.

"Well?" John said.

I ignored him.

Still puzzled, I shined my flashlight down along her shoulders and her back and over her buttocks. It was then that my light picked up a bit of blood around the anal region . . . and a bit of sticky yellow-white matter that could only have been semen.

Damn, I thought. She was having bondage sex with her killer when he garroted her. That would explain the position. But why had he cut the ropes and left them lying on the ground?

Could he have intended to move her body elsewhere? Or

were the ropes just a means of assuring him that she could not fight back? If so why cut them at all?

It occurred to me then that Jolene must have been looking for love in one of the wrong places they talk about in that song.

And if it had been Winston, why would he have screamed? Possibly to throw us off.

"Well?" Ned asked.

I looked around to find a whole slew of curious faces, most of them pale in the illumination of flashlights and lanterns and candles.

"It would appear that she was having a bit of kinky sex with her killer when he got a little . . . carried away," I said.

"Ah, shit, Maggie," Vivian said. "You mean Barb was just leading me on?"

I took a deep breath and decided not to answer that absurd question. Instead, I looked around at our dwindling competitors and said, "So where was everyone when Winston screamed?"

"I was asleep," Harmony said, and even in this dim light, I could see dark rings under her eyes and hear her slightly slurred speech. "John woke me up because he heard someone scream . . ."

Astaria frowned. "Well, don't look at me. We were asleep, too."

"As were we," I said thoughtfully. "But someone was awake, having sex with Jolene . . ."

"You sure it wasn't your old lady?"

"My old lady?" I said. "I'll have you know Vivian is not that old . . ."

"Ah, gee, thanks, Maggie."

"And she and I were up in our room when we heard the scream, and when we came down, we were nearly freight-trained by someone quite large . . ." I chose not to mention the semen . . . that was the only evidence that her last visitor was male, and since two of the three males left alive on this island were standing before me at the moment . . .

"Well, if it wasn't your lady," John said, "then the only one left is Winston himself. And he was standing over her when Harmony and I got here . . ."

"What?" I said. "You saw Winston?"

"Yeah. When I heard all the screaming, I woke Harmony up because I didn't want to leave her there by herself, and we came down to his room. He was tearing his clothes off like some sort of maniac and screaming like someone had fucked him hard, and when Harmony and I went into the room, he ran just like the guilty mother he is . . ."

I looked at Harmony. She stood with her arms across her chest, something clutched in one hand. "Is this true?"

"Well, yeah," she said. "I mean, I saw Winston screaming and he did run . . ."

"So Winston must have been pissed at his old lady because she was fucking with your old lady and decided to just kill her now . . ."

"Shit," Vivian said in a hoarse voice.

I turned. She was trembling like a new lamb. Damn, not now of all times . . .

"Vivian?" I said

She shook hard. I took her arms and pulled her over to the nearest chair. She practically collapsed into it. "Shit, he was fucking her . . . she thought it was some damn game, and he tied her down and fucked her and . . ."

"Who?"

"The killer," she whispered so low that I barely heard the words. "Maggie, the killer was screwing her, and she thought it was just a game until he . . . Ah, shit, Maggie. This sucks like hell . . ."

"Easy," I said, pushing her hair out of her face. "Deep breaths. Let it go."

Vivian closed her eyes and sat trying to gather herself.

"Winston . . . I bet it was Winston," Ned said. "They were into sick games like that . . ."

"How would you know?" I asked, standing up and looking over at him.

He went silent then shrugged. "I . . . saw them . . . once. They were doing some kinky shit with a mask and a whip."

"Too much information," Harmony whined and turned away. From the corner of my eye, I saw her push something into her mouth. She swallowed as I looked at her, and catching my gaze, she flushed and turned her back to me. Still, it was not hard for me to figure that she had just popped some sort of pill.

"Harmony, are you on medication?" I asked.

"Leave her alone," John said. "She's tired and she's scared."

"Like she's the only one?" Astaria said. "I am feeling some really bad vibrations in this room. Dark vibrations. Death. I'm getting out of here. Come on, Pumpkin."

Astaria seized Ned's arm and started to escort him out.

"Wait," I said.

"What . . ."

"We can't leave Jolene's body here. It will attract . . . vermin. We need to take her down to the icehouse."

"Mug and I can handle it," Vivian said.

"I'll come with you two," I said. "Harmony, you stay with Ned and Astaria. No one should be alone tonight."

No one argued with me.

I oversaw the "packing" of Jolene's corpse, which really consisted of wrapping her in her blankets and tying them with a couple of her own scarves. The head was just too close to decapitation to risk letting it lie loose in the blanket. Once she was wrapped and bound in a cocoon of blankets, John took one end and Vivian took the other.

"You want us to drop you off at the Wymans' room?" Vivian asked.

"No, I'll go with you," I said, though I was not about to tell her it was because I didn't like the idea of leaving her alone with John since there was a very good chance that he was the killer.

Of course, it occurred to me that Ned and Astaria now had Harmony in their clutches, and if they were the culprits, I had just left the poor girl to her doom. Then again, by my thinking, the Wymans were just disgusting, and that does not always equate with killer.

On the other hand, I had to remind myself that they could have been pretending to be New Age geeks. Ned had certainly turned on me awfully fast, I still didn't really know why. It made him look all the more guilty, now that I thought about it, all the more reason to go with Vivian and John. I certainly didn't want to be left with the Wymans. Harmony should be safe with them at least for a while. After all, if she was left in their care and something happened to her, didn't that make them the only suspects? They'd have to be as stupid as they appeared to do that, and the killer was a lot of things, but stupid wasn't one of them.

What if I was wrong, though? What if they were New Age cult types and these murders were a part of an elaborate rite of human sacrifice? What if they were back at the hotel sacrificing Harmony on some altar right then? It would have been all my fault.

I had only to remind myself that we were on an island reputed to have been the home of some ancient Aztec god who was in the habit of devouring his disciples to make me have second thoughts about the pair. They could have been cultist. Ruthless maniacs. There was a certain ritual nature to all the deaths. For one thing, they were getting worse.

My flashlight played over the ground as I led the way to the icehouse to store yet another body. The uneven ground required my holding the light down more than might have been wise under the circumstances, but I didn't want to risk any of us tripping over some root or rock, or the pair of bare feet that appeared in the path before me.

I froze. With a gasp, I lifted my flashlight.

"Shit," I heard John say, and Vivian added her curse to the mix.

Winston stood before me on the path. He was half naked, and through the rents in the remains of his clothing I could see that his body was a mass of scratches and bruises. His head was bleeding from several knots and cuts. Bits of greenery decorated his hair, which was frizzed out. He looked like some wild man of the woods, and he panted like a dog in hot weather.

"Winston?" I said.

His eyes were not focused on me. Instead, he looked over my head at Vivian and a sneer appeared on his face.

"You bitch!" he said. "You're to blame."

"Winston," I said firmly. "What happened?"

He looked at me, and the anger fell away. Tears were streaming down his face. "She's dead," he said in a whimper. "I . . . I . . ."

"Shit, he killed her," I heard John say. "He's confessing."

I ignored him. "Winston, what happened? Did you see who killed Jolene?"

"They came for me," he said. "Out of the dark . . . I don't know . . . I ran . . . I want my Jolene . . . Where's my Jolene?"

He sank to his knees, keening like a child in mourning.

"Shit, this is just great," Vivian said. "Look, I'm getting tired of carting this meat bag. Could you get Ken to move his whiny ass out of the way?"

"Vivian," I said and crouched. "Don't be so callous. I think he really loved her."

"That's a laugh," John said. "Let's put her down. My arms are getting stretched."

Vivian nodded and they lowered Jolene's corpse to the path. I leaned closer to Winston, looking at the masses of wounds he possessed. More than one graced his head. He could have gotten that falling down the stairs with Vivian . . . or just as easily from playing human pinball in the jungle.

Winston continued to whimper and whine. I reached out to touch his face when he suddenly grabbed my wrist.

"Don't touch me, you sick dyke . . ."

"Hey, I'm the dyke," Vivian said. "Maggie's the fem. Get it straight, will ya?"

I was not paying attention to Vivian's crack. I was looking at the blood that covered Winston's hands. He noticed the look, too. More tears streamed down his face. "It's hers," he said and let go. He held up his hands for my inspection. "I cut the ropes off her hands and feet . . . tried to pick her up . . . but she was . . . her head tried to come off . . . Why did he do that to her? Why did he fuck her and then kill her?"

"Who?"

"I . . . don't know," Winston said. "I was out walking, and I came in . . . and . . . there she was. Dead. I . . . I think I started screaming . . ."

"Damn right he was screaming," John said from behind me. "But it wasn't grief. It was rage. He was calling her all sorts of names and tearing at himself."

"What would you expect?" Winston lurched to his feet, nearly knocking me aside as he pushed past me to glare at Vivian and John. "She was a whore! A damned stupid, sick, kinky, whore I picked up in Denmark. But she was beautiful, and I loved her . . . only she couldn't stop being a whore! Videos, she said. "We'll make videos and call them exercise videos." But they weren't exercise videos. She made porno films, and she made me star in them with her, and she played all these little games. One day be the doctor, next day be the patient, or be a mean daddy or a bad little boy or . . . My life was hell, but I loved her. I thought if we could win the money, she would stop wanting to make those stupid films, but once a whore, always a whore . . . and now she's dead and . . ."

"I've had about enough of this," Vivian said.

She reached down to snag the corpse.

"Don't you touch her, you bitch!" Winston screamed and dove at Vivian. "Get your filthy hands off her . . ." He lunged at her, snagging her throat with his hands. I shouted and charged at him from behind, not sure of what else to do. He was trying to get a chokehold on Vivian, knocking her back into the trees.

Vivian, however, made a good account of herself for someone who'd been laid out cold by a blow to the head. She got her back against the trunk of one of the palm trees and rammed her knee hard into Winston's groin before John or I could intervene. Winston's scream actually went up several octaves, which I would have thought impossible. He fell back and tripped over Jolene's corpse when his head found a tree trunk on the other side of the path and knocked him out cold.

"Are you all right?" I asked Vivian, who leaned over to catch her breath.

"Yeah . . ." she said. "Come on, let's get Jolene on down to the icehouse."

"What about him?" John said.

"We'll get him on the way back," Vivian said. "I don't think he's going anywhere for a while."

John nodded. He and Vivian seized up the corpse in the blanket and started on.

I squatted at Winston's side and checked his pulse just to be sure, then hopped up and followed the other two. I sort of hoped he would still be unconscious when we got back.

No telling what would happen if he came to and took off again.

CHAPTER SIXTEEN: VIVIAN

Hetero sex is so sick; I don't know how you people do it. I know that what I saw and felt as I relived the last few moments of Barb's life almost made me vomit.

And there was nothing of any use in what I learned, nothing at all. So I went through the horror of her death throes apparently for fun. Not that I had actually stepped on the hot spot on purpose, mind you. The kill was fresh, the energy strong, and it was almost like it came looking for me.

The dumb-ass had thought she was with her husband. That he'd forgiven her and was ready to make up. That he had apparently dressed like the murderer and refused to speak was all just part of a game, and when he indicated that he wanted to tie her down she'd no doubt thought it was for the fun.

Till the wire had started cutting into her throat, and in that moment she'd known—or at least she'd been sure—that it wasn't Ken. As awful as her nearly decapitated body had looked, she had died relatively painlessly. It had been quick. Whoever her killer was, he was strong. Even I knew it took something more than normal strength to pull a wire damn near all the way through someone's neck.

So that more or less pointed to Ken or Mug on two counts, they were both strong, and they both had dicks.

We put Barb's body in the icehouse and Knight was still there, which I guessed was a plus.

When we got back to the spot where Ken had knocked

himself out—with more than a little help from me—he was sitting up, rubbing his privates with one hand and his head with the other.

"What we gonna do with him?" Mug asked Maggie.

"We can't leave him alone . . ."

"No, because he's the murderer," Mug said.

"I don't think so," I said.

"Why not?" Mug asked, more than a little agitated.

"Because she didn't think so, and I, well . . . He basically started doing her while he was killing her, and I think she'd know Ken's dick." That did it. I gagged, ran to the side of the trail and threw up.

"Beautiful," Mug sputtered.

Maggie patted me on the back; I'm not sure what good she thought it did. I had a feeling it was a holdover from raising kids, and feared at any moment that she would start poor babying me, which would only add to my embarrassment and make me hurl more.

It's not very butch to puke over seeing something gory.

"Are you all right?" Maggie asked when I'd lost something that looked like a body part and had obviously finally quit hurling.

It was a stupid question, and I gave her a stupid answer.

"Oh yeah, I'm fine," I said.

We all looked at Ken who was just sitting there curled up in fetal position and crying like a baby. You couldn't really blame him; he'd had a really shitty day any way you looked at it, especially if he was the killer because now everyone was watching him.

I knew we were all thinking the same thing, too. What the hell were we going to do with him? He was going to have to stay with someone or he'd be alone—easy pickings for the killer if it wasn't him. And no one was going to want him to bunk with them in case he was the killer.

Leave it to Maggie to come up with a solution that made things worse for us.

"We could tie his hands and feet together and he could stay with us at least for tonight," Maggie said with a sigh.

"I'm not going to let anyone tie me up and stick me in a room with you bitches. You might very well be the killers," Ken said, moving into a sitting position.

Maggie sighed again. She was no doubt as tired—though nowhere near as beat up—as I was. "Whoever killed your wife had semen, so that sort of rules me and even testosterone woman out."

I liked that handle. I decided to have it put on a T-shirt if I lived to make it home.

"She could have had sex with someone other than the killer before she was killed," Ken said. "We only have her," he pointed at me with a look of total disdain, "word that they killed her while they were having sex."

"Neither of us is strong enough to practically decapitate a grown woman with nothing more than even a very thin wire," Maggie said.

"She's plenty strong enough," Mug said pointing at me.

I grinned like an idiot and said a proud, "Thanks."

Maggie looked like she wanted to kill me.

"I think it's the only safe solution," she said with a sigh.

"It's not going to happen," Ken said, crossing his arms across his chest.

"I say we tie his ass to a chair and leave him in the kitchen. If he's the killer, nobody else will die, and if he's dead in the morning, well then we'll know he wasn't the killer," Mug said, and I swear from the tone of his voice he was dead serious.

"I said," Ken all but screamed, "I ain't letting any of you assholes tie me up. I'm not the killer. Why would I kill my own wife?"

"Oh I don't know," Mug said. "Because she was a lying, cheating, little slut, who bedded everyone who showed even mild interest."

Ken jumped to his feet ready for a fight and almost fell over. He staggered like a drunk for several seconds until he found some good solid ground and his head stopped spinning. "I'll just find a room and go to sleep. I'd rather take my chances alone than with any of you." He stumbled toward the house.

"Ken, the killer is watching us!" Maggie screamed after him.

"Shouldah tied the bastard up and left him in the kitchen," Mug mumbled and started after Ken.

"So?" Maggie asked as we started back into the house.

"So what?"

"Which one of them do you think is the murderer?" Maggie said.

I shrugged. "There's still the very real possibility that there is someone else on this island. Someone that Dead Kennedy guy hired to off us to get ratings," I said.

Maggie sighed. "Not that again. I'm leaning toward Ken," Maggie said.

"All right, I'll give you that he had a whole buttload of motive for killing his wife, but she didn't think it was him, and why is he killing everyone else?" I asked.

"Duh, a million dollars."

"Well, duh, then why did he scuttle the boats and why kill the cooks and Knight first? Why not leave the boats and kill John first? He was the only one of us likely to stay once someone had actually been killed."

"Well you do have a point besides the one on the top of your head," Maggie said. "What about Mugs then?"

"I think he'd kill someone and have breakfast, but what's his motive?"

"Again, why kill Jesus and Juan and Knight and why scuttle the boats?" Maggie said thoughtfully. "He could have very easily outlasted everyone but you and I . . . except that Jugs was more ready to chicken out than anyone else."

"Yeah, but there is no way he would have let her leave, and I have a feeling she doesn't ever go against what he says. It's the Wymans."

"Again I find myself asking . . . Do you have an actual reason, any evidence or do you just keep pointing the finger of guilt at them because they're a little annoying?" Maggie asked with a smile.

"Maggie, a hang nail is a little annoying, these people are bad hemorrhoids after judging a chili contest," I said. "I have a feeling that whoever is doing this is just as whacked-out as the guy who did the other murders. The Wymans are fruitcakes; let's say that it really isn't all an act. That they really believe the dribble that pours from their mouth and are crazy enough to sacrifice us all to Zippie Kotex."

"Xipe Totec," she corrected. "The Flayed Lord . . ." She stopped walking and looked up at the sky, thinking. I stopped and watched her, expecting great things, and I wasn't disappointed. "If the wire was sharp enough, and he had handles on it, and he put his weight into it—he could do it."

"And he has a dick . . . I think," I said.

"Of course this is all speculation. We have no real evidence on anyone, and from what we know of the past murders on this island, I think it's probably most likely that there is some crazy on the island with us. This house is a maze of secret tunnels and hidden cubbyholes. The island is nothing but jungle, and they could be hiding anywhere."

"Well that's a pleasant thought, what with us out here in the open at night and all."

Maggie shrugged. "I'd rather think that than that it's one of them. Not that I'm particularly fond of any of them, just that I think we're safer that way."

Maggie started walking again and I followed. We walked in the back door into the kitchen. It was one of only two rooms in the house that had electric lights. There were scattered lights around the house but not many, not enough to really give us decent or even adequate light, just enough to cast spooky shadows around the haunted mansion. "That's it . . . we knock out the generator and . . ."

"You're the one who told me the cameras run on batteries. You knock out the generator, and we lose the few electric lights we have and our refrigerator and cook stove. You know good and well that those cameras can film us in pitch black most likely."

She was right, of course. She's always right; that's one of her worst flaws.

I looked at the camera even now watching us. "I know it's you, Dead President Guy. You fucking people will do anything for ratings. Well, I'm betting you show this shit through sweeps and . . ."

"Vivian, yelling at the cameras isn't going to do any good, and please make up your mind as to who the killer is, you're giving me whiplash. Let's just go to bed and get some sleep, you're hurt and we're both tired."

"Mud!" I yelled out as I got one of my most brilliant ideas ever. I grabbed a pan and ran back out the back door.

Maggie followed yelling, "Vivian . . . your head injury, you need to rest and . . . what the hell are you doing now?"

What I was doing was putting dirt into a pot. "Mud," I said, then ran back into the house, went to the sink, and started mixing the water in the dirt, going for just the right consistency.

Maggie was giving me a look that said that she was afraid the whole thing had finally driven me completely crazy, or I had taken a much worse hit to my head than she had initially thought.

"Mud, Maggie, get it? Mud," I said, trying to make her understand. Truth is, I was more than a little brain fucked; between the fall down the staircase and reliving Barb's final moments, I was physically and emotionally drained. But that didn't mean that I hadn't just had the best idea ever in my life, it just meant I wasn't able to articulate what I was doing.

When I had the consistency I wanted I made a ball out of it, looked at Maggie and then the camera. "Mud," I explained again, and then threw the ball of glop at the camera, successfully covering the Lexan box over the lens and sensing eye.

Maggie smiled broadly. "Mud," she said, nodding her head approvingly. "But let's do it in the morning. Right now, I just want us to get back to our room and board ourselves in for the night."

"All right, give me a second." I washed my hands, picked up my trusty spatula off the top of the fridge, lifted a box, killed a roach, and picked it up with a plastic bag. "Fine, I'm good to go."

It's a good thing the killer didn't come after us that night. We had decided it would be safer for one of us to keep watch. Maggie let me sleep first and when she woke me up so that I could take my watch I stayed up for all of three minutes then I was out. I don't guess either of us stirred again till the sun was streaming in through the mound of shit we had piled in the veranda door and someone was screaming.

At this point I was getting so used to the terror that I almost rolled over and tried to go back to sleep. I guess Maggie was feeling the same way because she said lightly, "Should I get that or will you?"

"It sounds like one of the idiot Wymans," I said, and realizing this I really did roll over and try to go back to sleep.

"We still ought to see what's going on," Maggie said, getting up.

I grumbled something about if there was a God one of them was dead, and got up.

It took us the usual five minutes to clear our door, and the screaming had stopped.

"By the time we get there, whatever is happening will have already happened," I said, grabbing up a board and following Maggie.

"Would you rather leave the door unbarred? I mean after all, you're such a good watchperson."

"Very funny, Maggie. Christ, I was hurt pretty damn bad, you know. I'm lucky to be alive. I mean I did crash down a flight of stairs."

Maggie laughed. "Chill, I'm just giving you a hard time. I think the screaming came from the kitchen."

"The Wymans must have cooked again," I said.

"Except that's her I thought I heard screaming," Maggie said.

In the kitchen all seemed calm though the Wymans looked agitated. Both Mug and Ken were also present.

"Where's Jugs?" Maggie asked.

"She's taking so many God damned 'ludes I can't get her up," Mug answered.

"She shouldn't be left alone," Maggie said. "No one should be alone these days." She glared with meaning at Ken, who mostly ignored her.

"As long as I know where all you coconuts are, I know she's safe," Mug said.

"I told you, I think there is someone else on this island,"

Maggie said.

"Well, that is what you'd say if you were the killer. Don't you worry none about my old lady, you just mind your own business," Mug said.

"He's the killer, that's why he's not worried about her," Ken accused.

"I'm fixing to kick your foreign ass," Mug said.

"Could we just please not fight?" She-Wyman said, and it was now obvious that she had been crying. "If we weren't sure about the real culprit in this crime before, you should both know after what we just found in the pudding. Even my true love and I had begun to think that the killer was human, but after this morning you must all admit that the true killer is some demon right up out of hell."

"It's pudding, for God's sake. It had a worm in it, not the devil himself. Hell, this place is eat up with them, it probably just crawled in there," Mug said.

Male Wyman glared at Mug. "Some evil mystical power made this pudding, then stirred worms into its chilly goodness . . ."

I walked over and picked up the pan in question, holding the evil satanic pudding. I started laughing. "This isn't pudding, you dumb fucks, it's mud. I made it last night."

"Mud?" She-Wyman said.

Mug laughed. "Probably tasted so much like their own cooking they didn't even notice."

"Why would you make mud?" Ken asked.

"To knock out the cameras, see?" Maggie pointed up at the now-clean camera.

"Son of a bitch," I growled, and threw another handful of mud at the camera, then washed my hands. "This bastard is always one step ahead of us, and I was so hoping to be able to get my smokes back." I mumbled the last part.

"Vivian covered that camera last night before we went to

bed," Maggie told the others.

"It's a damn good idea," Mug said. "Give me that." I handed him the pot in spite of his bad manners, and he headed out of the room. "I'm gonna go check on Jugs and fix the camera in our room, keep the bastard from watching us."

He left.

She-Wyman was giving me a go-to-hell look. "Why would you just leave something like that in the kitchen?"

"Because I didn't think anyone would be stupid enough to eat it," I said.

"It was in a cooking utensil," Male Wyman defended.

"If I shit in a cake pan would you stick a candle in it and make a wish?" I asked. "No. On second thought don't answer that, it's still a step above the crap you cook."

"You," Ken said pointing at Maggie, his face suddenly going white. "You did it."

"Did what?" Maggie asked.

"You killed my beautiful Barbie."

"Me?" Maggie said incredulously—yeah, I can use me some big words when I need to. "Why on earth would I kill Barb?"

"If I have motive, then you most certainly do. She slept with your girlfriend, and you're a pathologist. You'd know how to kill her and make it look like someone else did, and again we only have your word that she died the way you say she did."

Maggie took in a deep breath then let it out. "All right, I see no sense in continuing this little ruse, Vivian is *not*, repeat *not*, my girlfriend. I'm not even gay. I said we were a couple to get on the show so that I could check this place out. Since I mostly retired from the forensics department I've written a couple of books. I wanted to come here to do research for my new book."

"Ix-nay on the not-a-couple-aye," I whispered in Maggie's ear, thinking that even if we lived, if Maggie didn't shut up we weren't going to be eligible for the prize money, and after all the shit we'd been through and still had as yet to go through, I wanted that damn money. I knew enough about law to know this was going to be a violation of the contract we signed and cost us the prize money. "Ah come on, honey," I laughed. "It's all right, you don't have to lie. No one really believes you could kill anyone."

"I'll kill you if you don't shut up," Maggie said, but not without a smile. "Look at us," she said to the others, "do we look like a couple?"

The others all looked from Maggie to me and then back, and said a collective, "No, not really."

"There goes the money," I said with a sigh.

"Now isn't the time to worry about money, Vivian," Maggie scolded. "We have to focus on figuring out who the real killer is and where they're hiding. More and more I am convinced that the killer isn't one of us . . ."

"It's some dark evil from the time before man walked the earth . . ."

"Shut the fuck up," I ordered Male Wyman. I was suddenly really depressed. The only thing that had gotten me through all the death I was forced to relive, the bodies stacking up, the physical trauma, and all the filth was the idea that I might actually make the big bucks. Now Maggie, who had insisted we do this whole stupid thing, had just ruined it for me. So I wasn't in the mood for mad Wyman's stupid shit.

"I think the killer came in with the crew, maybe he was even a member of the crew, and now he's hiding here, watching us and picking us off one by one," Maggie said.

"Who?" Mug asked as he entered the room all but carrying a very drugged-out Jugs. In that moment I half thought she had the right idea, and I think I actually would have killed for a beer.

"The killer."

Maggie recapped what she had been talking about, and Ken added, "They aren't a couple. They just said they were to get on the show."

"May I ask what your relationship is then?" Whine-man asked.

"We're best friends and business colleagues. You know that," she said, glaring at him, no doubt because he had known who she and I were from the start and had early-on made a point of telling everyone.

Mug made a face and looked at me. "But *you're* still a lesbian, right?"

"Hello, she slept with my wife," Ken said, and duh was implied.

Mug laughed. "Oh yeah, but apparently only one of them was cheating."

Ken looked like he was ready to rip Mug's throat out with his teeth. Then suddenly his features changed, and he looked at me. "You . . . you don't have anyone at home?"

"No," I answered simply. "I'm really sorry I banged your old lady."

"It's all right," he said. It was obvious that he meant it, and I knew immediately why. His wife was always cheating on him. So the fact that I had slept with her wasn't as big a deal to him as the idea that I had cheated on Maggie. Because he knew how it felt to be cheated on and had no understanding of people who cheated.

He was a tortured soul, a man in love with an unfaithful woman. This immediately put him back on the top of my suspect list.

Barb might have naturally assumed her attacker wasn't Ken because he loved her and wouldn't kill her, and after all wasn't a dick, a dick, a dick? Maybe there wasn't that much difference from one to another—I made a mental note to ask Maggie later. If Ken wanted to kill Barb and not be suspect, what better way than to make her just one of a long list of dead bodies on a haunted island?

If Barb had driven Ken crazy, there was no telling what he might do. Once someone was nuts murder might seem like a perfectly plausible way to end their suffering.

My brain had been working so hard on this scenario that I hadn't heard any of the conversation.

"Is that all right with you, Vivian?" Maggie all but yelled at me, no doubt noting my not-quite-there state.

"Huh?" I asked intelligently.

"We've decided to check the house and the island to try and find this guy. We figured by taking mud and knocking out the cameras we can keep him from watching us at least for a while, after all he isn't likely to come out in broad daylight and wash the cameras off. Mug and Jugs are going to take the south side of the island, the Wymans are going to take the north side, and you and Ken and I are going to search the house."

Great . . . she would assign us to go off with the man I was now sure was the killer.

"Yeah, fine with me."

The house really was a maze, and we found ourselves using the maps we had been given just to keep from searching rooms we'd already searched. I occasionally did what must have looked like modern dance steps to keep from stepping on spots where someone had been killed.

Wonderful place.

We were checking Mug and Jug's room when Ken said, "I think we should go through everyone's things. Theirs, mine, and yours."

"Good idea," Maggie said.

I looked up at the camera. "Look," I said, pointing.

The camera lens was clean, but there was mud and lots of

water on the floor under it, and mud behind the camera on the wall where it had splattered. I slung a new fistful of mud on the camera.

"That does it." Ken took in a deep sigh. "There *is* someone else on the island."

"What makes you say that?" I asked.

"Because we were all in the kitchen when Mug came back here to cover the camera, which he obviously did, and we all left from the kitchen afterwards," Maggie said.

"Oh yeah," I said, showing my massive intellect.

We didn't find anything of real interest in Mug and Jug's special effects, mostly a lot of porn magazines, a huge dildo (I was beginning to feel absolutely straight amongst all these obvious perverts) and tons of beauty supplies including a blow drier. I don't know what Jugs was expecting, but it certainly wasn't rugged living on a deserted island with dead bodies piling up around us. She'd even brought high heels and a formal evening gown. She seemed to have a lifetime supply of Quaaludes and Valium.

"This is how he was going to win even though he had the partner most likely to chicken out," Maggie said.

I nodded.

Their room was a big blank, but in the hallway right across from their room Maggie noticed a difference in the texture on the wall, and when we checked it out it turned out to be a secret door leading to a passageway. Flashlights in hand we entered the passage barely wide enough for one person to pass through. At one point Maggie—who was leading the way—stopped and bent down.

"What is it?" I asked.

"Blood and a partial footprint. I can't make out the pattern, though, it's smeared." She looked around for several minutes. "No clear print, but I'd say the killer's shoes weren't rubber soled—probably why he was slipping."

She moved a little further and stopped again. She looked up at me and smiled. "I've got a full print. I'd say a size eleven, and the smears are consistent with the robe pattern in the kitchen."

"I wear a size eleven," Ken said.

Great, and the bastard was standing behind me.

"But I only have running shoes," he said.

Maggie nodded, no doubt thinking what I was, that if you were the killer you probably wouldn't keep your props in the same room you slept and had your shit in. Maggie stood up and started moving again.

Ahead of us the hallway forked. "Which way?" she asked.

"Doesn't really matter. We'll have to go down both anyway," I said.

Maggie looked down at the floor with her flashlight. "The blood goes this way."

A few minutes later we were opening a door that led us into what had been Ken and Barb's room, where the air was still filled with the stench of her blood. Behind me Ken started sobbing.

"You want to stay here while we check the room?" Maggie asked Ken. He nodded and moved up the passageway a little as we entered the room. I quickly moved to coat the camera in their room with mud. In the light of day, Maggie found more of the footprints. They matched the ones we'd found in the secret passageway. We rummaged through Ken and Barb's stuff and didn't find much, mostly fitness crap, a dildo and some handcuffs with the keys hanging on a ring from them. I grabbed the handcuffs and pocketed them.

"What are you going to do with those?" Maggie asked in a whisper.

I looked at her with raised eyebrows and then before she could scream at me answered, "We might need them to restrain someone later, and I sure don't want *him* to have them."

Maggie nodded. "Go ask Ken if he'd like us to bring him his stuff."

I nodded and walked into the passageway, but Ken was gone. "He took off," I said, walking back into the room with Maggie.

"That idiot. I understand that he's upset, but . . ."

"I think he's the killer," I whispered.

"I wish you'd make up your mind who you suspect. Really, Vivian, your mind is like a spastic running around in circles." Maggie shrugged. "Maybe he went down the other passage. Well, grab his gear anyway."

I nodded and picked up the bag she had packed. We walked back into the wall and headed down the other side of the passageway, which wound up opening into the Wymans' room.

"What did I tell you, Maggie? It's the Wymans."

We checked the Wymans' gear and then the whole house, but we didn't find any real clues and we never saw Ken again. When we met the others in the kitchen that evening it was just starting to get dark.

Neither the Wymans nor Mug and Jugs found anything that would either help us off the island or that proved that there was someone else on the island with us. Of course if one of them were the murderer, or an accomplice, they would have spent the day sunning themselves on a stretch of beach and then just showed up to say they'd found nothing.

Of course all *we* had to offer were the secret passageway we'd found and some bloody footprints.

"Where's Ken?" She-Wyman asked.

"I wish I knew," Maggie said. "When the passage opened into his room he was very upset, so we left him in the passage. When we got back he had left—at least that's what I thought happened, but now . . . I'm starting to worry."

"That does it, that bastard's the killer," Mug insisted.

At that point I was thinking it was most probably Mug; like Maggie said, I changed my mind a lot.

Outside the wind started to kick up.

"Looks like there's a hell of a storm blowing in," I said.

"Wow . . . you are a detective," Mug said with a laugh. "So . . . are we going to eat any time soon?"

Maggie and Jugs started to cook something, to this day I'm not really sure what it was, but it didn't taste half bad. Jugs actually mostly just got in Maggie's way. She was so stoned at that point I don't think she was really aware of anything.

"That's how you were going to win the game!" Wyman yelled at Mug.

"What?" Mug asked.

"If we were still playing the game," he started in an accusing tone, "she would have been the first one to chicken out and you would have lost by proxy. So you were going to keep her drugged so that she wouldn't, *couldn't* leave."

I remember being more than a little pissed off because Maggie and I had already figured it out and now He-Wyman was acting like he was all smart because he'd figured it out.

Mug smiled then. "Who says we ain't still playing the game? *I'm* still playing. Someone's gonna take home a million bucks. Some lunatic is killing people, and I'm thinking you and your old lady ain't got a chance of living to the end of the week, so me and my baby will be rich." He laughed then and pointed at me and Maggie. "Hell, they got more of a chance of living than you two whackos, and they admitted they aren't even a couple, so they can't win."

I glared at Maggie. "If we live, I'm going to kill you," I hissed.

Maggie just shrugged, obviously not worried in the slightest.

We had just finished eating the whatever-it-was when the wind really kicked up. We could hear little pieces of jungle rot pounding into the outside of the building, and then a window broke.

Female Wyman screamed, and then because of the delayed reaction all the drugs were causing, so did Jugs. The rain started coming down then so hard and so fast that the sound was almost deafening.

Then the generator went out taking all the lights with it. Not that we were all living in fear at this point, but immediately flashlights clicked on.

"The wind must have taken out the lines running from the generator," I said.

"Or it just ran out of gas," Maggie said. "Has anyone thought to put fuel in it since the Mexican's died?"

"Jesus didn't die, he ran off. He might even be the killer," Ken said quickly.

And I shot Maggie a dirty look she couldn't see.

"I've been filling the generator," Mug said, then added, "it was a sure bet none of you numb nuts were going to remember that we aren't hooked up to the utility companies. The generator ain't out of gas; I just filled it this afternoon. There must be a tree down on the line."

"What now?" Jugs asked.

"I suggest we choose up sides and go to bed," Female Wyman said.

It was a good idea; we seemed to be safest in our own rooms. Except of course Barb who'd died in hers.

"I suggest you either change rooms or barricade that passage off," Maggie told Mug and Jugs.

"What about Ken?" Maggie asked.

"What about him?" Mug asked.

"He could be outside in this storm," Maggie said.

"Or worse," I said, "he might be the killer and be in here with us and we have not a clue where he is."

"Which is just another reason why it couldn't hurt to barricade those secret passages," Maggie said.

"The forces that haunt this domain, the evil being unleashed by this storm, will not be stopped by simple barricades," Male Wyman said in a voice rattling like a Baptist preacher in the middle of a hellfire and damnation sermon.

"Then I guess you better change rooms," I said.

We were lucky we'd chosen a room on the west, so a little water was running in under our barricade on the balcony, but at least rain wasn't driving all the way across the room as it would have been if we were on the other side of the hotel.

After we had checked our room for intruders, we barricaded the door then we gathered up all our dirty clothes and put them against the bottom of the barricade in the hopes of keeping the water from running all the way across the room and getting our bedding wet.

It was so loud you could hardly hear yourself think, and the light from our candles danced in the wind. It was some spooky stuff, and so I let Jake sleep in my bedroll with me. Poor little guy was scared practically to death.

I was on watch when the wind started to die down and the rain started to slow. I didn't know how Maggie had slept through the thirty minutes before that, because it had been awful. Glass was breaking everywhere, and I could hear trees snapping. This wasn't just some jungle storm; it was a fucking hurricane. I was just about to wake Maggie up when the voice started loud and low and deep. It was no human voice, but it sure as shit wasn't a ghost because . . . well, I've already explained about that a dozen times already.

Maggie woke up immediately. "What the . . ."

"Shush," I ordered and stuck my hand over her mouth.

Together we listened. "You can run, but you can't hide. Many come here but few survive. Come into my parlor said the spider to the fly." It said this about a dozen times and then it stopped.

"What the fuck was that supposed to be?" I asked Maggie in a whisper.

"Part of the game?"

"Maybe." I sat up, grabbed my flashlight, and did a quick scan of our room just to make damn sure we were alone. "Remember what Mug said? We're still playing the game. They were bound to have set up stuff just to scare the crap out of us, and it would run on batteries just like the cameras."

Maggie nodded. "It's got to be that. Unless the killer is doing it."

"Well, gee, that's a fun thought."

Jake had crawled into my lap. Maggie's own flashlight quickly whipped down spotlighting him, and I swear the little monster smiled. Maggie looked at me as if she were seriously worried about my sanity, which I defended by saying, "Hey, the little guy was scared."

CHAPTER SEVENTEEN: MAGGIE

That gecko was really starting to creep me out. More so than the rage of the storm outside, the weird disembodied voice, or even the chance of becoming the next statistic on the killer's list. And to make it worse, Vivian was actually treating the little creature like a pet.

On the other hand, I suppose it was interesting to think of her accepting an animal for a friend. She's always been such a clean freak. Now here she was making mud balls and playing with a lizard. I wonder what Freud would have said about that?

I shook my head. "You know, if that recording *is* the killer trying to mess with our minds and scare us out of here, then he has got to be somewhere around the vicinity of the control room right now."

Vivian looked at *me* like I had lost my marbles, and considering how things were going I don't think she would have been too far off base, but at least I wasn't talking to a lizard.

"And I suppose you think we should go and see?" she said.

"Would you rather sit here all night wondering when the killer is going to come after us?" I asked, and I glanced up to make sure our camera was still covered. Tempted as I was to shine my flashlight on it, I resisted the urge. The light might shine around the pack enough to reveal to the killer that we were up. The last thing we needed was the murderer figuring out that we were about to embark on an investigation.

"I would rather be on the mainland in a nice safe hotel with a real bed and some hot chick massaging my feet . . . for starters." Vivian squinted up at the camera in a longing manner. Jake charged up her shirt and into the breast pocket of the short-sleeved shirt she had been wearing over her tank top. I cocked an eyebrow. That *was* too weird . . . because Vivian acted as though he had been doing it all along.

I shook my head. "Well, if we make it off this island alive I'll pay the hot chick myself . . ."

"I'm gonna hold you to that, Maggie," Vivian said. "And I get to pick the chick. *And* you owe me a carton of cigarettes, too!"

"Fine," I said. Though if there were a way to get out of purchasing the cigarettes, I would find it. The last thing I wanted to do was feed Vivian's nicotine habit.

We gathered what we could for weapons. I saw Vivian stick the handcuffs into her pocket, and still didn't know what good they were going to do us. I wished I had brought my late husband's pistol with me on this trip. He used to take me out and make me learn how to use it when we were young, and I was a fair shot, but for some reason, a fencing blade always felt more at home in my hand than a gun. Working in a coroner's office, we were required to know firearms. Of course if I'd even tried to get a gun on the airplane I'd no doubt have been sitting in a jail cell in the States, which still would have been a damn sight better than where I was. I sort of doubt I could have convinced them to let me bring a sword, either. Even if I had gotten one through customs, no doubt the show's producer would have taken it from me when they searched our packs before we left for the island.

So I settled on a chunk of wood with a couple of nails in the end. If anything, it would serve to discourage attackers. I hoped.

With flashlights strapped to our arms using kerchiefs—Vivian's idea so we could keep our hands free for fighting—we carefully shifted all the broken boards and debris of our barrier out of the way. Then stealthy as a pair of ninjas—me looking more like one of the Ninja Turtles, I imagine—we started down the hall.

Vivian took the lead. She insisted. "I'm taller and more experienced at hand-to-hand combat," she said, as if shoving drunks out the bar door made her a judo master.

Maybe it was a good thing I *didn't* have the gun. No way I could have shot over her head.

Except for the storm, there was an eerie quiet pervading in the air. A lot of static electricity kept tingling my skin. This was a powerful storm, to be sure, and only a maniac would get out in such weather.

And of course, it occurred to me that there *was* probably at least one maniac out there in the weather somewhere.

"Wonder where Winston got off to?" I whispered.

Vivian signaled me to stop and be quiet. She pointed to the camera up in the corner. We shut off our flashlights, though part of me remembered that there were night-vision settings on those things. As we got closer, Vivian crouched and stayed close to the wall. I was not really sure *that* would work either, but I followed her example. We got directly under the camera when we came across the splotch of mud. I looked up and realized the camera was dripping.

The killer had washed off the lenses again! But how? They were too high to reach, and no one was supposed to have access to a ladder. The camera crew had taken those away. Except of course for the one in the vault.

Still, I think we would have heard someone hauling a ladder around, and the water looked like it had been sprayed over the Lexan boxes in a tight stream. Hmmm, there were no hoses around here, either, and certainly no sources of water anywhere but in the kitchen and bathrooms. I suppose he could be using a bucket and just throwing the water, but I somehow thought that would make a lot more mess, not to mention noise.

Vivian was already moving on, so I picked up the pace to catch up with her. When she hugged the wall, I did the same. We managed to get all the way to the stairs unchallenged. Once there, we took our time. Vivian clearly did not want a repeat of her earlier encounter with the attacker who burst out of the shadows. I didn't blame her. One concussion was more than enough, and a second was not highly recommended.

We reached the bottom of the stairs. Vivian risked turning on her flashlight and scanning the white beam over the room, still no one in sight. We picked up the pace now and crossed the room, heading for the next section of halls. Flashes of lightning scattered through windows, casting wicked shadows with each stroke.

We were making all the turns to head for the back hall, "the parlor," to be exact, when Vivian suddenly stopped and pushed me back into one of the rooms. First, I saw the flicker of candlelight that quickly winked out. Then a large shadow loomed at the end of the next corridor, and started up our way. The patter of flip-flops accompanied the gasping whimpers of someone who was obviously crying. Vivian and I crouched and watched as the shadow rolled past our hiding place, moving at a purposeful pace.

"Ned? Pumpkin Poo?" It was Astaria Wyman who waddled down the hall at a frantic pace.

Vivian and I traded looks. I *know* we were thinking the same thing.

Pumpkin Poo?

We stepped quickly out into the hall. "Hey, ASStaria," Vivian called.

The sound that erupted from Astaria was sonic and left a ringing in my ears. Vivian jumped back as the cry blasted her eardrums as well. Astaria spun around and floundered like a beached whale trying to keep her balance. Vivian's flashlight must have been a slap in the face, because she cringed, threw up her hands and squealed.

"Hey, it's just us," I said, using my "reassuring mother" voice.

Astaria lowered her arms and blinked in uncertainty. Only then did I see that she had something that looked like a stone fetish knife in one hand and a candlestick in the other.

"What are you two doing here?" she asked.

"We could ask you the same thing, ASStaria," Vivian said, making me want to elbow her.

"I'm looking for Ned," she said. "He . . . he went out over an hour ago, and I'm worried about him and . . . So what *are* you two doing out?"

"Did you hear a voice?" I asked.

She took a deep breath that raised and lowered her leviathan chest. The knife was shaking in her hand. Small wonder she wasn't able to keep the candle lit. "That's what Ned went looking for," she said. "He said he thought he knew who might be doing it. I was right behind him, but somehow we got separated."

I saw Vivian quirk an eyebrow. "I don't suppose he said *who* he thought it was, or how he knew," she said.

Astaria shrugged. "He . . . thought he saw someone outside earlier." Worry seethed across her face. "Look, I really should go look for him," she said. "I lost him quite a while ago . . ."

"Why don't we look together?" I said. As much as I disliked Ned Wyman, I could see how distressed she was. And I suppose it's not my place to determine why people fall in love with one another. Though I am starting to wonder if we should make it a law that certain gene pools be sterilized.

Vivian gave me the "are you insane" look and sighed.

"Just stay behind me," she said.

We both nodded.

The storm was starting to abate as we made the rounds. We reached the kitchen without finding anyone else. It occurred to me then that the number of folks on the island was now drastically reduced. I ticked the list off in my head: me, Vivian, John and Harmony, Ned and Astaria and Winston who no one had seen since we'd lost him the day before. We were down two cooks, one heir, and one slut . . . I mean, woman.

Well, maybe we were not doing too badly, then?

Right.

The kitchen door to the outside hung open and banged in the blasting wind. I marched over and dragged it shut, getting soaked in the process. When I turned back, I noticed the trail of sludge and dirt across the floor. Something—someone—had been dragged through here.

"Vivian," I said, and pointed to the trail.

She came around and looked at the floor. "Fine, I am not cleaning *that* up," she said.

I would have poked her, but the urgency in me now was to follow those marks. They led through the other door of the kitchen, the one that opened into the old dining room hall.

I left her still staring at the tracks and followed them. They led through the dining room, back into the hall. From there, I could see a flicker of candlelight in the parlor. Someone was in there, I thought.

Yep, someone was in there all right.

In the middle of the room was Winston, sitting in one of the old chairs. He'd been tied to the seat to keep him in an upright position. His hands were bound to the arms of the chair, and his fists were curled around candlesticks that were still burning. A strap around his neck kept him from slumping though his head rolled off to one side.

My eyes went to his chest. There was a huge hole, dark with blood that spilled down his chest. His heart was lying in his lap, and around him was a circle of blood.

"Ah, Christ!" Vivian swore. "Jesus H, fucking Mary and Joseph."

"What . . . is it . . . Oh . . ." Astaria stopped in the doorway, her chin resting on her ample breast in shock.

I took a deep breath and switched on my own flashlight as I carefully crossed the room. Years of training came into play. I would not disturb the scene of the crime more by habit than anything, but also because I could see that there was a camera primed on me and on the scene. *Bastard,* I thought. *I bet you're enjoying this.*

"Jesus, Maggie, you're not gonna . . ." Vivian said.

I ignored her and leaned down to get a closer look. Removing a human heart from a human chest is no simple task. People seem to think you can just cut it out. Well, you can't really, because there's a breastbone and several ribs in the way. On closer examination, it looked as though the killer had used a heavy tool—possibly bolt cutters—to snap the bones so he could get to the heart. The little door of flesh lay oozing under the heart, which looked as though it had been squeezed because there were imprints of fingers on the surface. I carefully raised Winston's head and looked into his bleakly staring eyes. They were dilated. Hmmmm. I ran the flashlight over the body as quickly as I could without missing much, circling the corpse. And was rewarded with the sight of visible needle marks in the back of the neck. Drugged, I thought and stepped back.

"Well?" Vivian said.

"He was alive when this happened," I said. "See how the blood on him is sprayed in an arc? Blood doesn't do that unless a heart is pumping at the moment of death. When the first incision was made to remove the ribs, he was still alive . . . but he

218

had been drugged so he probably didn't feel a thing . . ."

"Makes sense—there's no hot spot in the room," Vivian said.

I heard a whump and turned. Astaria had sunk to the floor in a faint.

"So, we're down to two possible killer guys," Vivian said. "Cause there's no way you are going to convince me that Jugs or ASStaria did this . . ."

"That, or there is still someone else on this island that we don't know about," I said. Then my flashlight played across something on the wall—written in blood were the words, "All Must Pay."

"Fucking beautiful," Vivian said.

"Looks like it was squirted on the wall," I said thoughtfully.

"We don't have time to investigate, Maggie," Vivian said, and gave me a hard look. "What now?"

"Blow the candles out and cover him up," I said, frowning up at the camera. Vivian was right; we didn't have time to investigate.

We found the slightly rotten remains of a fancy linen tablecloth in a cabinet in the pantry. Vivian snarled at me as the dust billowed when we unfolded it and tossed it over Winston. By then, Astaria was starting to rouse and the storm was beginning to calm down. The creaking and groaning and crashing of timbers abated as well. Which was good, because I really was tired, and needed a few hours more sleep.

So far, no one else had made an appearance, which was probably for the better. I closed the door to the parlor, not that there was a way to stop anyone from going in if they seriously wanted to. Old habits. If there had been anything resembling crime scene tape, I no doubt would have used that, too. Duct tape might work, but I suspect no one would respect it.

Astaria finally crawled to her feet. She looked as bone weary as I felt. Vivian was back in livewire mode. I suspected that once we got back to the room, there would not be much sleeping. She wanted to talk about this and apparently didn't want to while Astaria was around. Still, I didn't think it would be wise to leave her alone until we figured out where Ned was.

Assuming Ned was not the killer. I glanced at the stone *athame* that Astaria had dropped when she fainted. It was clean of blood. Still, she could have wiped that off. Carefully, I picked it up.

"That's mine," Astaria said, and practically snatched it from my grasp. Vivian raised her board as though planning to conk Astaria with it, but I shook my head.

"That's an unusual knife," I said.

Astaria cradled it close. "It's a ceremonial knife," she said. "Ned found it."

"Found it? Where?"

"There are some old ruins near the heart of the island," Astaria said. "Mostly broken down. I read in the description of this place that it once had a Incan temple . . ."

"Aztec," I corrected. "The Incas were further south, in Peru . . ." Mayans were in Yucatan. Chichen Itza, for example.

She gave me a look that said she was not pleased to be corrected. "Whatever," she said. "Most of the stones were used to build the original hotel here. What's left is rubble filled with jungle. Ned was looking around in there, seeing if he could find a clue or two, when he found an old cave that had been used for burial purposes. He said it was filled with jars and tools and what looked like the remains of a mummy, and a statue of Xipe Totec."

"Zippie who?" Vivian interrupted.

"The Flayed Lord," I said. "Remember, Aztecs made blood sacrifices to him." I really wish Vivian would actually listen when I talk to her.

"Yes," Astaria said as though confirming my words. "Anyway, Ned found what looked like an old stone altar, and lying at the base was this knife, and he figured it was pretty old and so he brought it back to me."

"Old?" I said. "That isn't old."

"What?"

"I've seen enough old Aztec and Mayan stone knives," I said. "They were made of obsidian. That's chert. It doesn't occur in this part of the world. Besides, the chipping on that blade was done recently. It shows none of the smoothing out that real Aztec stone daggers possess. Sorry, Astaria, but that's a fake *and* an imported one at that."

"So the ruins have been faked, too," Vivian suggested.

"I'd have to see them to know that for sure," I said. "But I'm willing to bet they are . . . part of the *game*. Maybe we better find Ned and get him to lead us there."

"But it's late and it's storming," Vivian said.

Astaria was busy examining the knife with a frown. I think it was dawning on her that Ned Wyman was not half as bright as she had believed. She lowered it with a sigh. "Yes, let's go find Ned," she agreed. "And maybe we should form an alliance like they do on those other reality shows. That way, we can work together and whoever wins can split the money, and . . ."

A distant crash interrupted her speech. Both Vivian and I jumped, and Astaria squeaked. Vivian and I played flashlights over the hall. Another crash sounded . . . like someone was overturning furniture. The sounds seemed to emanate from the direction of the sleeping chambers.

"Great," Vivian said.

A third crash sounded, fainter than before, as though whatever caused it was moving away. And then the moaning began. It started low, like a groan of agony, and rose in pitch. Behind it, I could hear laughter and that ominous voice taunting us with another riddle.

"Piece by piece, one by one, little nips until he's none . . ." the voice broke into maniacal laughter.

Astaria covered her ears and screamed, which made me cover *my* ears. Damn, the woman could have shattered glass with her voice, and she didn't seem to want to stop screaming until Vivian slapped her. Her shriek went from terror to outrage.

"How dare you hit me!" she screamed. "I'm telling Ned, and he'll fix you for good!"

She turned and bolted down the hall, lumbering like some mad buffalo.

Vivian looked at me. "We better follow her," she said. "I have a bad feeling about all this shit, Maggie."

I nodded, though I thought that was probably the understatement of the century. We loped after Astaria who had already managed to turn into the maze of corridors that led from the main part of the hotel to the rooms. She was moving pretty fast for a large woman. I let Vivian lead because jogging had never been one of my specialties. Ahead of us, we could hear the thunder of Astaria's footsteps and the wheezing whimpers of her troubled breathing.

And then her screams.

Vivian picked up the pace. She charged into the secondary hallway where the stairs were. For a moment, she was out of my sight. Frantic, I hurried around the turn and skidded into Vivian.

Astaria was on her knees, a crumbled ball of weeping. Vivian was staring ahead, though when I collided with her, she turned an ornery look in my direction.

"Piece by piece," she said and pointed.

I followed the direction of her hand.

Ned Wyman was dangling from the railing by a length of rope. He was naked . . . not the most attractive sight, especially since little triangles of his flesh had been snipped away.

I sighed and stepped closer. Someone had taken a pair of garden shears and snipped pieces of his flesh off. His penis had been trimmed by inches and the little rounds of flesh had been carefully laid in a line on the floor beneath his feet with his balls to either side. I looked up at him, dangling by his arms. The cuts were everywhere, but they showed a lack of serious bleeding, a sign that the heart was stopped when the majority of the mutilations took place. It was possible he had died of shock when the first cut was made . . . or that he had been killed then mutilated. Or like poor Winston he had been drugged. Still, there was duct tape over his mouth, holding in what looked like one of his own socks. And the gardening sheers had been thrust through his eyes and protruded from his face. The torture must have been too excruciating for his delicate constitution.

As I looked at him, a small part of me could not help but think of the pain he must have gone through. It's really hard to explain what a mutilated corpse looks like. Only one who has been involved in such a process can know the pain and terror he must have gone through.

And whenever I'm feeling particularly low, I call it to mind . . . and I feel so much better, because as far as I'm concerned, he deserved every little snip.

But for the moment, there was another death to add to the list. And it wasn't terribly pretty.

"Damn," Vivian said, pointing to the mess on the floor. I notice she was keeping back as though fearing she would find out what Ned *had* gone through. So I was guessing she could feel a hot spot, which would mean Ned had known at least part of what was happening to him. "Is that what I think it is?"

"Yeah," I said. "Though I wasn't sure you'd ever seen one of those."

Vivian sneered. "What happened, Maggie, did your pet rock die?"

I made a face at her and turned.

Astaria was on her feet again, backing toward the door.

"You did this," she said.

"What?" Vivian and I turned toward her.

"You did this! Both of you! You hated him! You killed my Pumpkin Poo."

"What the hell is Pumpkin Poo?" Vivian barked back at her. "Get your head out of your fat ass, woman, and listen up. We did not kill the Whyman . . ."

"Murderers!" she shrieked and turning, she ran. I could hear her screaming over and over as she fled, and then silence.

I looked at Vivian. "What made her think we did this?" I said.

She pointed to the stack of clothing.

Stacked on top of Ned's shorts was a copy of my last book. And across my picture on the back cover someone had written "murderer" with blood.

CHAPTER EIGHTEEN: VIVIAN

"They sort of look like beads," I said looking at the pile of pieces of Wyman's dick.

Maggie sighed, "Do you think you might try being serious for a minute? You know what this means, don't you?"

"He didn't have much dick to start with?"

"Dammit, Vivian . . ."

"You're right, I'm sorry."

Maggie and I looked at the body, the damning evidence against us, and then at each other, and said in unison, "Mug." Well, actually Maggie said John, which was of course the guy's name, and his I actually *do* remember now because . . . Well, you'll see.

Jake acted like he wanted down, so I took him out of my pocket and put him onto the floor.

"Got to be," Maggie said in a whisper.

"The way Ken died was sort of a dead giveaway. He was tied to a chair just like Mug wanted us to do."

"I'd bet money he isn't working alone," Maggie said thoughtfully. "Someone's working those cameras then calling him on the phone telling him where to go and when."

"Could it be Jugs?"

"Christ, Vivian, do you think you could just work on getting at least one person's name right?"

"I've got yours right," I answered with a smile.

"I don't think it's her. She's obviously drugged completely out."

"Someone else on the island?" I said. "Someone besides us as we've suspected all along."

"Yes, remember your visions . . . The same man committed both of the other massacres. The lunatic was never counted among the occupants of this island. Maybe he's come back."

"He'd be in his seventies now, Maggie. Christ, that's as screwy as something the Whinemans would come up with . . ."

"Not with John for an accomplice."

"But what's Mug's motive?" I asked.

"Same as before, money. He wins the prize for the stupid-assed show if we're all dead, and maybe lunatic guy is rich and he's giving him a bundle . . ."

"That sounds like a story straight out of the *Sun*. I'm telling you it's Dead President Guy. He's doing it . . . all of it, for the ratings."

"Yes, my explanation is ridiculous while yours is perfectly plausible. Really, Vivian, murder for the ratings . . . They are hardly going to allow any of these killings to be on the air."

"You don't watch much TV, do ya Maggie?"

"No, not really but . . ."

"I rest my fucking case. They'll air it. There will be a warning in the front of it just like they put on any show with gay content, and they'll air it in its entirety," I said. Then I realized why Jake had wanted down so bad. The bloodthirsty little bastard was chewing on a piece of Deadman's dick. "Jumping Jesus on a pogo stick, Jake." I picked him up by the scruff of the neck and shook him till he let the piece of meat go. "Bad, bad, bad lizard," I scolded, and stuck him back into my pocket.

"That does it, you've gone completely round the bend. You, the queen of clean just stuck a bloody lizard who'd been chewing on a dead idiot's penis into your pocket."

"These are desperate times, Maggie, in case you hadn't noticed."

"Yes, they certainly are," Mug said as he walked into the room with Female Wyman in tow. The stupid bitch had run to get him, and, yes, we being the idiots that we are had stood there talking and bitching at each other till she had come back with the murderer.

Mug shook his head. "Hell, you guys aren't even trying to cover your trail now. Little triangles, that's a gay sign, isn't it? And your book—he must have written murderer on it as he was dying."

"That would sort of be impossible since he's hanging over there a good five feet from the book," Maggie pointed out.

The look on John's face confirmed what we already knew, because it was obvious from his expression that he had just figured out that far from this implicating Maggie and I, it more or less proved we weren't the killers since this was obviously staged, and why would we implicate ourselves? Of course I didn't want him to know that we'd figured out that he was the killer, so I attacked him on another level. "Triangle is some gay sign isn't it? God, that's got to be the same brand of logic Jerry Falwell used to conclude that the fucking tubbytubber was a queer."

"Teletubby," She-Wyman corrected.

"Every time there has been a murder you two have been right there," he accused. "How do you explain that?"

"Just lucky?" I said with a shrug.

"So have you, and so has she," Maggie accused, pointing at them both in turn.

"Me . . . why would I kill my sweet Pumpkin Poo, or anyone else for that matter?" She collapsed onto the floor in a lotus position and buried her face in her hands. "We just wanted to free this place of the evil spirits that haunt it, my poor, poor baby, how he must have suffered."

I had taken hold of the back of Maggie's shirt and was slowly moving both of us further away from John and the Whywhore and closer to a door. Maggie knew what I was doing and why, and she followed my lead.

We were both sure that John was the killer. Each killing was more brutal than the one before, and even if he had been perfectly sane when he'd started his killing spree, he couldn't possibly be sane now. You couldn't be a man and cut up another man's privates with pruning sheers—even an asshole like Whyman—and not be fucking crazy on some level. She-Whyman had decided that we were the enemy and had gone to John for help, so there was no saving her even if we wanted to. As for Jugs, she was either already dead or drugged out in her room. Either way we couldn't help her, either. In my opinion it was high time to save our own asses.

There was only a day and a half left before the game would be over and the boat would come for us from the mainland. No doubt we were all supposed to be dead by then, and John would make his getaway on that damn boat we couldn't find because of course he knew exactly where we were and what we were doing.

He was running out of time. That's why he had killed Ken and Whyman so close together. In his estimation they would have been the hardest to kill. The way I figured it, that made Maggie and me next on his list. No doubt this was why he'd tried to frame us. Maybe to get She-Whyman to help him capture us, tie us up, stick us somewhere, and then he could come back and kill us at his leisure.

John seemed to notice that we were moving then and in which direction. "Where the hell do you two think you're going?" he asked, and I knew from the smile on his face that he knew that we knew he was the killer and he didn't care. He wasn't worried in the least about being caught. No doubt because he was sure he could kill us. Dead people don't talk.

Except of course to me.

We were still too close to him, and he probably would have gotten at least one of us if the mysterious voice hadn't picked that moment to speak, which distracted John.

"One of you isn't what you seem. Is this reality or just a bad dream?"

Assateria let out a hysterical scream the minute the voice started, and in all the confusion caused by the two outbursts Maggie and I took off running down the hall, me basically dragging Maggie along by the arm. John came running right after us as Maggie yelled out, "Run, Assateria! John is the killer."

Me, I wouldn't have bothered to make the effort. I guess Maggie's just a better person than I am. In fact, I know she is.

John was going to catch us; it was only a matter of time. I'd run into him once on the stairs—I was now sure it was him since the other two were dead—and I knew I couldn't fight him. We were basically screwed. Then I saw a doorway and the board Maggie still clutched in her fist. I had stupidly laid my own weapon down somewhere. I pulled Maggie into the doorway and grabbed her board away. Maggie gave me a "What the hell are you doing now look," and I mouthed the words "batter up," and moved over to the door. John didn't come, and I was afraid for a moment that he was going to be waiting just on the other side of the doorway if I looked around the corner, so I jumped out, ready to swing, but he was nowhere in sight.

"What the hell?" I muttered.

"He's the killer, Viv, and by now he's figured out that we're going to be harder to kill than he thought, so he isn't going to wait around anymore. He's gone off to get his costume so he can kill us without being seen."

"So . . . what we going to do, Maggie?"

"We have to get the hell out of this house, that's for damn sure. The storm's all but over. We'll be better off outside. There are fewer cameras, more places to hide out of their vision."

"I don't think we can chance getting our gear." I gave Maggie back her board and looked for and found another one for myself.

"No, he'll expect us to go back there."

At least we still had our flashlights because we had tied them to our arms. Of course we were afraid to turn them on so they didn't do us much good right then.

We were whispering, of course, but I still wasn't sure that whoever was watching those damn cameras didn't know every single thing we were saying. I whispered as much to Maggie who asked, "What?"

"Damnit, Maggie," I cursed. "Let's just go."

We wound up going out a broken window. It was still raining buckets, and as we walked out from under the eves we were immediately drenched by the rain that poured off the roof.

"Where are we going?" Maggie asked.

"Don't talk, just follow," I hissed back. "You brought me to this fucking hell on earth, now we do things my way for a while."

I led her through the jungle to the shed the generator was in. I grabbed two of the gas cans and left the building. I put the cans down at Maggie's feet then went back into the building. I found a half dozen glass bottles, some old coat hangers, a couple of old dresses, what was left of an old framing hammer—no handle and only one claw—and a piece of tarp that was only about five foot square and all but gone. No decent weapons. But what we had would have to do. I wrapped everything up in the tarp then tied the tarp closed with a coat hanger and carried it out to Maggie. Then I went back inside and poured the last can of gas on the generator and everything else in the building. I walked out, tossed the can back through the door, then touched it off with my lighter and took off running. I grabbed one of the cans of gas and the bundle while Maggie grabbed the other can and we headed into the jungle.

That's the thing about Maggie, she isn't stupid, so you don't have to waste time explaining what you're doing. She just catches on and goes along for the ride . . . most of the time.

The building went up making a nice little exploding sound as the flames hit the generator's gas tank. "Now he can't fix it, and he has to rough it just like we do. It should also cause enough of a diversion for us to get away."

"Maybe they'll see the fire from the mainland and send help," Maggie said hopefully.

"Maybe," I said, but I sort of doubted it. We had been sent here to die. No one was coming till the game was over. Besides which I doubted that in this rainstorm it would burn long after the gas was gone.

We didn't use our flashlights, just stumbled through the dark and the rain without talking. We knew that it would be hard to see us on the monitors under these conditions, and as long as we didn't talk the killers weren't likely to find us.

It was slow going. There were trees down everywhere and we couldn't see our hands in front of our faces, and of course there was the rain.

Just before the sun came up we found a large area where several trees had gone down taking the only camera in the area down with them. When we were sure that the camera had been crushed beyond repair we put our loads down and stopped to rest. It was a good spot because the trees being down the way they were allowed us to hide in the middle of the mess, but we could still see through it to see if anyone was coming.

We were wet, but it wasn't cold, just uncomfortable.

I sat down on the trunk of a fallen tree and Jake climbed out of my pocket and down my arm to sit on the log beside me. All hint of Wyman's blood had been washed from Jake's face in the rain, and I chose not to remember the incident.

"That's sort of creepy," Maggie said, pointing at Jake.

"Huh?"

"That thing, the way . . . Well, it acts like it actually likes you."

"Is it so hard to believe that something could actually like me?" I said, more than a little pissed off. "I mean you like me. I have friends, the customers at the bar like me, the people I play ball with . . ."

"Wow, hold there, Viv," Maggie said with a laugh. "What I meant is that he's a lizard, like I said before they have very small, primitive brains."

"Oh . . . well not this one." I opened my makeshift pack and pulled a couple of the bottles from it. There was water running everywhere and I easily found a small "stream," and washed the bottles then filled them with water. I was glad the bottles were brown, because I couldn't really see how dirty either they still were or the water was. Even though we'd been rained on for hours I was still thirsty. I handed one of the bottles to Maggie and I drank from the other. The water actually tasted pretty good—a little gritty, but not bad.

I decided to take lots of shots as soon as I got home, if I got home.

"So, why'd you take the gas?" Maggie asked.

"Mostly I just didn't want them to have it, but then when I saw the bottles . . . I figure we can make some Molotov cocktails."

"Good idea," Maggie said. Suddenly she looked distant.

"What's wrong?"

She laughed. "You mean besides the fact that we're trapped on an island with at least one madman and the dead bodies just keep piling up? I'm wet, I'm tired, I'm hungry . . ."

"Yeah, we should have tried out for *Survivor* instead of *Chicken Shit.* All you have to do there is not get voted off and try to find stuff to eat which is actually the least of our problems here on Death's Own Island," I said, only about half kidding. I figure I could have made it on *Survivor,* and even if I didn't make it to the end I would have made it long enough to make a bundle of cash. Of course they don't actually allow dykes on *Survivor,* flaming queens, yes, but dykes, no. And what the hell is up with that anyway? I mean believe it or not I know a lot of gay people, and I know dykes that would kill to be on that show. Hell, half of them have sent in tapes. I don't know even one gay man who has any interest at all in sitting around in the dirt, eating bugs. For that matter come to think of it neither do I, but as long as I have to do it anyway . . . But I digress. Let's see . . . we were in the jungle and I was talking about *Survivor* and then Maggie said . . .

"I . . . just want to see my kids again, even that puking, shitting, grandbaby. I want to be bored on a Friday night with nothing to do and nothing decent on TV . . ."

"That's your problem," I said with a laugh. "You keep wanting to watch something decent."

Maggie mostly ignored my wisdom. "I want to sleep in my own bed and take a nice bath and wonder why the newspaper boy can't hit my porch. I want to worry about you smoking and drinking too much and being way too loose. I don't want any of . . . this. I'm way too old for this shit. And you, you're my best friend, and you didn't want to be here at all." She looked at me and all traces of humor left her face. "I'm so sorry, Vivian, so sorry for all of this. This is all my fault."

"No," I shook my head. "It's not your fault. If we'd come here and I'd wandered around studying hot spots, having dreadful headaches, and tripping over spectawhatagrams the whole time, that would have been your fault. The fact that I have no cigarettes, that's your fault. But the rest of this isn't your fault. You didn't know there were going to be real monsters on this island any more than I did. In fact, I would have been the first one to insist that we were perfectly safe. If you had known our lives were going to be in danger, then in all honesty I might have still said let's go, just for the money, but you never would have gone for it. Any of it." I drank the rest of my dirty water down. "You and I aren't going to die on this island, Maggie, unless we get killer dysentery from drinking this shit. Everyone else might, but not you and I. You're too smart, and I'm too mean, so it just flat isn't going to happen. So you can save your little speech for some future date when one of us really is going to die."

Maggie nodded. "So what now, Kemosabe?"

"Ah . . . I had my big leadership moment. It's your turn," I said with a smile.

"It's so peaceful right now, with no storm, so quiet. You could almost sit here and forget that there's a mass murderer and six corpses just through the trees. It's hard to believe that anything bad much less evil could happen here, and yet it has, over and over again."

"Bad land?" I suggested.

We heard a blood curdling scream echo through the jungle.

"Bad land," Maggie said.

We made a funnel out of a palm leaf and poured one of the bottles full of gas then stuffed a rag down in it tight enough that not much gas could leak out even if we shook the bottle too much.

We filled two more bottles and fixed them the same way.

"This is a crazy plan," I said again.

"Probably, but I don't see a lot of options," Maggie answered.

I nodded. As hopeless, reckless plans went, it wasn't as bad as most. Hell, I've done stupider shit just to get a date.

Which means I'm not too damn bright or my libido is just way too active, most probably some combination of the two.

Maggie walked around picking up sticks and swinging them around as I used some of the coat hanger wire to lash the busted hammerhead to a three-foot long stick. I was thinking that a mace worked a whole lot like a baseball bat, and if I could swing one of those I ought to be able to use my contraption the same way. I had visions of that one claw sticking in John's skull. I had just finished when Maggie came back with a stick. I looked at it and made a face.

"It's big enough," she said. I just shrugged and lashed my pocketknife to the end of it. She took a couple of stabs in the air, made a face and handed it back. "Don't say a word, just take it off," she said, and went off to find a bigger stick.

We had figured out that we were actually only a few hundred yards from the house, which was making us jumpy as hell. At any moment John or his accomplice might figure out where we were by figuring out where we weren't. Truth is I'd been just fine—in fact seriously considering a nap—till Maggie had insisted on pointing that out to me.

"How do you suppose he's washing the mud off the cameras?" I asked, suddenly very curious.

"I've given that a lot of thought. He's a big man but nowhere near tall enough to reach the cameras in that Victorian monstrosity even with a chair. If he were dragging a ladder around, surely to God one of us would have seen him, heard him. I realized he's got to be doing it from the ground, but how? There is no running water except in the bathrooms and kitchen, and you could hardly drag a hose all through the mansion without being caught any more than you could drag around a ladder. Besides, as far as we know there isn't any hose, either. Then it hit me—a squirt gun, probably one of those the kids run around with now that you pump up and it shoots twenty feet. Quick, easy to hide, easy to use, silent."

"That's a good answer, but why would he have brought a squirt gun? You aren't going to convince me that they figured out in advance that we'd figure out how to cover the cameras with mud," I said.

"No, but if he planned to paint with blood . . ."

"That's how he wrote the message on the wall with Ken's blood."

"Precisely," Maggie said smugly.

I nodded my head, excited at my own revelation. "That morning we found the mud washed off the camera in his room he just mudded the camera and then immediately washed the mud off. Jugs wouldn't have even noticed because she was completely stoned out of her gourd."

Maggie nodded. "The problem is the accomplice. We still don't know who he is or where he's hiding. Is he one of the players or a wild card?"

At that point I just rolled my eyes because I was sure I knew and that he wasn't even on the island, but Maggie and I had already had that argument and I had apparently lost. We made camouflage of palm fronds to cover our clothing. By the time we were done our clothes were almost dry, and it was still hours before it would be dark enough for our lousy camouflage to work.

With nothing to do but keep watch for John and wait, my stomach started bitching about all the food I hadn't eaten.

Jake was starting to look really good.

CHAPTER NINETEEN:
MAGGIE

I don't know whose stomach was making more noise, Vivian's or mine. Anyone out in the jungle just then might have mistaken us for a pair of snarling tigers . . . but of course, there are no tigers here, maybe a wild pig or two. I suspected it would not be wise to mention that to Vivian. She'd want to hunt it down and have barbeque. Then again, barbeque didn't sound half bad . . .

But thinking about roasted boar was only making my stomach hurt more. The temptation to chew on the palm fronds was kept at bay only because I had some vague recollection that they might be poisonous.

"Coconuts," I muttered as I tripped over yet another snarl of roots. "Why aren't there any coconuts now? We were tripping over them the other day when we were walking around looking for the boat and now nothing . . ."

"What?" Vivian stopped and gave me a hard look.

"Sorry," I said. "I'm thinking food at a time like this, and I shouldn't be." I shifted my bundle, which now held a couple of the makeshift Molotov cocktails, and I heard the tarp tear a bit more. At this rate, there would be little enough of it left and I would have to learn to juggle again.

"You're not the only one," Vivian said as she turned back and continued to wend her way through the growth. She was carrying both gas cans. "I keep thinking that Jake on a stick might be tasty . . ."

"You wouldn't eat that poor little gecko after he befriended you . . ."

She stopped again and looked at me like my marbles were spilling from my head. "I don't eat friends," she said, then her mouth spread with such a wicked smile. "Okay, so maybe I *do* eat friends . . . but I'm not in the mood for sex right now. I'm in the mood for a steak with a baked potato . . . a really big one . . . Though I would settle for one of those coconuts . . . if there were any . . ."

I saw her glance wistfully up at the heights of the trees as though hoping the coconuts would magically appear. But there were none to be seen. Besides I remembered that they were a lot harder to crack than people thought. I sighed and wished I hadn't thought of coconuts. I mean, this was a tropical island, and there should have been other things besides coconuts and mango groves . . .

"Mangos," I said just as Vivian started to move again.

"Damn it, Maggie, are you trying to drive me insane talking about food?" Vivian turned and glowered at me.

"There was a mango grove over by the shore!" I said excitedly. "I remember seeing it as we were coming off the boat!"

Vivian didn't look like she believed me, but she settled her shoulders and nodded. "Okay," she said. "Let's go look. If I'm going to have the trots from the water, what does it matter if I do the tutti-frutti two step, too?"

I rolled my eyes, but at least we shifted directions and started for the shore. The palm fronds rustled around us, clattering when we picked up our pace.

"You know," I whispered. "Too bad the pits from the mangos are not hard . . . otherwise, we could rig slings and use them for a weapon . . . Then again, I think the bark is poisonous . . . and so are the leaves and the wood . . . And in India, they say that mango trees grant wishes . . ."

"You know, you're just a shit-load of good news and interesting facts, Maggie," Vivian said. I could hear the teasing in her voice as she said that.

"Sorry," I said and grinned sheepishly. "It's the hunger talking . . . Of course, if the mangos are too green to eat, they *will* be hard enough to knock a man out."

"Ah, now you're talking," Vivian said. "Food and weaponry . . ."

We reached the edge of the jungle without incident. Out here it was a lot easier to dodge cameras and hot spots. Vivian crouched in the shadows, and I stooped beside her, putting my bundle down.

"So where is this grove?" she asked.

I looked at the dock and tried to remember what it had been like when I walked ashore and spotted the grove. I had turned to my left . . . not far from where we were crouching, if I remembered right.

"That way," I said and pointed toward the path to the house. "It was just over there . . ."

Vivian nodded. We backed into the trees. At her suggestion, we pulled the palm fronds up over our heads and stayed close to the ground to take advantage of the vegetation—in case there was a camera aimed in our vicinity. Move. Stop. Move. Stop. Vivian was in no hurry, in spite of being hungry. I probably looked like one of those jungle leaf-cutter ants that carries a leaf over itself to keep the rain off.

A few more yards and we were in the grove.

The storm had done a good bit of damage and had even torn down some of the mango trees. The sweet odor of mangos was everywhere, because there were a ton of them smashed on the ground, already attracting a host of insects and vermin. Well . . . at least they looked ripe, I thought, and scowled at the mess.

"Yuck," Vivian groused. "I don't eat fruit with bugs on it."

I pointed to the limbs of the mango trees. "There are still a few up there that didn't fall."

Vivian nodded and stretched up on her toes, trying to grab one of the rosy and green fruit lobes, but she was not quite tall enough. I frowned and stuck my stick with her knife on the end up and chopped. Took a couple of tries, but I managed to hack the fruit loose. Vivian caught it before it could join its kin on the bug-infested ground. A couple more fell to my stick. Jake, meanwhile, had crawled out of Vivian's pocket and was making short work of the grubs, flies and beetles that were not fast enough to escape his gecko reflexes. We stuffed the mangos in our pockets, working swiftly. Vivian captured Jake who was gulping down a grub, and we took off back into the depths of the jungle to hide and devour our feast.

We washed the mangos in a creek. I told Vivian not to mess with the sap coming out of the stems.

"Dermatitis," I said. "That sap will eat your skin off if you leave it there.

"Dangerous fruit," Vivian said. "You gotta love dangerous fruit."

"Don't eat the skins either," I said.

Vivian rolled her eyes. We unwired her knife from my stick and used it to peel them while keeping an eye out on our surroundings. Every snap of a twig had both of us twitching like a pair of spastic limbs. The mangos were not as ripe as I would have liked, but they were edible and put our hunger to rest. I felt better now, ready to tackle the tasks at hand. Like figuring out a way to stop John and whoever his cohort was.

I'd been tossing the theory around in my head. Vivian was right. The killer would have been in his seventies. I kept remembering all those pictures in the book, the victims whose faces did not match the killer, in spite of the authorities' conclusion that in each case the killer had butchered them all and then taken his own life.

Since we did not dare stay in one spot for long, we finished the mangos on the walk. Right now, life was a game. Stay alive. Sitting in one spot would only make us easy targets. Besides, if I had the plan down right, we were going to try and burn down the mansion as we had the generator house.

Of course, moving through the jungle trying to haul everything under the sun that Vivian had thought we *might* have a use for was no treat either. The idea that I was balancing on my bum a bunch of bottles filled with gasoline and stuffed with rags was not my idea of fun—or even terribly intelligent. I was just wondering if I should carry it in front of me when the tarp ripped again, and I heard something thump to the ground, one of the bottles by the sound of it. I turned to look, and sure enough, one of the homemade bombs was rolling off the path. I ducked back to catch it before it got away.

"Maggie, keep up," Vivian hissed, glancing back at me.

Which was a mistake. She took a step and suddenly hissed, "Oh shit!"

There was nothing there . . . well, not entirely nothing. I glanced down and saw that the ground was splattered with blood. Fresh blood. Oh, hell, someone had died here . . . and Vivian was about to be a witness to their last moments.

Vivian gasped as I carefully settled my load on the ground, and scrambled over to her side. She dropped the gas cans, jerked and clasped hands to her chest as though someone had hit her there, and then dropped like a stone to her knees. I caught her before she keeled over totally, but I knew from the stiffening of her limbs that she was seeing someone's death. There wasn't much I could do except hold on to her and whisper over and over, "It's okay, it's all right," as though comforting one of my own children.

"Ah, fuck," she snarled. She shook me off, got to her feet,

grabbed the cans and moved quickly away from the spot before setting them down again.

I helped her over to lean against a tree. I looked around, making certain we were still alone, then fetched one of the water bottles. Using her knife, I slashed the tail off my own shirt, and then dampened the cloth down and washed her face. At length, Vivian opened her eyes, looked at me and sneered.

"Damn that cow ASStaria," she said. "She died here."

"John?" I asked.

Vivian shook her head. "No . . . she was running up the path, wheezing like an old horse, when this little old man stepped out of the trees. She stopped and looked at him. God, Maggie, he was thin as a stick and had white hair . . . and the skin of his jaws was sagging down to his knees. I don't know what she asked him, but he suddenly pulled out a gun with a silencer and shot her in the chest . . . Couldn't have happened more than an hour ago . . ."

"Whoa, back up. A little old man shot Astaria?"

"Yeah . . . a butt-ugly little old man. He looked like one of those gnomes you see in one of those fairytale books, all wizened and skinny and . . ."

"I was right!" I said cheerfully.

"What?"

"I was right!" I repeated. "I told you John wasn't working alone. I told you there had to be someone else here . . . and that it had to be someone who had been here before. Someone who would know this island like the back of their hand . . . someone who had killed before and was now coming back to kill again."

"But John . . ."

"Had to have an accomplice," I said. "Someone who knew about all the other murders, someone who could watch the cameras for him. I knew that John couldn't do it alone . . ."

"Yeah, yeah, that was a given," Vivian said. "We need to get up to the mansion and finish what we were going to start."

Looking as surly as ever and spoiling for a fight, I got up and gathered the bundle, tempted to say, "Why don't *you* carry this for a while?" But in truth, I knew the gas cans were heavier and it was better to have her leading the way if we were attacked.

Or not. We hardly went a hundred yards, and Vivian was pushing her way through some low limbs when I got a brief glimpse of the corner of the mansion through the trees. Was that someone at the balcony window? Our balcony? The idea that someone was in the room, probably scrounging through my backpack and seeing my notes on this affair distracted me. Damn, I should not have left my pack behind. Everything that I had collected here to put in my book was in that backpack, including the book with the pictures of the victims . . .

And Vivian's sketches.

Vivian cursed and stumbled, and I stopped to see what had gotten in her way now.

A mound of lacerated flesh was the best description I could give for what had once been Astaria Wyman. I wonder if she had felt as much pain as her sweet Pumpkin Poo?

CHAPTER TWENTY:
VIVIAN

Maggie seemed to have side-stepped what I thought was the main problem with the old man. That old psycho had a gun. As far as we knew, John didn't. The gun worried me a hell of a lot more than the fact that the old fuck had found the need to cut She-Wyman up after he'd killed her.

"The gun had a silencer, that's why we heard Assateria scream, but we didn't hear the shot," I said again, just to emphasize the whole gun issue.

Maggie just shrugged, saying we already knew that and leaned closer to the body seemingly intent on checking out every cut, abrasion, and piece of *shmutz*.

"These are all postmortem trauma," Maggie announced as calmly as if she were looking at some cadaver on a slab in her old forensics lab.

"Well, duh, Maggie. I told you how she died. If you and I don't get a move on *we're* going to be postmortem, too."

"It's very interesting. What makes a man do things like this?"

"He's a fucking psycho," I hissed. "Now let's go."

She nodded, stood up, and one of the Molotov cocktails fell from her makeshift pack again. It was no good. I was going to have to fix it before we could go any farther or she was going to lose everything. I said as much to Maggie then sewed the tarp back together as good as I could, using coat-hanger wire for thread.

Yep, no doubt about it, I should have been on *Survivor*.

We stopped in a clump of brush away from any of the cameras. Night was just starting to fall, casting shadows across the land and the house. I looked up at the rising full moon in the clear sky, and frowned, so much for cover of darkness. Behind me Maggie sighed.

"What?" I asked in a whisper, knowing all too well that particular sigh meant something was wrong, something more than the full moon. Since everything already sucked rocks I was afraid to hear her answer.

"The mansion . . . it's all cut stone and concrete with a slate roof."

"So?" I asked with a shrug, thinking that now was not the time to worry about the architecture.

"Rock doesn't burn, knucklehead," Maggie said in an angry whisper, spraying the side of my head with spit.

I lifted a shoulder and wiped the spit on my shirtsleeve. I ignored what normally would have caused my flesh to crawl because there were so many things worse than a little spit to worry about just then. "I'd hold off on the name calling, Maggie. After all, you didn't remember the house was rock till just now when you were looking at it."

"The inside would still burn," Maggie said thoughtfully.

"Maybe, maybe not. The floors are stone, the walls are lath and plaster, and gasoline . . . well, it flashes. The vapors burn and lots of times doesn't even catch the wood. I was camping once and tried to light a fire with gas. To make a long story short, the wood was hardly charred, but I didn't have any eyelashes or eyebrows for about three months."

Maggie smiled a good kind of smile, the one that meant she'd thought of something. "The real problem is the damn cameras and those stinking monitors, right?"

"Right, we could get Jugs and just hide out till the boats get here if we could just knock out the monitors so that they couldn't watch us."

"I've got a plan," Maggie said.

Her plan included her carrying one big gas can and her makeshift weapon, while I had my hammer sticking in my back pocket with the head wedged uncomfortably against my right butt cheek and the handle stuck up over my head. I was carrying two Molotov cocktails in one hand and my lighter in the other. We hadn't gone far when we rounded a corner and there was John in his "costume." Turned out it was nothing more elaborate than one of those *I can see out but you can't see in* masks that kids wear at Halloween—as I'd already known—and a cloak made of a solar blanket. Its reflective surface no doubt played hell with the cameras' lenses.

John was carrying a large axe. From the rust that covered the head I assumed it was something he had found on the island, and I was a little pissed at God for letting him find the good weapon while I had a pocket full of broke hammer.

He didn't speak now, no doubt because that would have broken his cover. He raised the axe high and ran at us. I didn't hesitate. I dropped one of the bottles so that it hit my foot before it rolled onto the floor, then I lit the other one and tossed it at him. The bottle shattered at his feet and the solar blanket caught fire, covering John in flames.

I felt a little better about my weapons.

Expecting that his gun-toting accomplice would be on his way when he realized John had failed, I picked up the other cocktail and we ran toward the vault. John was screaming in pain, and Maggie stopped. I shoved her gently on the shoulder.

"No time to be a nice guy, Maggie," I said. She nodded and we kept moving.

At the vault door we stopped and started stripping off our "camouflage." Maggie stuck one of the fronds under the door and held it as I gently started pouring the gas. Just as Maggie had theorized that it would, the gas was running under the door and—hopefully—pooling on the vault floor.

"That's got it," I said as I poured out the last of the gas.

Maggie nodded and I helped her get up off the floor. She laughed a little.

"What?" I asked, thinking this was hardly the time for humor.

"I was just thinking that I haven't thought about my impending birthday or menopause since I got here," she said with a shrug.

"Great, so what you're saying is that for you, murder and mayhem is a great way to fight melancholy and hot flashes."

She smiled helplessly. "I just thought it was funny."

"Are we ready?" Right then I didn't think anything was funny.

Maggie sighed. "What a terrible waste—all the spectrawhatzits and Trecklespinulators. Well, I'll just never be able to afford equipment like that, and it's just going to be wasted, and . . ."

"Let's get this fucking show on the road," I said, and started back down the hall dragging Maggie along with me. I let go of Maggie, lit the rag in the top of the bottle and hurled it toward the vault door. There was a very satisfying explosion. Maggie looked like she wanted to cry. "Buck up, little camper," I said.

Maggie frowned at me and shook her head as I fought to remove my weapon from my back pocket. I know I wound up tearing a little triangle-shaped piece out of my ass. Lucky for me—as crispy John had pointed out—it was a gay sign.

I finally got my weapon free and we started back the way we had come at a brisk pace. We hadn't gone far when there was a second, larger explosion followed by several smaller ones.

"I hope that's what I think it is," I said.

"Monitors exploding? I've got my fingers crossed," Maggie answered.

"Go get Jugs?" I asked.

"Yes."

"Where?" I asked.

Maggie shrugged. "Try their room. If she's still alive and still drugged out of her gourd, that's where she'll be." There was another explosion. "And let's hurry. It would be just our luck to actually start the house on fire when we weren't trying to, with us in it."

I doubled my pace, though I was still very careful to step around hot spots and keep my eyes out for the old man with the gun. In truth I was more afraid of him than I'd ever been of John. After all John at least had a motive. The old guy just liked to kill people. He got off on it. In fact to this day of all the murderers that I've seen none have looked as sinister or made my blood run as cold as this guy.

It galled me no end to think of all of the lives he had taken while he had gone on to live a long and full life. He hadn't used a gun back then, but age had made him too weak to commit the murders the old-fashioned way, so he was just going to hire a big goon to kill them for him and then use a gun when they needed to speed up the killing.

The gun, that was the real problem, he didn't need to be strong or even particularly skilled. It was basically just a "point and pull the trigger" sort of thing. I guess that's why they call guns the great equalizers.

We got to Mug and Jug's room without incident, so I knew something was going to suck. She wasn't dead, but she might as well have been. She was in a drug-induced haze.

"He's gonna kill me," she slurred out. "That's what he said. Saving me for last because I'm easy and stupid. He said I was worthless."

"Well at least he's right about one thing," I mumbled.

"Vivian," Maggie said in a scolding tone.

I stood watch at the door. "We have to leave her," I told Maggie.

"We *can't*, Vivian, he'll kill her."

John was toast, so I knew she was talking about the old man, and I knew she was right. I went to the blow-up mattress and knelt down by the girl, keeping a half an eye on the door. "Why couldn't we have had one of these?" I said, pointing at the mattress, suddenly as tired as I had ever been in my life.

"I hardly think that's the point right now, Vivian, can you get her up?"

I slapped Jugs hard across the face. "Come on, chick, wakey wakey."

"Christ on a crutch, Vivian," Maggie said, shoving me aside. "I hardly think giving the poor thing a concussion is going to help."

"Couldn't hurt," I said, looking into Jugs's totally unresponsive face.

"Help me get her up," Maggie said.

And that was when I knew I was going to have to carry the bitch. I sighed when Maggie suggested it and reached into my shirt pocket. "All right, here, hold my lizard."

Maggie made a face, but took him and stuck him in her shirt pocket. I was afraid he'd get all smushed when I picked up the trollop.

Now, she was a small woman—except for the breasts—and I'm a fairly big girl and I know how to do a fireman's carry. But let me tell you something—that bitch got heavy fast.

"Maybe you're right, maybe she has had a boob job."

"I'm sure that's relevant right now," Maggie whispered back. Since my only weapon was once again in my back pocket and my hands were full of woman—not normally a problem for me—Maggie had taken point with her makeshift sword jutting out in front of her.

"It is, because if they're not real we can cut them out and lighten my load by fifty pounds."

"Yes, oh yes, this is a perfect time to make a joke," Maggie whispered in a scolding tone.

"Or we could talk about your fiftieth birthday and your hot flashes," I countered. At that moment I don't think I was kidding about cutting her tits off, my back felt like it was breaking.

We got out of the house without incident, and this only made me more sure that we were about to be shot at any moment.

"Where do we go?" Maggie asked.

"How the fuck should I know? You're the smart one; you choose. Just go wherever you're going fast. I can't carry this chick forever."

Maggie nodded and started for the dock.

"Are you fucking nuts? We'll be in the open there."

"I figured we'd hide in the jungle around the beach where we can see the dock. That way as soon as the boat gets here we can run down and warn them."

Damn, she *was* the smart one. I hadn't even thought of the possibility of the old fuck killing the boat and camera crews as soon as they arrived. He no doubt had brought his own boat to the island, and God alone knew what he might have at his disposal. He might have a high-powered rifle with a scope so he could just sit up in a tree and wait for them to dock.

"This sucks," I said as I followed Maggie.

We were just about to leave the path for the jungle at the edge of the beach when something that smelled a whole lot like when I'd burnt my eyebrows off jumped out of the bushes into the path in front of us.

John definitely looked the worse for the wear. There were burns all over his face and hands and his hair was all singed.

"You fucking bitches," he swore. The axe didn't seem to have been hurt in the slightest.

I thought fast, don't ask me why. I think a combination of being scared shitless and being more pissed off than I'd ever been in my life. I tossed Jugs onto the ground like a discarded feed sack and started pulling at the hammer in my pocket. The pocket ripped away and I held my weapon with both hands.

John laughed at me. I guess I did look sort of ludicrous with a broken hammerhead wired to a piece of stick for a weapon.

"Maggie, run," I ordered, and was glad—if a little disappointed—when she didn't hesitate to leave me to face the crispy critter myself. John momentarily looked toward Maggie as if wondering which one of us to come after first, and that was all I needed. I swung at his head for all I was worth. He spun around and caught the blow on his axe head, so I cocked back, found a second target and slammed that one claw into the side of his knee. He crumpled to the ground screaming as I tried to free my weapon. It wasn't coming out, so I had to let it go. I tried to grab John's axe, but even hurt he was incredibly strong and he wasn't letting go.

"You fucking bitch. I'm going to kill you. Let go, let go!"

"You're going to kill me no matter what, you fucking lunatic. *You* let go." He brought his good leg around and kicked it up, hitting me square in the middle of my chest and sending me flying. As soon as I hit the ground I jumped up and took off running straight for the dock. I could hear John's limping form right behind me. When I reached the water I jumped in and started to swim. A few seconds later there was another splash as John hit the water, and then a loud bloodcurdling scream— saltwater hitting all those fresh wounds. I smiled and kept swimming toward the shore. But all pain had done was slow John down a little, and he was on me in seconds. He grabbed my leg, and I spun around slamming a fist into the burns on his face. He screamed, took hold of my shoulders, and pushed my head under the water. We were now in water about waist deep. I splashed around but couldn't get out of his grasp, and I couldn't seem to get my feet to take hold in the sand. Then my finger found the hole the hammer claw had made and I slammed my finger deep into the wound. He twisted, fell, and let me go. I took off again but didn't get far before he had me again. This time both his hands went around my throat and he started throttling me. I pounded at him with my fists but it didn't seem to do much good. I got a good angle and kicked him in the nuts hard. He made a choking sound and pitched forward on top of me. At first I marveled at the power of my kick, but then I saw the blood staining the water as it flowed freely from his body. Under the water I saw the ragged bullet hole in his chest as I swam out from under him.

Crazy old guy, apparently John had outlived his usefulness. I swam under the water as long as I could then popped up just long enough to get some air. Not too unexpectedly a bullet grazed the water close to my head. I dove back under and made for the relative protection of the dock. I didn't come up again till I was under it. I listened as the old man started walking on the boards above me.

"Oh, do come out and play. It's no fun if you won't come out and play. Everyone has to pay," he said, and I realized his voice wasn't the voice on the tapes. No, that was just some actor the show had hired to try to scare us into leaving the island. He was never part of the game.

"What about your friend?" I asked. I quickly moved to another position as the bullets ripped through the board above where I had been. I figured I could run him out of bullets and then the old fuck would be easy to kill. All right, so it wasn't my brightest moment, but you tell me if you think you'd have had a better plan.

"Friend? Oh . . . you mean that moron. He ruined everything for me, everything. It was like a dream come true. No one had been here in so long, and I never dreamed I'd have a chance to relive the glory." He laughed. "*Gory* days of my youth, much less have it all on tape, but then some moron decided to tempt fate. All I had to do was wait till today, bring my boat in as I had done before and kill everyone. But that idiot had already killed most of you. He ruined it. It's bad enough I have to resort to this crude gun to do my killing, but then to have someone else kill all my prey. Well, I still have you two to take care of now, don't I?"

Two. That meant he'd already killed either Maggie or Jugs. I hoped it was Jugs.

"You ain't got shit yet." I moved again, and this bullet got closer than the last two.

"You're a truly great adversary, but alas it only works if you're dead. All must die."

"Why?" This time I moved quickly while I was talking. This seemed to screw him up, and his next shot wasn't even close.

He laughed then, the most unpleasant sound I have ever heard. "I'm going to take a wild guess and say you've had a rough life. A life filled with total assholes who parade in and make your life a living hell, but you can't kill them. No!" He was screaming now. "No you can't kill any of the people that you'd like to because the fact that you want to kill them makes you a suspect. It's a lot of anger to carry with you, year in and year out. So . . . I came up with this. I went to the resort and killed everyone. I never would have dreamt that people would just keep giving me the opportunity to relieve myself in the same spot over and over again. It's so nice for them to accommodate me. Killing people in really brutal ways every twenty years has allowed me to live a normal—and one might even say an admirable—life."

"You're a fucking lunatic!" I yelled, and again I moved. This time the bullet was so close I could actually feel the heat.

"You're a clever girl. You think I'll run out of bullets. But you see I have a whole pocketful, and . . ." I heard the bullets hit the deck above my head. I heard a sound like a knife thumping into a melon and then a loud scream followed by the thump of a body. I carefully crawled out from under the dock and I saw Maggie standing over the old man's body. The knife with the stick tied to it was sticking out of his chest. I ran around till I could jump up on the dock, and then I ran over and hugged Maggie. Yeah, I was glad she had saved my miserable life, but between you and me, I was happier to see that my best friend wasn't maggot food.

I let go of Maggie and grabbed up the gun and the bullets. I carefully loaded the gun then pointed it at the old guy's head.

"Vivian, for Christ's sake, what are you doing?"

"Making sure this fucker is dead. This guy . . . You know what he is, what he's done without guilt . . ."

"And he's already dead." Maggie pulled out the makeshift weapon, and dark blood oozed from the wound.

I looked at the old man's body and realized what she said was true. Maggie had attacked the psycho with the skill of a fencer and the accuracy of a forensic pathologist. He'd turned when he heard her. Startled, he'd dropped the bullets, and she'd stabbed him in the heart by thrusting up at an angle under his breastbone.

"John still had to have had an accomplice," I whispered, and started shoving Maggie in the direction of the beach. She went but not very quickly.

"The accomplice isn't here. The only place you can see the dish is from the dock. That's why he didn't put it there till after we were here. Once he had started killing people no one was very likely to notice something like the addition of a satellite dish." Maggie pointed to the roof of the house where I could just see the outline of a small satellite dish.

"The satellite dish you saw in the vault," I said then grinned. "So I was right."

"Yes," Maggie hissed. "Yes, you were right." She sat down on the end of the dock and rested her face in her hands. I sat down beside her. Jake crawled out of her shirt pocket and scampered across the small space that separated us. I picked him up and patted his head.

"The old fuck . . . He was so evil, and now we'll never know what really made him do it," I said.

"The police will be able to tell us who he was. I'll check his background and we'll see what we can find out, but . . . no, we'll never really know why people do things like this. Why some people can go through a trauma and come out the other side virtually unscathed and others have something minor happen and it makes them psychotic. You OK?"

I rubbed at my throat. "I been better, but yeah, I'll be OK. You?"

Maggie just nodded silently.

"Should I pull John out of the water?" I asked.

"So *now* you finally remember someone's name," Maggie laughed.

I shrugged. "Hey, the lunatic tried to kill me. I can't very well call him by a pet name anymore."

"Hey, guys! Where did everyone go?" I damn near shot her. Jugs stood in front of us rubbing at her eyes. "I had the weirdest dream, and then I wound up back there in the jungle. Thank God I heard you guys talking or I would have been lost."

Apparently the old man had thought she was dead.

"Have you seen John?" she asked.

I got up took her hand and pulled her over to us. "Why don't you sit down? Maggie has something to tell you. I just have to go fetch something out of the ocean."

"Chicken!" Maggie accused.

We found John's cell phone in his pocket, but somewhere

between fire and water it had been rendered completely nonfunctional. We would have to wait till the boat arrived in the morning to get off the cursed island. We drug the old man off the dock and pulled him over next to John. Then we went back to the house, got some food, the blow-up mattress, Maggie's notes and our gear, and went back down to the dock and set up camp for the night right there on the dock. The three of us lay down on the mattress covered with our mosquito netting and in spite of the fact that we had to all lie sideways, the bugs buzzing over us fighting to get through, and the dead bodies scattered across the island, we fell asleep. When I think about it now, I think we stayed there that night because it was the one thing that seemed somehow detached from the rest of the island.

We awoke to the sound of a boat's motor, and a more beautiful sound I have never heard. We all stood up and waved excitedly at the boat. They waved back and I could see the glare of the camera lenses.

"Hey, what the hell's going on?" the director—though I'd wondered from the beginning how one went about directing something like *Chicken Out*—asked as he stepped off the boat, looking at the bodies.

I looked at him, smiled, and said, "Let's just say I think you're going to win in sweeps this year."

CHAPTER TWENTY-ONE:
MAGGIE

The camera crew came spilling off the ship like rats deserting a bilge. Raymond Kennedy was staring at the bodies on the beach in awe.

"Damn," he said. "Just what's been going on here?"

"Like you don't know?" I asked in return. "Oh, but that's right, you don't know since your accomplice was killed and we screwed up your monitoring equipment."

He looked at me, cocking one eyebrow. "What on earth are you talking about?"

Funny what some food, a good night's sleep, and the realization that land is just a boat ride away will do for me. Granted, I know this whole affair was my idea, and that I had come here for the sake of my book. And in doing so, I had endangered Vivian's and my own life. Of course, I had no idea what I was getting us into. All I wanted to do was ghost-hunt and solve an age-old mystery. But I'm getting off track.

Seeing Raymond Kennedy standing there looking like he had swallowed a sugar cube—all Mr. Sweetness and Nice—just set me off. Before Vivian or any of the show's crew could stop me, I stepped up and seized him by the nape of the neck—an astonishing feat for a woman of my short stature—and forced his head around so he could see the mansion.

"Just what does that look like?" I asked and pointed to the satellite dish on top of the structure.

"I don't quite know what you . . ."

Okay, I could not resist. Normally, I leave the rough stuff to Vivian since she's taller and better at it than I will ever be. But I had just spent several nights on an island with a couple of crazy killers, and I wanted the truth to be known. I let go of his neck and smacked him up the back of the head. He cringed and yelled, "Hey! What was that for, you stupid . . ."

"The satellite dish, Mr. Kennedy," I said harshly. "There is a satellite dish on top of the buildings."

"So?" He rubbed the back of his head. "The workmen must have forgotten to take it down."

"Except it wasn't here when we first landed. All that recording equipment in the vault—it wasn't so you could record and edit later . . . it was computerized. You lied about no satellite feed, you were watching us all along. You knew what was happening, and it was you who kept John informed as to where we were and what we were doing."

"That's ridiculous," Kennedy said.

The director was now ordering the cameramen to aim their cameras at Kennedy.

"We'll see how ridiculous the Cancun police think it is when they get here," I said. The director immediately pulled a cell phone from his pocket and started phoning the police on the mainland, as if realizing for the first time that with at least two dead bodies, this was indeed a matter for the police.

"*Chicken Out*," I continued. "It wasn't about the prize. It wasn't about the ghosts. It was about the ratings. Put a bunch of people on an island and scare them silly. That's been done. There are a lot of 'scare the contestant' shows on the air already. No, Mr. Kennedy, you wanted something special . . . you wanted a show filled with all the horror of human nature that could be revealed."

"You wanted the one thing they haven't figured out how to do yet," Vivian said, actually playing with the gun hanging out of the top of her shorts. "You wanted real honest-to-God murder."

"What?"

"You wanted a show where people would really die. Such a show would no doubt make ratings history. You'd make millions," I said.

"Sunstroke," Kennedy said and laughed nervously. "The little lady's got a touch of tropical sunstroke . . ."

"Sunstroke my ass," I said, and grabbed him by the lapels of his Armani suit. "I am trying to tell you that you, Raymond Kennedy, are a cold-blooded murderer."

The sound of the ocean was all anyone heard for a few moments. Then murmurs whispered back and forth.

"I don't understand," Kennedy said. "You're accusing *me* of murder? I mean . . . I've been on the mainland. Dozens, possibly hundreds, of people saw me on the mainland. How could I possibly have . . ."

"You might not have performed the physical acts," I said, "but you are still the person responsible. That satellite dish proves it. That and the bank of computers probably burned to a crisp since Vivian and I torched the control room . . ."

"You torched millions of dollars of equipment?" Kennedy snarled. "I oughta sue you . . ."

"I think the police will agree that a little arson pales in comparison to the atrocities you set us up to suffer."

Kennedy looked like he was going to bolt, and that's when Vivian knocked him to the ground and—with the help of two of the camera crew—pulled off his belt and bound his hands behind his back. When he tried to squirm away she pulled the pistol from the top of her pants and stuck it against the base of his skull.

"Go ahead, give me a good reason," Vivian hissed, sounding like a really bad Dirty Harry imitation. I got the impression that

Kennedy was not very well liked by his staff, they were just too quick to believe he was capable of murder. Too quick to help Vivian pistol whip and handcuff him.

"What the hell!" he protested. She frisked him none too gently. When she found a small gun hidden under his arm I don't think there was any doubt in any of the crew's minds that what I was saying was true.

"A little insurance?" I asked and didn't wait for him to answer as Vivian and a stout man hauled Kennedy up off the beach. "It must have been extremely disconcerting when you knew he," I pointed to the body of the old man, "was here, and you lost your ability to watch us all. For the first time since we left the mainland you had no idea what we were doing. For the first time since John installed the dish on the second day, you couldn't watch us. You went suddenly from knowing exactly what you would find when you arrived here this morning to having to walk in here blind with no idea of the outcome of 'the game.' "

I saved the rest of the story till a few minutes later when the police showed up in force and boiled off the boats.

"Knight wasn't supposed to let anyone but John in the vault. He thought John was just there to help him play his role. Knight was supposed to go down and get us whatever we needed from the room; he wasn't supposed to let us in there. But he was never part of what you and John had planned. No, as far as he knew, he was just there to try and scare all hell out of us. Lead us to places and tell us scary stories. Go down to the vault and play a scary recording every once in a while. But after Eduardo had been murdered he no longer wanted to play the game. He was as scared as the rest of us—maybe more so, because part of his family had been brutally murdered here. *He* wasn't expecting anyone to die on this island, not this time. He truly believed you were just going to scare us until one couple remained, but the killing of the cook, and then the sinking of the boats, jolted him too much.

"Since he thought the game was over, and he just wanted to find a way off the island as bad as we did, he didn't see anything wrong with letting me into the vault. That's when I first saw the satellite dish. It's one of those usually put on the roof, which was why it didn't make sense for it to be sitting in the control room. I'm thinking that's what tipped Knight, too, and what got him killed so early in the game. I noticed the missing satellite dish when I returned with Vivian to get some equipment and thought it strange, but then we found Knight's body and I quickly forgot all about it till last night when I looked up and saw it on the roof. John must have killed Knight and then immediately gone to install the satellite dish. If those banks of equipment were just for recording, or for Knight to know when to scare who, why would you need a satellite? The answer was simple—you needed to keep track of what was happening so you could tell your ape there who to kill and when, and I imagine even how."

"This is just ludicrous!" Kennedy shouted looking at the police appealingly.

"John was a plant. He was sent here to be the killer. I'm guessing everything he'd needed had been stored here in some hidden spot long before we arrived. I'm guessing when they do a thorough search of the house and the grounds they're going to find a laptop with a remote wireless modem, and we already have the cell phone—all means of communication that the rest of us were denied. You told him what moves to make, who to kill, when to kill them, all from the comfort of your office where I am willing to bet there is recording equipment filled with all the deaths."

"That's absurd," Kennedy said. "You're talking nonsense."

"That's what I thought when Vivian kept saying it was you

and that you were doing it for the ratings. It just sounded crazy. It's more than crazy; it's obscene that human life is so cheap to you. That's what I kept telling Vivian, and that's what you were hoping for. That what you were doing was so unthinkable that no one would ever know that you were behind everything or what your motive was."

"The whole idea was to push everything to the limit. Shove the ratings as high as possible. Give them real blood. Give them real death. You knew about Knight's family history. You knew the island had a previous history of murder before the Knight family took over, and you wanted to play the 'kill everybody' angle to the hilt. Your very own *And Then There Were None.* Only in the beginning, John sort of made a mistake. I don't think we were supposed to start dying right away, but I'm guessing Eduardo saw John scuttling the boats." I looked at Vivian then, "That's what he and Miguel were arguing over. Eduardo probably wanted to tell us, and Miguel wanted him to stay out of it. Anyway John had to get rid of both of them right away so he killed Eduardo and made it look like Miguel had killed him, then he hunted Miguel down and hung both bodies in that tree knowing that a missing body was going to scare us more and he needed for everyone to keep thinking that Miguel was the killer."

Vivian nodded.

"Knight had to go next because when he saw the satellite in the room he knew what that meant, and he'd gone to confront John. Of course we were all supposed to die but John. What Kennedy wanted was for the crew to get here this morning and John would no doubt be gone. No one the camera crew found would be alive. The fourth boat—we looked for it but of course we never found it because again John knew where we were because you told him and told him when to move it. Had he succeeded in killing us all and was still alive he would have taken the fourth boat and gone. They'd count the bodies and one would be missing, but I'm thinking that a tape had already been made weeks beforehand of John being killed by our mysterious, masked, cloak-wearing villain and his body maybe tossed into the ocean. Tape would also show that the boat had been missing since the very first day, and his piece would be carefully placed in so that it looked like he died later. We keep saying *tape* because that's what we're all used to, but all of this technology is digital, so it's very easy to move footage around and have no one be the wiser. He'd get away, go to a foreign country where his money would be waiting for him. I'm guessing the payoff was more than the one million in prize money, but what does a top-ten prime-time show bring in these days? You probably planned to pay less to John than you'd make for one commercial.

"But in order to ensure the big bucks you needed splashy. You weren't happy with the deaths you were getting, so you had John step it up a notch, didn't you, Kennedy? Going for the highest ratings possible. A knife in the back—face down in the enchiladas—that wasn't going to do it for you, not when there is more brutal stuff on the 5:00 news every day. John should have killed us first, but we were just too good to be true, weren't we? Me running around collecting evidence, seeming to be more upset about not getting to do my research than I was with all the murder. Vivian talking to lizards, mooning the cameras, having sex with Jolene, and a dozen other really stupid, but sometimes heroic things."

"Hey!" Vivian protested.

"I said sometimes heroic," I said quickly, and she went to mumbling things I couldn't hear.

"You're crazy, lady," Kennedy said and laughed, but no one else was laughing.

"A little respect, scum sucker. Maggie was solving lots tougher crimes than this when you were still shitting your diapers," Vivian said.

I glared at her, then turned back to Kennedy and said, "This was all your doing, all your script, except for two things. You didn't count on Vivian and me actually being able to foil your plan, and you couldn't have prepared for the real wild card—the murderer who killed everyone in the hotel then butchered the Knight family twenty years later. He was still alive and still crazy, and he felt like you gave him something and then took it away. You see I have been researching this particular island's history for a book for a long time. I have all the details, all the books, all the pictures. I suspected all along there had to be a connection other than the mumbo-jumbo about ancient gods and human sacrifice. When Viv kept hitting hot spots and seeing the past, it all made sense. One killer. One killer who no one knew was here. It's an easy trip from the mainland even in a small boat. Vivian saw the killer, then the same killer twenty years older."

Vivian shook her head. I knew what she was thinking. *There goes Maggie, and we're both gonna end up in a loony bin.* I ignored her and went on.

"You wanted to re-create the murders, but you didn't realize the real killer was still alive. He came here to collect his prize, and your pistol-whipping bully-boy had already killed most of us. I guess the horrible irony is that if you had just left everything alone you would have gotten the show you wanted and you wouldn't be going to jail now."

"There's no way you can pin this on me," Kennedy said.

"Oh, no?" I said and held out my hand for John's cell phone. Vivian handed it to me. "I'm willing to bet that your direct private number is programmed into John's cell phone."

Kennedy sneered. "And just how are you going to prove that? From the looks of that phone, you couldn't call 911 with it, let alone hit redial and get a number."

"I won't have to," I said. "The police have only to get a court order and check all the phone records. And cell phone companies keep excellent records. All they will have to do is pull the records for your phone and see how many calls you made to John while he was here on the island, and that's all the evidence they're going to need to put you away for life."

His face turned the shade of a ripe plum as he backed away from me. "Why you . . . stupid . . . you. I know what this is all about, you're pointing the finger at me because you're mad that you can't win because you're not actually a couple."

I smiled then. "You're right, Mr. Kennedy, we're not a real couple. But how did you know that? Since I never told *you* till now, and since the only way you could have known was if you'd actually seen my confession in the hotel's kitchen. That in itself rather implicates you," I said. "You know everything about us. You did background checks on all the contestants. I'm just wondering if you knew John before or if you found him in your contestant search. The psych profiles they no doubt did on us would have told you who might be willing to go along with your plan. You picked all of the rest of us because we would make for entertaining TV. You knew that I'm a mostly retired forensic pathologist who writes books about paranormal activity at crime scenes, and that Vivian is a police sketch artist with a special gift. Only you thought she was just a fake—or worse yet a total flake—and that I was just some old woman who was so blinded by love and perhaps a need to believe that there is something beyond what we see that I believed her. But you seemed to overlook one thing . . . we both investigate crime for a living, and we're really good at what we do. Your biggest mistake was underestimating us. In thinking I was over the hill and that Vivian was just some hapless flake."

The members of the film crew kept filming, but they were forced to step aside as more of the police stepped forward. Kennedy was calling them all names as they took hold of him and dragged him onto one of the police boats.

"I think you better come down to the station and let's sort this out," the captain said. He frisked Kennedy himself and found his cell phone.

He looked at Kennedy's phone, then held out his hand for John's. I gave it to him, knowing full well they would have trouble getting prints on the thing. It was too badly damaged on the surface to hold any clear ones. Vivian handed him the gun she'd taken from Kennedy.

"He had this," Vivian said.

The captain looked at Kennedy and said in his broken English, "And see? I'm thinking an innocent man doesn't carry a gun to go make a TV show."

"The old man had this one. It's the one he shot She-Wyman and John with." She seemed reluctant to hand the gun over, though it was hard to tell if it was because with all that had happened she just felt safer holding the weapon or if she was afraid they'd find more of her prints on it than his. I knew she was safe because she hadn't fired the gun and they'd no doubt check all of us for gunpowder residue.

He took that gun as well and nodded. "We need to make a thorough investigation of the island. You will all have to leave." He looked at Harmony, Vivian and me. "We will take you to a hotel room where we will take your statements. I see no reason to take you to the station. I think you've been through enough."

As we were following the camera crew onto the boat, Vivian poked me in the ribs.

"I was right all along!" she said loud enough for everyone on the dock and beyond to hear. "I told you it had to be Dead President Guy."

"Vivian, at one point you thought it was everyone—including the lizard."

"Hey, but I was right!" Vivian yelled. "You think I'm going to let you forget that?"

"No, I guess you're not," I said. "Come on, let's get out of here . . ."

We grabbed what portions of our stuff we had managed to salvage, and got on the boat.

"Hey, Maggie, you know . . . we're rich."

"Yeah," I said. "We're still alive . . ."

"No, I mean, we're rich. We're the only surviving couple!" she added rather loudly. "She was just kidding about us not being a couple, all just a way to catch Dead President Guy. Come on, baby, give me a big kiss."

I didn't kiss her, just sighed and shook my head.

The first bath felt like heaven. The second was just for fun. Real food. A real bed. I could have slept for a month, but we had to catch a flight back to the United States after only a couple of days. Seems like once I had outlined everything for the police, they decided we were no longer needed. I guess the evidence really spoke for itself. Don't get me wrong. They were happy for the assistance but admitted so only in private. As far as they were concerned, they had solved the case the moment they stepped on the island.

The good news is that Kennedy's calls to John were on record. Furthermore, John had been keeping a sort of diary on the laptop, detailing how he killed this person and that, and grumbling about Kennedy's orders. I have the feeling John thought he would be able to sell his story after all this was over—or use the diary to blackmail Kennedy.

Oh, yeah, they confiscated Kennedy's near confession on camera, too, and pointed out that it was their evidence. They also found the rather damning recording of John's supposed death.

In a way, I was glad to be heading back. I was tired, and I had a book to write. A good one about murder, and how the secret of the island's mysterious serial deaths was that the killer was still alive after all these years—or was. They let me off the hook with self-defense. The coroner said I would have to come back for the inquest—assuming there was one. But for right then, I had a story I could write about, and I felt pretty good about that.

I didn't feel so good about the immediate return of my hot flashes, but I guess if you weigh it all up I'd rather deal with those than death and dismemberment. Especially when I'm one of the targets.

Still, it was annoying.

Vivian and I were sitting on the plane, being served what passed for dinner on a long flight—which was actually a bag lunch that we had to grab before we boarded—when I saw Vivian break off a bit of her sandwich and drop it inside one of the zipper pouches on the outside of her bag. I cringed.

"What are you doing?" I asked. "That'll rot in there."

"No it won't," she said, and did not look at me as she pushed some of the food quickly into her own mouth.

"Vivian, what have you got in the bag?"

She shook her head. "Just my stuff," she said.

I looked down at the bag. The zipper pocket where she had stowed the bit of sandwich wriggled slightly. I glanced at her, my mouth gaping.

"You put Jake in there," I said. "You know he's going to show up on the X rays."

"No he won't," she insisted. "I'll put him in my pocket while we go through customs—just like I did when we boarded. Now don't spoil it for me, okay, Maggie?"

"He's a gecko," I said. "Why are you taking him home?"

"Well . . . I've grown rather fond of him, that's all."

"You, the Queen of Clean, have grown fond of a *lizard?* A bug-eating lizard?"

"Hey, you said they ate roaches and spiders and stuff, and I figure he'll come in handy. Besides, how could I leave him there after all we've been through together? That would be like leaving my mother on a desert island . . ."

She paused in that statement.

"Then again," she said.

I rolled my eyes.

I just hope I'm not standing close should the customs officers decide to pat Vivian down . . .

Chapter Twenty-Two:
Vivian

So . . . that's basically it. We went through all that shit and we didn't win the money because of Maggie's big mouth.

Would it have actually killed her to kiss me on the mouth? For a million bucks I would have screwed She-Wyman . . . well, maybe not.

For the record, Maggie didn't come through with either the hot chick or the carton of smokes. Guess it's just as well—on the cigarette side anyway. I actually did quit smoking.

You guessed right, the bimbo who'd spent most of her time in hell too drugged out to know what was going on won the million bucks. Contracts are contracts, and while I argued that the contract didn't specifically say that we had to be a "real" sexually involved couple, the network lawyers were quick to point out that it *did* say that the couples had to be romantically involved. I said I was willing to have sex with Maggie, but Maggie screamed that there wasn't enough money in the world for her to have sex with me and the lawyers quickly pointed out that it wouldn't really count after the fact anyway.

Maggie and I got *Chicken Shit* T-shirts and $5,000.00 each. We saved the bimbo, killed a serial killer, and figured out who was behind the whole plot, and we get not even enough money to pay for the therapy we're going to need and some crappy T-shirts while Bimbzillia gets a million bucks for sleeping through the whole thing.

Worst part—try as I might I couldn't convince Jugs that she

was gay or that she was madly in love with me. I think she's just in denial, but her lawyers issued a restraining order against me, so I guess I know when to take a hint.

We got medals from the Cancun government, and of course I smuggled Jake home with me, but except for that all I got for my trouble was a giant raging migraine headache that lasted for three days and ruined any chance of chasing half-dressed women up and down the beaches of Cancun before we had to go home.

On an up note I haven't seen a single bug in here except the crickets I buy Jake at the pet store since I brought him home. Cleaning up little piles of Jake crap seems like a small price to pay, and they've come out with those really great antibacterial wipes that are perfect for cleaning up the mess. They even have some in little individually wrapped packages so you can carry them in your pocket.

Of course I get calls daily from some crank or another wanting me to solve this murder or that one. If I did them all, I'd burn my brain out in less than a year. Besides, none of these people are offering me money for my services. They think my gift is God-given, and I ought to burn my brain out for free.

Bull shit!

They took lots of pictures and called us heroes, but no one's giving us barrels of money, and I'm figuring we deserve barrels of money after what we went through.

Maggie has finished *Bad Lands*. It's already been printed, and it's getting rave reviews. She's promised to give me twenty-five percent of what she makes on the book, which wouldn't amount to much, except . . .

Well, after a lengthy court battle and pay-offs to the family members of the dead and the government of Cancun—Yep, even they made more money than Maggie and I—the Lynx Network has won the right to air all fifteen episodes of *Chicken*

Out, including the murders, and no doubt my making a total ass of myself on several occasions. They have promised me that I will be one of the most pixilated people ever on TV. It doesn't really matter. Even if they showed every stupid thing I did I'm thinking all the great footage of me being like Superwoman are going to be enough to override the stupid shit. Just being on TV is going to assure my getting laid on a fairly regular basis for a considerably long-ass time.

I made up a bag of popcorn, put on my Testosterone Woman T-shirt, and me and Jake are sitting on the couch kicked back getting ready to watch the very first episode of *Chicken Out.* I'm thinking by tomorrow the girls will be lining up at my door, and Maggie's book will be jumping off the shelves.

I hope I look good.

ABOUT THE AUTHORS

Selina Rosen is insane; there is no other explanation for the things she does or what she writes. Her hobbies include gardening, carpentry, fencing, sculpting, and drinking large amounts of beer. Her short fiction has appeared in *Sword and Sorceress XVI, Such a Pretty Face, Thieves World . . . Turning Points and Enemies of Fortune,* and *Turn the Other Chick,* to name a few. Her novels include *Queen of Denial, Recycled, Chains of Freedom, Chains of Redemption,* and *Strange Robby.* She created the Bubbas of the Apocalypse universe for Yard Dog Press.

Laura J. Underwood is the author of several novels and numerous short stories in the fantasy field. Her work has appeared in various volumes of *Sword and Sorceress,* Marion Zimmer Bradley's Fantasy Magazine; *Turn the Other Chick; Bubbas of the Apocalypse;* and many other anthologies and magazines. Her books include *Ard Magister, Chronicles of the Last War, Dragon's Tongue, The Hounds of Ardagh* (also from Five Star Press), and the collections *Tangled Webs and Other Imaginary Weaving* and *Magic's Song: Tales of the Harper Mage.* Her novel *Wandering Lark* is forthcoming. When not writing, Underwood is First Assistant at the Carter Branch of the Knox County Public Library System. In her copious spare time (whatever that is), she has been known to hike, bike, play harp and guitar, embroider, string beads, study folklore, draw, meditate and play with swords. A former state fencing champion, Underwood now limits her swordplay to her writing, and to trading blade strokes and jibes with author Elizabeth Moon and others as a member of the SFWA Musketeers. She is an Active Member of the Science Fiction & Fantasy Writers of America.